The Caribbean Job

A Case Lee Novel

Book 3

By Vince Milam

Published internationally by Vince Milam Books

WANT TO RECEIVE MY NEWSLETTER WITH NEWS ABOUT UPCOMING RELEASES? Simply copy the link below into your browser:

http://eepurl.com/cWP0iz

Other books by Vince Milam:

The Suriname Job: A Case Lee Novel Book 1

The New Guinea Job: A Case Lee Novel Book 2

Acknowledgments:

Cover Design by Rick Holland at Vision Press – *myvisionpress.com*.

Vicki for her love and patience. Mimi, Linda, and Bob for their unceasing support and understanding.

We sleep soundly in our beds because rough men stand ready in the night to visit violence on those who would do us harm.

Chapter 1

A pinpoint of light on a Nassau night signaled bad news. The button-sized red dot wavered across the casement window's glass pane. It hovered, sought, and flashed toward my half-out-the-window body. A laser gun sight. With a high-powered weapon on the other end.

A frantic split-second fling backward accompanied a brittle crack as bullet pierced glass. No boom, no loud report. The killer used a silencer.

I hard-smacked the tile floor, tumbled upright, and pulled my own silenced pistol. A quick leap tucked me among the room's steel cabinets. Hidden, surrounded with dead bodies. Trapped in the massive old Princess Margaret Hospital's first floor morgue in downtown Nassau, Bahamas. Great. Just freakin' great.

This guy wasn't a pro. Sloppy work. As a former Delta Force operator, I'd know. And my weapon was drawn. Unlike this clown I wouldn't miss. Advantage, Case Lee.

Another mental warning flag waved. This guy had a partner. Professionals worked solo. Clean hits, leave the scene. Non-pros brought a sidekick, for whatever reason. Support, insurance, bolstering of courage—the rationale didn't matter at the moment. What did matter was a second hitter lurked somewhere.

A simple job, Case. Investigate the deaths of two high-net-worth individuals. Rich dudes. Low profile, baby. Safe and easy. Man, I was an idiot.

The morgue door stood five paces distant and led to a quiet hallway. The hospital crowd was minimal this late at night, huddled and waiting near the emergency room entrance. Several options presented. Wait for the shooter to show at the window, his sidekick a dangerous unknown. Or move, hunt. Delta training dictated the latter.

A breeze waved the oleanders outside the window while distant palm fronds rustled in the Caribbean night. The hum of refrigerated body drawers, chemicals, and still death filled the air. The Glock maintained an aim toward the open window as rapid steps gained the door. Cracked open, a quick glance confirmed the large old colonial building's hallway stood empty. A silent slip through, the door shut behind me.

The hospital's morgue area held dim illumination late at night, every fifth overhead incandescent light lit. It made for a dark cavernous setting.

Cones of light as spaced circular stages in both hallway directions. The remnant aroma of a disinfectant mopping came as a welcome relief after the confined odor of death.

The pistol slid into my jeans front waistband, covered with the untucked shirt. I might encounter hospital staff during my hunt. The hidden pistol would avoid setting off verbal alarms. But I could produce the weapon, aim, and fire within a half second if needed—a strong likelihood.

I opted for the shorter hallway segment toward the building's rear. Around the darkened corner, exit doors. But I'd depart the hospital through another window before that option. Approaching footfalls altered my plans.

He turned the dark hallway corner, twenty-five paces away. Ubiquitous blue-green hospital scrubs, no weapon evident. I continued, prepared for a smile and nod at a passing physician or nurse. Friendly, benign, presenting little reason for recall if this hospital staff member was later questioned. Questions concerning dead hit-men.

A large man, his shoulders sloped. A surgeon, maybe. A career spent leaning over an operating table. The dim light created a challenge discerning more detail. But as we approached each other he passed through a cone of light and the danger claxon sounded. No natural arm movement accompanied his gait, hands locked along his side. As we closed distance it became clear he'd pulled the scrubs over his pants. And he wore leather sandals. Not hospital footwear. My shooter's partner. Had to be.

I stayed left. Bahamians drove and often walk left. I timed my stride so we'd meet in the shadowed area between lit circular stages. Five paces apart, then three. The internal steel spring compressed, muscles tightened, nostrils flared. We locked eyes, any pretense of a casual greeting long gone as the scene signaled killing conflict. At the final step we came abreast and he shifted toward me, attacked. A leftie. Too quick a move for the half-second pistol draw. The knife, hidden against his wrist, flicked dark and keen. He snorted an exhale and grimaced as the well-practiced motion drove the blade toward my neck. A sucker strike. But he'd never tried the killing move against a former Delta operator. Too bad for him.

The natural reaction, the human reflex—jump away. And get killed. His side-step and momentum relied on this reaction. Years of training and real-life experiences propelled me toward him. Inside his move. Right hand grabbed his knife wrist, left fist drove two explosive punches into his throat. The first damaged his windpipe, the second crushed it.

A half-second interlude. One of those weird pauses within extreme violence, a split-second mental collection point. I maintained a wrist grip. Eyes bulged, his free hand cradled his throat, mouth open as lungs sought air through a damaged pipe. Condensed, hyper-fast thoughts drove action. A dim hospital hallway. A shooter somewhere at my back. A simple push-away, Glock pulled, a silent head shot a quick and sure option. Drag the body into a nearby office.

But scattered blood and brain matter threatened a clean exit. It would draw attention from any casual passer-by. And my exit strategy consisted of a boat. I required lead time, a slipping away. And the hitter with the laser site remained in play, the clock ticking. So I'd take this guy out without a mess, without blood and with minimal struggle.

The knife first. I twisted his wrist and slammed a knee into the elbow of the knife-wielding arm. The long blade clattered on the hard tile floor. Noise. Damn. A lightning-quick slide behind him as frantic gasps for air consumed his being. I applied a sleeper hold, restricting blood flow to the brain via the carotid arteries. He was unconscious within seconds. I held it longer—much longer—than necessary, eyes down the long hallway seeking movement. All quiet. While I stood there exposed, squeezing the last bit of life from a guy. Not good.

I dragged him across the hallway. An unlocked door opened a cleaning supply closet. Dumped him inside. With a crushed trachea and too-long restriction of his carotid, he wouldn't wake up. Nasty stuff, but the guy *had* tried to kill me.

The hallway remained still. No alarms, no alerts. I retrieved the dropped knife, backtracked, and entered an empty office several doors down from the morgue. An office with a window. The colonial-style opening proved well-maintained—the hinges silent as I cracked one side of the casement window and waited.

Slipping away was an option considered and rejected. Such action left a killer with a laser-sited weapon after me. And I was headed toward the docks. The shooter, not finding me dead or wounded, might guess as much. I didn't relish the idea of a small electric-red dot seeking my back while exiting this Caribbean island. So I waited, pistol drawn, and listened through the open window to near-area silence. It wouldn't last. A few minutes passed since his attempted kill shot. The shooter would follow up, creep to the morgue window, and check the outcome. Freakin' amateur.

Chapter 2

Breaking into Caribbean island morgues wasn't a hobby of mine. Part of the gig. The investigation of untimely and so far unrelated deaths of two wealthy guys—Bettencourt and Whitmore. Earlier that day I'd left the Abaco Islands—second home and last-breath location of Mr. Joseph Wilkins Bettencourt, dead rich dude. I boated the four hours to Nassau and enquired at the morgue about tissue samples from the recently expired Bettencourt. When an American citizen dies in a non-US Caribbean island, diplomatic protocol dictates delivery of the coroner's autopsy report with tissue samples. The morgue personnel lied about possession of any such samples. Facial expressions, body movement, lack of eye contact. You can tell. You can always tell.

Bettencourt died at his house on Abaco, the body transported to Nassau, capital of the Bahamas. A coroner's report issued—death due to natural causes. Heart failure. The body cremated. They'd tossed his ashes into Nassau harbor, as per the instructions of his less-than-bereaved widow, Mrs. Elizabeth Bettencourt of Fifth Avenue, New York City.

A phone call to Mrs. Bettencourt several days earlier kicked off this little Caribbean jaunt.

"Mrs. Bettencourt?" I asked, voice low and empathetic. She'd suffered a deep personal loss. "My name is Jack Tilly, with the Providence Insurance Company."

The name held a solid, upstanding ring. Jack Tilly. Something about an insurance claim.

"Talk with my lawyers," she said. Ice slid and clinked inside a highball glass as she finished off the drink.

"Yes, ma'am. I will. I have their information," I lied. "But due diligence dictates a short chat with you. First and foremost, I'm so sorry for your loss."

"I'm not." High-heels struck marble floor, a silent pause as she crossed over a rug—oriental and expensive no doubt—followed with more footfalls. Additional ice plopped in her glass along with the glug of poured liquor.

All righty then. A less than close bond between married partners. "Well, okay. May I ask you if your husband was ill? Any health issues?"

"He was a sick bastard. More so in the last ten years."

Bettencourt was sixty three when he died.

"Okay. Sick as in poor health?"

"No. Speak with my lawyers. I don't want to think about him."

"Okay. I will. But allow me to ask you about the disposition of the body. Did you request cremation?"

Cremated bodies hid a host of ill-intents. More heel-on-marble footfalls and an aside command. "Get off there, Bovy!" Her dog or cat. A lighter flicked as Mrs. Bettencourt lit a smoke. An easy visual—drink and smoke in hand, looking down upon Central Park. And, dependent upon personal character, looking down upon her lessers scuttling about.

"Mrs. Bettencourt? The disposition of his remains?"

She took a drag and exhaled.

"A hospital down there contacted me. I told them to toss him in the ocean."

"I take it they declined your suggestion."

"The next option was cremation. So I said yes."

"And they sent you the ashes?"

"No. Flushing them down the nearest toilet comprised my second suggestion."

True love. A marvelous wonder.

"I take it they declined this suggestion as well."

"They said they'd dump his ashes in the harbor. Which suited me just fine."

"Mrs. Bettencourt, did your husband have any enemies? People who would do him physical harm?"

"Speak with my lawyers." She hung up.

Fine. An accepted part of the deal. This held the earmarks of a low key investigation. High-net-worth deaths and 'go talk with my lawyer' admonitions. No skin off my rear end. It was a dramatic departure from my past engagements. A safer, less violent vocation.

My last two jobs delivered physical and mental wounds. Bullet holes, shrapnel, an arrowhead driven into my chest. And head flotsam. The psychological scars of engaging my retired Delta brothers in violent activities with nebulous outcomes. A personal promise made—no more high-danger engagements from my client. A promise broken right out of the Caribbean chute. I clearly hadn't dialed in the low-key and safe concept.

A Miami flight followed the short phone call with Elizabeth Bettencourt about the disposition of her late husband's remains. Fine by me—cruising the

Caribbean sat a far distance from hard times. I leased a sea cruiser with a false ID and a credit card tied to a Cayman Islands bank. Procured the silenced Glock and scoped semi-automatic rifle through underground contacts. Visited a Miami quick-print. They set to work creating business cards and a three-foot wide banner, plastic, with *Dawn Reckons* in flowing black script. While the print shop performed their magic, a brief shopping trip stocked the larder with necessary items. White marine tape, a marine GPS unit, groceries, latex gloves, and Grey Goose vodka—my drink of choice.

The rented vessel afforded two advantages. One, an exit strategy. The first thing I focused on when entering an operational area was a way out. When it hit the fan, such efforts saved me more than a few times. And second, I could arrive well-armed. Locked and loaded. Credit my vocation, the bounty on my head, or a healthy dose of paranoia. Take your pick.

The boat leasing company representative smiled and waved as I left the boat slip and headed east. Once out of sight and well offshore, I switched to autopilot and handled a few chores. The white tape covered the hull's registration numbers and secured the plastic banner across the stern. It covered the boat's actual name, *Sundancer*. The name change wouldn't pass close inspection, but would do at a distance. Unplugged the boat-equipped GPS so it could no longer acquire navigation information or store my route and whereabouts. Activated my own GPS unit. Jack Tilly of the Providence Insurance Company traveled incognito.

I wadded up a paper grocery bag and tossed it overboard and cut the engines. Once I'd drifted a hundred yards away, sighted the rifle's scope, popping the paper bag. It took five shots until I was satisfied with the weapon's set-up. Mr. Tilly was good to go. Then made a vodka-rocks drink and started in earnest the six hour leg for Bettencourt's Bahamian getaway—the Abaco Islands.

The Caribbean Sea. About as fine a stretch of salt water as anywhere on this good earth. Water with such clarity it amazed. Cobalt blue washed the deepest portions, azure as the water shallowed. And celeste blue, inviting as a dream, washed beaches that ranged from white sand to black rock. Take a handful of pebbles and sow them across a sandbox with a single toss—the resulting placement would resemble the geography of the scattered islands. Islands as independent countries, and islands as territories of the US, UK, France, and the Netherlands. Each unique, each with their own flavor and feel. But with common denominators: warm water, sunshine, stunning scenery, wonderful people. A person could do a heckuva lot worse than working a Caribbean job.

A job, a contract, offered by my client. A murky outfit called Global Resolutions, based in Zurich. International arrangers for below-the-radar activities. They would select requests from business, government, or private clients. Dole them out to the appropriate contractor. I never knew the payee, the initiating client, and they would never know me. The lone exception—my last job in New Guinea. I'd been hired and played by the Company. The CIA. But under normal circumstances, I performed a job, filed a report, and collected my fee. And Global Resolutions took full advantage of my Delta background, with gnarly-leaning gigs offered.

After New Guinea I'd explained to Global Resolutions, via encrypted messages, the termination of high-risk jobs. Finito, Benito. So when this offer came over the transom, it held sedate sleuthing promise. Two dead rich guys. One in the Caribbean, one on Long Island. No known foul play. A walk in the park, Case.

☐

Chapter 3

It was simple enough finding Bettencourt's place on Abaco Island. Thank you, internet and Google Earth. Large sturdy docks extended from the expansive lawn. The mansion, seashell pink, dominated the immediate surroundings, which included a large swimming pool. I never understood the pool thing. Crystalline Caribbean waters—seventy steps from your back door. As I secured my vessel a young man strutted down the lawn and yelled toward me.

"This is private property!"

I waved back, smiled, and completed the tie-up. A small flotilla of jet skis bobbed nearby. And a very classic and very expensive mahogany-decked "dinner boat." A requirement when one wished to dine at a nearby shoreline restaurant and conveyance via vehicle or, God forbid, walking was simply too pedestrian. I didn't begrudge the super-rich their toys—hell, I'd like owning a dinner boat—but there came a point where things left the realm of "Man, that would be sweet," and drifted into plain silly.

The young man stomped onto the pier and repeated his earlier statement.

"I'm well aware of this property's situation," I said. "Jack Tilly. Providence Insurance Company. Arriving at Mrs. Bettencourt's request."

A large lie and great kick-off point.

"What does that bitch want?" Nineteen, maybe twenty, he stood, hands on hips. Crisp linen pants ruffled with the breeze. Bling—diamond-encrusted bling—hung from around his neck. A bright orange scarf hid the chains. A loop earring completed the ensemble.

"The bereaved widow asked for an assessment of her Abaco holdings." I pulled an embossed business card from my shirt pocket and handed it to the kid. Amazing what a good print shop could do for you. Very official, very professional, and very fake. The card listed a false address in Omaha, Nebraska. The phone number fed an electronic forwarding exchange, encrypted, and would ring my satellite cell phone. Until I turned off the exchange.

"Her holdings?" He paused and digested the card's information. "Joey told me this place would remain under the foundation's control long after he passed." He delivered an expansive wave toward the grounds and mansion accompanied by, "His sanctuary, he called it. His blue diamond. The crown jewel of his existence."

"Joey?"

"Mr. Bettencourt." The kid's hands returned to his waist, his stance resolute. It was damn near comical. What wasn't funny was the young man's eyes. His countenance. A mean streak lay buried there, and not deep. Along with a touch of fanaticism.

"What's this foundation?"

"He established it last year. Some kind of trust fund. In Nassau. To ensure his dream carried on."

Joey. Mr. Joseph Wilkins Bettencourt, rich dude. Sunglasses lowered, I locked eyes with the young man. Trinidadian, his accent lacked a Bahamian smooth slang or the clipped style of Barbados. A tighter enunciation. As for the foundation's status, it would remain between the solicitors in Nassau and Mrs. Bettencourt's bevy of attorneys. Good times for the bill by the hour lawyering business.

"If you feel this alleged foundation has a legal claim, I'd suggest you address it with Mrs. Bettencourt's law firm. Such matters are outside my purview. Meanwhile, let's follow appropriate protocol. I will survey the house and its condition. Ask questions. Are you capable of answering my enquiries, or should I engage someone better suited for such an activity?"

The kid's mind raced, weighing options. White flannel flapped, the Caribbean waters choppy. He chose cooperation, albeit a bit on the surly side, in case I might be an ally down the road. A conniving survivor and one never trusted.

"I can show you around. And answer questions."

"And your name?"

"Tig."

"Does Tig have a last name?"

He started a lip curl, then controlled himself. "Roberts."

"The Dread Pirate Roberts. Great." I extended an arm toward the mansion, indicating he should lead the way. He didn't catch The Princess Bride reference but turned and led the way across the lawn.

Pretty girls, pretty boys. Young, littered about, languid, waiting and hopeful and hostage. Jeez. Ol' Joey owned a private Caribbean playpen. You'd think Bettencourt—at sixty-three—well past orchestrating this act.

As we approached the pool where a half-dozen young people sunbathed, I asked, "First question, Tig. Why did you address my client in such a manner?"

"Your client?"

"Mrs. Bettencourt."

"Because she was horrible." He stopped and turned and pleaded his case. "Joey told me all about her. She is mean. Mean and bitter. She came here once." He shook his head, recalling the incident.

"When was this?"

"Last year. She just arrived. It was a surprise visit."

"Okay."

"She'd never been here. Joey never invited her."

"His wife required an invitation?"

He failed catching the incongruity. "She went crazy. Started screaming at everybody. Yelling at poor Joey. It was horrible."

"Yeah. I can well imagine." I brushed past Tig and chatted with several young people on my way toward the opened French back doors. The boys were of Caribbean origin. The girls, Eastern European. Albanian, Romanian, a real grab-bag of accents and inflections. Ages ranged from thirteen to eighteen, tilted toward the younger side. Very nice, Joey—you pedophile son of a bitch. I wished they *had* fed his body to the sharks.

The mansion displayed rich décor and professional interior decorating. Wealth oozed from every room. The garage held several Mini-Coopers so, I supposed, the kids could scoot about the island. A convertible Rolls Royce for when Joey wished a tour of the local environs.

"Did Mr. Bettencourt have a private study? A place strictly his own?"

"Yes. This way."

We climbed the expansive teakwood circular stairway. A pop song played from a closed-door room. Someone rattled pots and pans in the kitchen. An occasional half-dressed kid would wander past, cast an inquisitive look my way, and continue on. Looking lost, waiting for instructions.

"Let's take a detour for the bedroom," I said. "Quick look."

"I don't think you need to go there."

I leaned into the kid's face. "The bedroom. A quick look."

Jaw muscles clenched, Tig strode down a hallway, opened a door, and stood aside, arms crossed. Nothing unusual inside. A large bedroom with a king-size bed. Fresh sheets, the room recently cleaned. An adjoining expansive bathroom, off-white tile, and stacks of expensive towels. The medicine cabinet held few surprises.

"You don't need to look in there!" Tig said. Arms still crossed, he'd followed me into the tile cavern.

"Well, Tig. Where I do and don't look isn't your business." I shot him a hard stare. "It *is* my business."

The usual toiletries, over-the-counter pain pills, sundries. Two prescription bottles. A statin, for cholesterol control. And an industrial-sized bottle of Viagra. Atta boy, Joey. I held up the Viagra bottle, shook it Tig's direction, and raised one eyebrow. He snorted, turned on his heel, and walked away.

The private study held the usual unread leather-bound books, an antique world globe mounted on brass spindles, and a large desk. One wall displayed an oversized map of the Caribbean and Central America. Several stickpins were pushed into Costa Rica. Maybe the location of Joey's next planned retreat.

"How did he die, Tig? What were the circumstances?"

"It was terrible. Terrible. I couldn't wake him."

"You came to his room that morning?"

"Well, not exactly."

"Okay. You slept with him. Who else?"

There was no point avoiding the reality with this little slice of bacchanal heaven.

"She's gone."

Yeah. Gone. Earmarks and vibes painted a picture of tawdry life and unexpected death. Lots of folks may have wanted him dead, including the less-than-bereaved widow. A part of me couldn't blame her. But why not divorce the guy? An iron-clad prenup, social ostracizing, a strange sense of loyalty? I'd never know. And maybe he did die of natural causes. Or my personal tour guide Tig, with his eyes on a promised prize, had a hand in whacking his bosom buddy and lover Joey. I sighed—a weird, sad lifestyle. Money spent in pursuit of warped personal happiness, lapping at a perceived fountain of youth.

"So they took the body to Nassau. The coroner. Right?" I asked.

"I suppose so."

"Where he was cremated."

"So I understand."

"Was he feeling ill, Tig? Any physical complaints?"

"No. I mean, the usual aches and complaints. He was short of breath sometimes. A wonderful, wonderful man."

A peach of a man, Tig. A stellar human being.

"Did Mr. Bettencourt deal with any personal conflicts? Arguments either in-person or over the phone?"

"No. Well, with the hellbitch occasionally. But nothing else."

Mrs. Bettencourt, the hellbitch. So, here's the deal, Tig old buddy. If it came to a throw-down between you and her, my money stayed with the hellbitch. I perused the large desktop and opened drawers. Nothing of interest.

"How about business calls?" I asked. "Any regular contacts or conversations in that world?"

Tig spun the globe. The axis squeaked as it turned. "Jordan. He talked with someone named Jordan. Business stuff."

"Does Jordan have a last name?"

"I don't know it. But Joey lived here to, well, live. Relax and enjoy life."

"Yeah. Got it. What's the deal with Costa Rica?" I pointed toward the wall map. Tig shrugged, uninterested. "Any friends here on Abaco? Regular visitors?"

"We were his friends. All of us."

The globe stopped spinning. Tig set hands on hips again, challenging. The pop music down the hall changed songs. The view from the study window returned Caribbean crystal-blue water, manicured landscaping, a soft steady breeze waving palm fronds. Paradise.

"How did you get here, Tig?"

"I was hired."

"How long ago?"

"It has been two years. I did a Skype interview with Joey. He hired me right away."

"From where?"

"Nassau."

Why he'd lie didn't plop on my interest radar. He didn't wish revealing Trinidad as his origin, and I didn't care. I posed several more questions and sought insight or clues or a sense of foul play. Each question responded to with a "don't know" answer. Maybe I was missing something. Maybe not.

"Okay. I've seen enough."

"What now?"

"I'll head for the Nassau morgue. Talk with the coroner."

"I'm going to contact Joey's Nassau solicitor. That bitch isn't touching this place." His hands moved to his sides, an air of pissant righteousness radiating.

"Do what you gotta do, Tig."

At the bottom of the stairs, a teenage girl no more than fifteen and wearing a string bikini padded toward us. The breeze blew long white diaphanous curtains into the entrance hall. Someone dived into the outside pool, the splash audible over the call of gulls.

"Should I do something?" she asked Tig, a finger pointed my way. Her Eastern European accent was Ukrainian, perhaps Bulgarian. Both hotbeds of exporting sexual slaves.

"No. Not a thing," I said, preempting Tig's response. But what was there to say? Leave this place, young lady. Seek a path elsewhere. A sad moment, made more so with my lack of solid input or heartfelt advice. This girl had a father somewhere. Who would have a helluva lot more to say than no, not a thing. Tig strode toward the open front doors, and I handed the girl a business card. It was all I could think to do.

"Call me if you need anything."

A bright smile returned, teeth flashing. A kid's smile.

What a hollow and sad freakin' place. As I pulled away from the docks the strong breeze stirred the gin-clear water. Tig stood at the pier's edge and watched. Lips pursed and a lone finger tapped his mouth as he thought, cogitated, connived. I headed for Nassau and the morgue. Ten minutes later I killed the vessel's twin engines and drifted on the blue sea, Abaco bobbing in the distance. Stripped down to my birthday suit and dived in. I needed a bath.

Chapter 4

So there I knelt in the Princess Margaret hospital, waiting for my would-be killer. A fresh breeze stirred the office's curtains, my senses cranked. The latex gloves—donned when breaking into the morgue—remained. No fingerprints. A full-senses focus toward sounds and movement while biding deadly time on a Nassau night. It was a short wait.

The dry rustle of clothing brushing against oleander bushes signaled his approach. He'd shown patience, waiting for his murderous sidekick to show and provide a verbal report. Hate disappointing you, buddy, but your friend's speaking engagements were canceled. Light Nassau traffic sounded, a car horn's single short bleat far distant. Voices of a strolling couple outside the hospital grounds carried across fresh salty Caribbean night air.

The rustling stopped. He'd peek through the open window, his pistol's red dot laser moving around the room, prepared for a snap shot. A full minute ticked past before shoes scraped against the exterior wall, combined with a muted grunt. He hefted himself up and through the opening, into the morgue. My turn.

I slipped through the window and exited the oleanders onto the expansive lawn. Crept on grass alongside the landscape plants and stopped short of the morgue window. Then eased back through the foliage and pressed against the hospital wall. And again waited, ten feet from the morgue's window. The killer would stick his head out after determining I wasn't dead or wounded or there.

He turned on the morgue lights. The open window illuminated the immediate outside area, and I parked at its edge. Scooting back another ten feet afforded hidden blackness again. It made for a twenty foot nighttime headshot. Not a challenge.

Drawers and refrigerator doors opened and shut. The hitter mucked about, likely searching for the tissue sample—marked "Bettencourt"—now tucked in my jeans' front pocket. Then soft shuffling and a deep exhale. A final look around and, perhaps, resignation. The morgue lights flicked off. A motor scooter puttered down a nearby street. A lone ship's distant horn sounded. And my killer staged his final exit from this good earth.

I reconsidered a reprieve. Take a chance he wouldn't head toward the docks—my next destination. A pardon from the governor, buddy. Your lucky day. This little sortie already claimed one man. One soul.

The angst and mental musings damn near got me killed. The hitter heaved himself onto the window sill and perched. Prior to dropping on the ground, and for a variety of reasons including bad luck, he looked my way and recognized a dark figure. I remained frozen as a statue, the pistol at my side. The weapon's heft and grip of cool metal provided deadly comfort.

"Well, mon," he said, voice low and matter-of-fact. "We have a situation."

Seconds ticked by. Another scooter made its way down the street. He remained still, feet dangling. My prolonged silence became problematic, with the potential of initiating an unwanted move on his part.

"Yeah. Yeah we do."

His chin lifted, a slight head shift. Strong odds he attempted visual confirmation I was armed. With the pistol tight against my leg, deep darkness wouldn't provide him sufficient visual clues.

"We could keep this simple," he said.

"Simple is good."

"Toss me the tissue sample. Then you can walk away."

So I could get shot in the back. No thanks. But I held no burning desire to whack this guy. So I tossed him a life preserver.

"Here's a better idea. Release your weapon. Let it drop on the ground. Then you climb back inside."

I could scoop up his pistol, leave him unarmed. He wouldn't pursue. And the Bahamas chapter of this job would wrap up. But his growled chuckle sounded as a starter's pistol at a foot race. This was going down.

With a collected motion he dropped from his perch. The red dot laser flicked on and the thin beam of light whipped through the foliage as he brought his gun hand toward me.

I didn't hesitate. The Glock spit its restrained pop and the killer fell. He crumpled among the landscape bushes, splayed and still. I crouched, silent, for several minutes and ensured no observers, no foot traffic, no awareness among the citizens of Nassau. Retrieved my fired round's ejected casing. Then strolled away, across the lawn, and blended into the Nassau night.

The leased 40-foot ocean cruiser lay quiet under starlight. No other people moved about the docks at the late hour. I slipped the lines, slipped from the dock, and headed into the night, running lights off. The large twin engines could push the vessel at forty knots if needed, a more sedate thirty knot cruising speed the usual pace. Clear of the harbor, I firewalled the throttles, the engines responded, and the 200 miles separating me from south Florida began disappearing. I put the vessel on autopilot and went below. The tissue sample swapped places in the freezer with a bottle of Grey Goose. I knew a Miami toxicologist who owed me a favor and would analyze the sample.

Back on the bridge, vodka-rocks in hand, I checked the radar. Scattered traffic—the usual ships, cruisers, fishing boats. One vessel tracked my course, running parallel, a mile north. The Nassau to Miami run was well traveled, but this boat, like mine, showed no running lights. A dark and nebulous image when sighted through binoculars.

I kept the throttles pressed forward. A Bahamian police vessel would have approached full bore, cop boat lights flashing as the international waters boundary approached, twelve nautical miles away from land. But the dark vessel continued its track and matched my speed and heading.

A well-honed sense, much more than a gut feel, said I was a target. Situational awareness—too much didn't jibe. The other boat assessed me, the circumstances, and the odds. He'd consider firepower, mine and his, and weigh options. The possibility of pirates loomed—the real deal. The Caribbean was a hot-spot for piracy. Among the watery Caribbean turf, the Windward Islands—Dominica to Trinidad—held the largest number of high seas desperados. But they could appear anywhere.

The pistol wasn't my lone weapon. A quick trip below produced the semi-automatic rifle. But the weapon's scope provided no further defining features of the tracking vessel, the distance too great.

A mile into international waters, I cut the throttle back to a creep. Two or three knots, as the Caribbean rollers lifted and slow-rocked the vessel. If pirates, they'd make their move now. International waters, their quarry wallowing among the sea swells.

But the radar indicated the dark vessel slowed as well. Its onboard contingent planned and weighed the next move. Lurked. We rolled through swells together for five minutes. My slow-down sent a dual message—I'm aware of you, and I'm not running. Bring it on. A weird game of high stakes saltwater chicken.

The dark vessel turned and goosed its engines. The radar displayed the electronic reflection pull away, headed back toward Nassau. Enemy, pirate, disinterested party—I might never know. But the scoped rifle stayed with me.

I pressed the throttles and cruised at thirty knots. The dark vessel disappeared over the radar's horizon. I held a powerful dislike of such unknowns. Unknowns affecting the health and wellbeing of Case Lee, Esq. Unknowns such as who arranged the two dead hitters. That little turd Tig topped the list as the person who'd called ahead. But he wouldn't setup my morgue greeting committee. I couldn't see it. No, he contacted a boss, an arranger. So no clue who drove this little conspiracy regarding Bettencourt's demise, and it sat well outside the scope of this engagement. My job—assess and paint the landscape picture. If others wished further action from my findings, fine. It wouldn't be me.

I boxed away the dark vessel and the dead killers, relishing the glorious swath of horizon-to-horizon stars, and refused dropping into contemplative mode. Soon enough I'd hit Miami and drop the sample off with the toxicologist. Slip into my own dark movements, off the radar. The Bahama leg of this gig was now over and done.

My dearest friend from Delta days, Bo Dickerson, would say it rolls and tumbles. Life. Take it for what it is, even if it means along for the ride, a languid hand draped over the wheel, bearing life's ocean rollers with aplomb. So I attempted a door slam on the blues, tried bolting the hatch closed against introspection. Tried adopting a Bo mindset and revel in the here and now. A good and fine place, cruising the Caribbean, black night, with wind and saltwater and isolation. And thoughts of two more dead bodies racked up, courtesy of Case Lee.

A simple gig with a few minor wrinkles. Piece of cake, Case. No worries, other than someone now wanted me dead. Well, nothing new there.

Chapter 5

I dropped the tissue sample with the toxicologist in Miami and caught a Norfolk flight. Rented a car and disabled the vehicle's GPS a mile from the rental car terminal—a lesson learned from my last engagement. Returned to my boat tied in Chesapeake. My home, the *Ace of Spades*.

The *Ace* presented an image of what could be termed "well used." I preferred a different perspective. She possessed a certain panache. A comforting home and a bit worn around the edges and steadfast. She got me from A to B, every time. A blue tarp stretched across the foredeck, shielding my throne from the elements. The throne—an old La-Z-Boy recliner patched with duct tape. Heirloom tomato plants lined a railing, accepting sun. The wheelhouse was small and cluttered and equipped with bullet-proof windows. As much as I appreciated the sleek fiberglass Caribbean cruiser, there was something about an old wooden boat. A feel, a sense, a soul.

The *Ace* also held my armory. So I loaded the rental vehicle's trunk with select weaponry. A change of plans, the Long Island flight canceled. An eight hour Hamptons drive waited. I would arrive well-armed—a luxury unavailable for air travelers. An overreaction, sure, maybe. But Nassau changed my immediate outlook on the here and now.

The engagement's mission hadn't changed—provide my client a thorough investigation of two deaths. Two still-unrelated deaths. Bettencourt dead of natural causes as per the coroner—although the morgue assassination event pointed elsewhere. Someone wanted his tissue sample locked down. But the violence and killing and ugly undertow of Bettencourt's death might be contained within the Bahamas. Or the Bahamas and NYC, where no doubt Elizabeth Bettencourt held a stable of high-priced lawyers locked and loaded. A messy combination of hurt feelings, anger, chosen lifestyle, and upcoming legal fights. A toxic combination that brought out the long knives. And an attempted whacking of me. So be it.

But the chance Bettencourt's demise stood boxed as an isolated event was thin gruel. This Global Resolutions job sought a relationship between Bettencourt and the Long Island death. So, yeah, decent odds these two expired rich dudes connected. Figure it out, report out, haul ass out. Get back to cruising the Intracoastal Waterway. The Ditch.

The *Ace of Spades* and the Ditch afforded dual opportunities. A wandering lifestyle, sedate, solid. And it kept me a moving target. A big deal. I carried a million dollar bounty on my head. Courtesy of an unknown sponsor we'd mightily pissed off during our Delta days. A bounty that cost me my wife, Rae. A Damocles sword dangling over me and my family and my three former Delta blood brothers. Some of us handled the hanging reality better than others.

But even with the attempted murder of yours truly, I took comfort knowing I worked a job without spies, global gamesmanship, or professional operators and hitters coming out of the freakin' woodwork. Which drove my initial hesitancy at contacting Jules of the Clubhouse when I decided to take this job. It held no tingles of geopolitical intrigue, no scent of spooks. No CIA, no Russian FSB, no Chinese MSS, no MI6. Nope. A plain vanilla sleuthing gig. But with the ante upped, plans and actions changed. So I contacted Jules and asked for an immediate meeting. Her web stretched across the globe, and little escaped her watchful eye. Clubhouse information had saved my butt more than once.

Jules replied to my message—encrypted, deep web—with her usual tight manner. *Drop by. Now.* After Nassau, it was important venturing forth with someone on my side. Someone minding the informational store. Just in case. She rarely disappointed.

So a quick trip to Spookville lay in store. A world and collective mindset filled with gamed scenarios, lies, and shadow. The incongruence of a Clubhouse visit for a supposed gumshoe gig wasn't lost on me. Jules didn't simply wade in clandestine waters, she lived in them. Deep down.

Before the Clubhouse visit, I set up the next day's Long Island agenda. Geoffrey Whitmore was seventy-three when he drowned in his Hamptons pool. The widow, Melinda Whitmore, was now parked at their estate. She also owned a NYC place—not far from Mrs. Bettencourt's digs—and an AVI getaway. The American Virgin Islands. She hadn't raised suspicious hackles at the Jack Tilly, Providence Insurance Company line. I worked through both a housekeeper and personal secretary to chat with her.

"What may I do for you, Mr. Tilly?" Mrs. Whitmore asked.

"Just a few simple questions, ma'am. I assure you there's nothing wrong with the policy, everything is in good stead. We're required to make a few enquiries. A few loose ends. It's company protocol."

"Fine. I have a moment now. But only a moment."

A high-end accent, taught and affectated. Filled with style, class, and a humanizing lilt. I liked it.

"Actually, I'll be in your neck of the woods tomorrow." Your neck of the woods. Simple, homey, nice. Non-threatening. "May I drop by? Nothing beats face-to-face. At least in the insurance business. It won't take long, and my apologies for the inconvenience."

"A moment, Mr. Tilly." She cradled the phone against her body, the call to her secretary muffled. "Sally, what's my schedule tomorrow?"

An indiscernible response from Sally. Then back to me.

"Mr. Tilly? Between one and two in the afternoon. Let's remove those loose ends." It came with a soft touch of humor. A nice lady.

I signed off with an innocuous "Thanks for your time, and I'll see you tomorrow." A routine visit required of the insurance business. It would salve any suspicions she might possess and prevent a call to her law firm or a quick internet search for Mr. Jack Tilly or the Providence Insurance Company. I'd arrive the next day, we'd chat, and I'd leave. Melinda Whitmore saw it as routine. No big deal.

I parked and headed toward the Filipino dry cleaners below the Clubhouse. A rough part of Chesapeake and the usual scenario. Door handle bell rang, emotionless eyes stared, the Glock placed on the counter and covered with someone's dropped-off dress shirt. Through a side door, up squeaky wooden stairs, and two knocks on a steel door. A metallic lock mechanism clanged. Remote controlled, it announced the Clubhouse was open for business.

She squinted down the sawed-off shotgun's twin barrels, elbows on the desk, her one eye bright and capturing.

"He arises as the phoenix, new and improved and bristling with vigor. Empty your pockets and turn for me, dear."

I did. Her fingertips displayed a sealant sheen, preventing the spread of fingerprints. Her eyepatch band still lost among the short unruly crop of self-barbered hair. But an unexpected addition threw me. The fly-away ends of her coif were dyed. This was new. And unlike the popular colors of blue or pink or red often applied to spiked tips, she'd chosen white. Sheet white, bright, suspended above indeterminate-age gray. It lent a halo-like affect, or a medusa presentation—both applicable dependent upon her mood and moment.

"He presents before me a reformed man, a staid businessperson," she said, cheek pressed against the shotgun's wooden stock. "A quick question, dear. And not as an opening salvo to breach closed doors, mind you."

I completed my pirouette. One hand held a money clip of Benjamins. The Clubhouse was, above all, a place of business as the old abacus resting on her wooden desk indicated.

"Shoot. Figuratively speaking."

She chuckled and asked, "How shall your new life stance mollify your wild side?"

"No wild side left, Jules. New Guinea took it out of me."

She gestured with her shotgun toward two uncomfortable old wooden chairs. I sat. The shotgun returned to her desktop near the embedded KA-BAR knife. The knife was a permanent fixture. Desktop décor.

"You returned a legend, Odysseus. Polished bright. The web exalted your accomplishments."

She didn't mean the internet web. She referenced the Jules web, sticky filaments spread across the globe with collected information on the outcome of my last contract.

"And I must add," she continued, opening a drawer and producing a long thin cigar. "My admiration for your efforts knows no bounds. Quite the little jungle fandango."

"Ugly, pointless business."

A wry smile was her sole response as the sealed tip of the cigar twirled against the KA-BAR knife. The Cirque de Soleil poster still occupied one steel wall, the lone item considered true decoration. My statement, which I regretted, stood inappropriate in The Clubhouse. Depending on a person's perspective, Jules often dealt with ugly, pointless business. Maybe it was the hair. It rattled me seeing her with any stylistic affectation. White tips. Bright white. Mercy.

"I understand you and your friends suffered several injuries. And carry the ache of a lost opportunity."

She fired a kitchen match along the arm of her chair and leaned back, assessing her client. Cigar smoke wafted around her head. The lost opportunity referenced a brief chance to identify the bounty's funding source. Jules cracked open the door for my spook-filled elaboration on the subject. I declined.

"I'm avoiding that world from now on. Hence the staid businessperson."

"Hmm. When might I meet your compatriots? They represent exceedingly handy individuals by anyone's estimation."

Catch and Bo, who'd accompanied me in New Guinea. A Clubhouse opportunity, new clients, fresh meat for the clandestine grinder. But Catch couldn't stand spooks of any stripe. And Bo—well, Bo wasn't a draw-inside-the-lines individual. By any stretch of the imagination.

"Don't think that's happening, Jules. Like your hair."

She inspected the cigar's smoldering end. "Apparently the change was quite disturbing for my downstairs tenants. One of the elderly Filipinos crossed herself upon viewing my new look. I wasn't aware it would have an ecumenical affect."

"Still figuring if it lends style or statement."

"Both. A style reflecting connectivity with current cultural mores. The statement is, well, open to interpretation."

I smiled. Not at her claim, but at the whole package. Jules of the Clubhouse. "A simple and honest broker of information," she often described herself. Buying and selling information, with an emphasis on the government clandestine variety. But she also kept a finger well-dipped in the industrial espionage pie. And for this reason, she might provide me value.

"I've received a new contract offer."

"A gentle sidestep. Less vigorous than a tango. A waltz perhaps."

"What?"

"You bypass an opportunity." She puffed again, blew smoke toward the ceiling, and scratched beneath her chin. "An opportunity to edify this poor creature regarding the final events of your last engagement. A pity." She used her non-cigar hand and felt the tips of her white spikes, ensuring, I supposed, they were still there. "Allow me a moment to recover from the hurt."

One eyebrow raised, she cast a tight smile. Her second attempt at pulling more information from the New Guinea job remained on the table. I held a monetary credit with the Clubhouse—more actionable information delivered from past jobs than consumed. It wouldn't hurt padding my side of the ledger.

"Okay. I'll share. But only if it's worth something to you, Jules. Don't want your time wasted."

She scowled, my statement a broadside reference to payment for the download. The old wooden abacus was lifted, shaken, and the black balls realigned across the top railings. I did a brain dump and filled her with details. Jules listened and absorbed the highlights and lowlifes, the treachery and ugliness. Five black abacus balls slid down their respective rails during the discussion.

"I shall use an expression beyond trite, but most applicable," she said. "You are lucky to be alive."

"And now a sedate sleuthing career. Case Lee, private investigator. Stolen art, misplaced yachts, dog rescue."

"Which shall last for the shortest of periods. You are not of that ilk, Poirot."

"Am now."

"Then why are you here, dear? Other than to place me deeper in your economic debt."

She eased open the selling side of the store, the Clubhouse ledger's debit side waiting entries.

"Thought you might have information regarding the demise of two high net worth individuals."

"I sit with bated breath." Her eye squinted with focus, the chair's arm supported her elbow, chin nestled in an upright palm. Smoke drifted from the cigar in her other hand.

"Joseph Wilkins Bettencourt. Of Fifth Avenue and the Bahamas. He died in the latter. The paperwork says natural causes. The two guys sent to whack me in Nassau would indicate otherwise."

"May I surmise you have ventured forth without first engaging my services?"

"A cut-and-dried job, Jules. Two dead rich guys. And all I'm looking for is background. And possible connectivity."

"I can hardly hear you, dear. The shock of bypassing our protocol roars in my ears."

She stared at the Cirque du Soleil poster, an affected expression of hurt troweled thick.

"A simple contract. Hardly up to your standards," I said.

"Simple? When will you learn the one big item?"

"Big item?"

She wafted a hand, dismissive. "But here you are. Seeking succor and nourishment from this hurt creature. After venturing off without so much as a fare-thee-well."

"Attempted murder of yours truly adds a layer of intrigue. A small, thin layer."

"Perhaps it is time I head to pasture."

"Jules."

"A valued client and dear man no longer requires my services."

"Jules. Can we get back to Bettencourt?"

"Care to share the events in Nassau?"

"When I return from Long Island. Then I can provide big picture."

"Fair enough, I suppose."

"Bettencourt?"

She adopted a business-like attitude, the hurt act's point taken. "Old money. But old money does dabble in the wrong ponds with regularity. Go on."

"Geoffrey Whitmore. Long Island, New York City, American Virgin Islands. He died on Long Island."

"Industrialist. Shipping, oil, real estate. High net worth, indeed."

"Anything more definitive, Jules? Something actionable?"

"You ask me to acquire backstory and connectivity between these two gentlemen?"

She smiled and raised the abacus parallel with the desktop.

"Yeah. That would be great."

Tilted vertical, my five-abacus-ball credit disappeared up the rails. Transaction sealed. I didn't mind. Sprinkling the Global Resolutions report with her insight would help pave the way for future and perhaps more sedate private investigator contracts. All good.

"Done and done. Do provide me a few days," she said.

"I'm heading to Long Island. I'll check back after that visit."

"A solid timeline. I look forward to our next convocation. Now, are you healing well? From your last little foray?"

"Aches and pains. The usual."

A hidden button was pushed and the metallic click of the door lock sounded.

"Perhaps this current engagement is a good thing, double-oh-seven. A pause before your next deep dive."

I stood and turned toward the door. "Deep dives are off the menu."

"For today. Meanwhile, tip your fedora to the downstairs ladies. And do endeavor, for once, to accept the big item."

"Okay, fill me in."

"A jaundiced eye cast toward your world. Regardless of the endeavor."

"Don't know how that would help, Jules."

"Much greater than mere help. It's life enabling. For nothing is *ever* as it seems, dear."

She puffed the cigar and tilted her head. We locked eyes, I sighed, and she smiled.

"Now depart. Eyes in the back of your head, Mr. Lee. The big item requires it."

Chapter 6

Six long road hours with the intent of finishing the Hamptons trip the next day. I hugged the coast until Wilmington, Delaware then joined crowded interstate traffic. Nothing relaxing about that leg of the trip. Past Philly, into New York City, and onto Long Island. I parked it at a hotel two hours from the Hamptons. A call from my Miami toxicologist arrived as I left the hotel room's shower.

"Hey, I've got your results," he said. The carbonated snap of a beer can opening came over the line. "You do run with a strange crowd. No doubt about it."

"How strange?"

"Well, first the good news, if you can call it that."

"Okay."

"Your guy was poisoned. So there's that working for you. If you're looking for skullduggery."

"The guy died in his sleep. At least according to a witness."

"I believe it. Yes, indeed."

So Bettencourt was poisoned. Less than a surprise given the Nassau goon squad greeting.

"Not following you," I said.

"A small injection of this stuff would put him away in seconds. No fuss, no muss."

"What stuff?"

"Tetrodotoxin."

"Okay."

"It's derived from either the blue-ringed octopus or puffer fish."

"Either of those in the Caribbean?"

"Puffers."

"All right. A local poison. Instant death. Got it."

A towel wrapped around my waist, I stretched out a few kinks. Recent wounds barked back.

"Not so fast. You haven't heard the cool part."

"Not sure there's a cool part."

"Yeah there is. Oh, yeah. This tetrodotoxin was altered in a high-end lab. The result creates a much more rapid reaction. Instant adios."

"So a pro did it. Or supplied it. All right."

"Yeah, maybe. It would have to be one hell of a pro. The only other time you see this stuff is with government hitters."

Nope and no way. Not headed down that rabbit hole. The toxicologist clearly wanted to speculate about James Bond stuff. No siree, this was isolated to a Caribbean hit based on greed or anger or a business deal gone bad.

"Let's stick with pro."

"You can bury the ostrich head, but I'm telling you. CIA, Mossad, FSB, MI6, MSS—the usual cast."

Nope. Not this time. Clandestine concerns wouldn't enter this engagement.

"Okay. Got it. Thanks."

"No problem. It's cool stuff. I mean, I don't run across exotic toxins often. The point is, you'll want to keep your head low."

"A regular practice, but thanks." I signed off.

Bettencourt was murdered by a hired hitter. That took money and contacts. Elizabeth Bettencourt owned the former, but I couldn't see her with the contacts. It opened the door for several possibilities. A soured business deal or a simple whack job tied to the Abaco trust fund Tig mentioned. But a high-end toxin was rare, so a real pro had his or her hand in the mix.

An outside hitter wouldn't deliver the lethal injection during the dead of night. Too risky, given the several bodies draped across the bed and the crowd of kids living there. So the poison was delivered by someone at rancho pedophilia. A proxy killer. Tig shared the top of the list along with the other "she's gone" bed partner.

It would go in the Global Resolutions report. Someone else could figure it out. Meanwhile I would capture information on part two of the puzzle from Melinda Whitmore. She was too far from the Caribbean for grave hitter concerns. Unless both Bettencourt and Geoffrey Whitmore held joint business dealings in conflict with major players. Major players who used murder as part of their business model. In which case Long Island no longer presented benign turf.

But I held no hyper-alert moments. This was the Hamptons. Playground of New York wealthy. Old, old money. Toss in a few celebrities for added spice at the yacht club parties. Hardly shoot-'em-up central. Besides, my vehicle held enough armament for any local threats.

A glorious day dawned, and I dropped thoughts of toxins, murders, hit men, and dark trailing boats. Spent the morning headed toward the Hamptons, passing sweet beaches, farms, and quaint tourist villages. Each village boasted an art scene, albeit a bit contrived. Handsome folks walked, meandered into shops, and sat at outdoor cafes. High-end sunglasses were aplenty. I enjoyed the air, the feel, and spent an hour at an outdoor table, back against the bistro's exterior wall taking it in. Pleasant and fine and cause for consideration that this contract—other than the Abaco and Nassau ugliness—could be all right. Yessir.

Estates. Mercy, were there estates. Hedges or expensive faux-rustic fences or both surrounded the individual kingdoms. Each estate was prepped and manicured. Summer had arrived and the Hamptons were in full social swing. Folks poured from the city for the Season. Then back to New York for the fall and maybe later a Hawaii or Caribbean estate, avoiding the bitter winter winds. Make the social loop, season dependent, and do it again, year after year.

The old money lifestyle was well and good for them, but you couldn't help wonder what anchored their lives. What would they reflect upon once old age hit, the grim reaper knocking? What thoughts and remembrances would they relish? Parties, soirées, cocktails with their fellow Big Money travelers at charity functions where writing a large check salved a few pangs but failed to fulfill? I'd never know. But listed high on their positive side—they didn't mess with Case Lee. And I reciprocated. Live and let live, baby.

I'd sussed the Whitmore estate on Google Earth. Twelve acres, nestled against an Atlantic Ocean inlet. A massive house, pool, and a couple of ponds—situated between other similar abodes. But satellite views fail to do the ground-level experience justice.

Approaching the estate I passed a parked sedan, the male occupant staring at a map. Who looked at maps with a navigation-enabled cell phone handy? But the guy's head remained down, studious, lost among the wandering estates. A UPS truck exited an estate driveway, took the usual right turn, and ground down the road. A breeze blew, my windows down, the air crisp and salty. I'd donned slacks and a light linen sports coat. Appropriate attire for a business visit. And appropriate attire for hiding the Glock-filled waistband holster.

The intercom at the Whitmore's gated entrance was reachable from the car window. I pressed the button, a voice enquired, and the gate swung open for Jack Tilly with the Providence Insurance Company.

The entrance road was plain vanilla concrete, which wouldn't do. So the builders set cross-patterned bricks along the narrow road's shoulders. A sea of manicured lawn, well fertilized and dark emerald green. Somewhere, a riding lawn mower fleet sat waiting for a call to action. At tasteful lawn intervals were architected landscape islands. Trees, shrubs, flowers. I was a bit of a sucker for landscapes, and the lawn islands were photo-capture worthy.

The mansion was over twenty thousand square feet. Single level, it ate a substantial chunk of real estate. But the building architects had performed an amazing job—the structure invited rather than intimidated. A beach house. One helluva beach house.

A housekeeper answered the front door, smiled, and stepped aside. Behind her, a well-dressed and officious young woman approached, hand extended.

"Mr. Tilley. Sally Richards. Mrs. Whitmore's secretary."

I smiled and nodded a "Hi" as we shook.

Sally cut right to the chase.

"Mrs. Whitmore is terribly busy. I would hope you will respect her time."

"Of course."

"And respectful of the terrible loss she recently suffered."

"An unfortunate aspect of my job, Ms. Richards. Dealing with the bereaved. I assure you, my unbounded empathy." Delivered with an understanding nod, grim, heartfelt.

I cleared the Sally Richards litmus test, and she signaled me to follow. We weaved through the house toward the back ocean-view rooms. White. White walls, white ceilings, white comfortable furniture. Light blonde hardwood floors and subtle patterned flat-weave rugs. Fresh cut flowers rose from massive vases, tasteful artwork placed at irregular intervals. The interior decorators pulled off an impressive feat. The vast interior space did, for a fact, possess a weekend beach house look and feel. Comfortable and inviting. Maybe not old shoe comfortable—we were talking Fifth Avenue footwear—but neither daunting nor off-putting. Damn impressive.

Melinda Whitmore rose from a cushioned wicker chair, one of many arranged across a playing-field sized covered back porch. Tables and chairs placed as unique sitting areas created a collection of lounging rooms across the vast open space. More fresh cut flowers, more white, more old money covered with a patina of our simple little beach house. It brought a smile—craftsmanship in the interior decorating field, done this well, deserved it.

"I hope I interpret the smile correctly, Mr. Tilly." She approached with her own smile and hand extended. "You appreciate my little abode."

"Spot on, ma'am. Well done you and your decorator."

"Melinda. Please. And may I address you as Jack? Or do your friends use another moniker?"

Mid-forties, lissome, and comfortable in her own skin. Slacks, silk blouse, her styled hair perfect. And a real smile, genuine. A striking woman.

"Jack is fine. And first and foremost, my sincere sympathies for your loss."

She nodded toward Sally who turned and clacked away on the hardwoods. "I'm well past that, Jack. Let's not dwell on my feelings."

She extended a hand and offered a nearby chair. A small glass-topped table sat between us.

"What may I provide you in the way of something to drink?" She signaled into the large interior room as she sat. Another housekeeper appeared. "And please don't refuse the offer. Let's forego the requisite sense of manners and business protocol."

"I'm fine, thank you." I placed a Providence Insurance Company business card within easy reach in case she wished to peruse my authenticity.

She delivered a fine semblance of a controlled Barnard College laugh, light and lilting. "I just reviewed my stance on the matter. A position clearly falling on deaf ears. Now once again, a chilled beverage? Ice tea? Beer? Cocktail?"

"A beer sounds great. Thank you." Delivered with my own genuine smile.

"Lager, pilsner, or stout?"

The offer of a stylistic beer selection at a private domicile was a first.

"Lager, please."

She nodded at the housekeeper and added, "I will join Mr. Tilly. An afternoon beer. It does sounds marvelous."

Returning her attention to me, she asked, "Now, how may I help you, Jack?"

31

Melinda orchestrated with a firm velvet-covered hand, all class and appeal and comfort. I was sucked in and didn't mind it one little bit.

Chapter 7

Melinda waited with a pleasant smile and upright posture.

"A bit of a painful endeavor, I'm afraid. May I ask a few questions about your late husband?"

"We've addressed the emotional aspect. I'm well past any pain. Please ask away."

I did. "I understand your husband drowned in the pool."

"Geoffrey often swam. It was a component of his fitness regimen."

"At night."

"Yes. He would often do so prior to retiring for the evening."

"Anyone else here that night?"

"I'm afraid not. I was in the city. A function, with my attendance required. And we have no overnight staff."

"Who found him?"

"Poor Sally. Early the next morning. It was terribly traumatic for her, without doubt. The local constabulary were immediately engaged of course."

"Was your husband in good health? I mean, any illness or heart issues that might lead to his death?"

"He was seventy-three, Jack. By no means a young man such as yourself." She locked hands over a crossed-leg knee. Her off-white slacks held tight creases. Tiny fine lines crinkled with interest at the edges of her eyes.

The housekeeper entered and placed two tall lager beer glasses between us. The liquid bubbled light gold, the soft foam head perfect. Man, I could get into this lifestyle.

As the housekeeper slipped away, Melinda continued. "In lieu of your standard litany of questions, may I suggest covering background? The complete picture as it were. A rather mundane picture I'm afraid, but it may help settle whatever angst your company maintains over Geoffrey's insurance policy. Then we may all move on."

"That would be great. Thanks." The beer was excellent. The swimming pool and expansive lawn lent an air of summer tranquility. The lawn ended at a short wrought iron and brick fence adjoining the beach. The Atlantic cast easy waves onto the shore, and the interior view across the small table showed better than fine. The lone board member of Case Lee Inc. voted a hearty aye for this new and improved business model.

"This was Geoffrey's third marriage. My second. We both came from old lines of industrial wealth. Beginning in the 1800s." She sipped her beer and used a folded linen napkin to pat the remnant foam from her upper lip. "I suppose it's familiarity that drives such marriages. It is the same for our circle of friends. You see, money isn't an issue for either party."

"You married inside your tribe. Nothing new there."

She smiled and cocked her head. "How well put. Our tribe."

Melinda laid the we-were-both-rich card, dismissing potential motive for wishing hubby dead. Fair enough. As far as I knew, he'd died in a swimming accident. The police report and autopsy showed no signs of murder. But I did share a small parcel of Jules's jaundiced worldview and wouldn't put anything past business activities in the rarified air of multi-billion dollar deals. And I held no illusion of crime-solving acumen if one was committed. But besides determining connectivity between the two dead men, part of my job was to ascertain the simple matter of natural vs. inflicted death. I did know a bit about that.

"And perhaps tribal familiarity bred contempt," she continued. "Geoffrey became bored with our relationship. But at his age, I didn't fear the muss of closet mistresses."

I nodded and appreciated the candor. I hadn't asked for this level of personal detail and sat there unclear of the purpose. Meanwhile, I couldn't let go of the guy drowning in his own pool. It wasn't that large a pool, and he could have made one of the sides without much effort.

Melinda appeared contemplative while delivering an unblinking stare. I didn't have the foggiest notion where her thoughts rambled. Lots of options there, but I wanted to keep the train on the tracks.

"Do you folks own a dog?"

Head cocked, she raised an eyebrow.

"What a peculiar question."

"I know. Sorry. Just capturing the situation so we can push the policy through."

Situational awareness. Hammered into us during Delta Force training. Weather, flora, fauna. Cultural attributes, individual behavioral tendencies. I already knew the weather the night Geoffrey died. A light summer rain, quarter moon, minimal wind.

"I'm afraid we don't own a dog. Or cats. Or ferrets, snakes, or parakeets." She chuckled and took another sip of beer. Man she was the whole package. Alluring as hell. "Now tell me about Jack Tilly. A touch of quid pro quo if you don't mind." She bent forward and patted my leg.

Well, Melinda Whitmore, not a lot to tell. Live on an old wooden boat, plying the Intracoastal Waterway. The Ditch. So no home address. And no cocktail parties, charity fundraisers, or yacht clubs. And as gorgeous as I find you, there's this little matter of a bounty on my head which you'd find a tad off-putting. The whole people trying to kill me and collect thing.

"Live in Omaha. Single. Like golf and reading. Pretty boring stuff."

"Now why in the world are you single? From where I sit there is absolutely no excuse for such a situation."

She took another sip and scoped me stem to stern, aware I watched her perusal.

"Maybe I'm too boring. Don't know."

"No. No, there's something else behind those eyes. A glimmer of wildness. Do you have a wild side, Jack?"

Only when I'm forced to kill people, Melinda. Things get pretty wild then.

"Nope. Sorry. Plain vanilla, I'm afraid."

"Hmm." She didn't buy it, but left backgrounds and proclivities alone. "Anyone your late husband might consider an enemy? Anyone who would wish him harm?"

"Not unless you consider spats with other board members at the yacht club. The latest was something about the harbor master. Hardly a death struggle." She laughed again and those ice-blue eyes bore into mine with serious connectivity.

Sally approached, her flats padding across the interior room hardwoods. She stopped at the porch opening. "No offense Mr. Tilly, but there is a schedule Mrs. Whitmore must adhere to today."

"A few more minutes," Melinda said.

Sally retreated. I drained the beer.

"Did your husband maintain a study? A place where he conducted business?"

She took a final delicate swallow of her brew, patted her lips again, and slid upright. A wry smile and bright eyes accompanied, "He did. It's on the other side of the house. Would you care to escort me there?"

35

We drifted away from the professional realm and into the personal with upper crust style. Nothing blatant or overt but signals and signs aplenty. Even for a social idiot like me.

"Love to." I regretted the wording and tacked on a follow-up. "If it's not too much of an inconvenience. A little final due diligence. Then out of your hair."

"It is hardly an inconvenience, Jack."

She locked an arm with mine and led us indoors. A social gesture, full of bonhomie and familiarity and something else. Oh man.

We passed Sally near the main entrance hall and headed for the mansion's private quarters.

"Sally, Mr. Tilly wishes to inspect Geoffrey's study. Please don't disturb us."

"The Bryce-Coddington affair starts early, ma'am."

"As I'm well aware. Arrange for hair and makeup in an hour, please." She continued directing me down a wide, white hallway. More flat-weave patterned rugs, more comfortable hallway furniture, more masses of cut flowers filling basket-sized vases. "And please don't disturb me until then," she added over her shoulder. Sally didn't reply.

Chapter 8

Whitmore's study abandoned the beach house look. It held subdued light due to dark paneling. I rubbed a hand across the soft leather of a wingback chair with matching ottoman. A massive desk built from old timber filled one side of the room. Odds high an old sailing ship's timber. This was old-school décor. Paintings of fox hunting scenes, the dogs and horses and gentlemen riders anticipating a rousing day afield. And paintings of stormy seas with tossed sailing ships battling the elements. There was a large stone fireplace, logs arranged and ready for the match.

"Nice study."

"I find it rather stuffy. But this was Geoffrey's room. This, and his own bedroom."

I wasn't walking the Geoffrey's own bedroom trail so I sidled over to the desktop. Mont Blanc pens were left in casual order, a few papers, a glass-bottled three-mast schooner. And a folded map.

The map opened to a detailed topographic representation of Costa Rica and Panama. With a hand-drawn line in bright felt-tip marker from coast-to-coast across Costa Rica. Bingo. Whitmore and Bettencourt held an interest in Central America business. Whether I could hitch their deaths to this endeavor remained a TBD.

But I held an ace in the hole. Jules. She'd fill the empty spaces. Produce connectivity, expose a trail. Meanwhile, I held a sliver of hope the Nassau greeting committee remained related to Bettencourt's estate and lifestyle and nothing else. Lots of room for killing motivation there. Otherwise, events moved to a larger stage.

"Did your husband discuss Central America business interests?"

"No. Or not that I'd remember. We seldom discussed such things." She floated about the room, straightening a painting and adjusting the spines of leather-bound books.

"Did he mention any names? With regard to business dealings?"

"Only the usual. We do tend to conduct business with known acquaintances. Our tribe, as it were."

She replied over her shoulder, arms crossed and wearing a casual expression.

"So no nefarious third world dictators? Pirates of the Caribbean? Asiatic opium merchants?"

We both laughed.

"I'm afraid not."

"May I take this map?"

"I'd rather you didn't. At the moment, Geoffrey is gone and I'm contemplating new adventures. Meanwhile, you strike me as the type of man who stirs things up. So please leave the map and leave suspicions and conspiracies tucked away."

She approached, eyes filled with possibilities. Another blouse button was now released, performed no doubt while viewing the hard-bound books.

"I shall toss you a bite, a nibble. And no more," she said. "There is something else I wish to show you."

This would be interesting. Both the nibble and the something else.

"He complained once or twice about a Pettis. Geoffrey simply referred to him as Pettis. No first name. He was new money, a Californian as I recall. A bit on the aggressive side apparently. A nouveau riche attitude, one might say. An individual not to Geoffrey's taste."

She took my hands and eased well into my personal space.

"Okay. Pettis. Good. Thank you."

"Was there anything else, Jack? I do fatigue of this."

"The Bettencourts. Did the two of you associate with them?"

"A bit. We brushed against them at functions. A shame that Joe also passed." She edged a few inches closer. "I believe Geoffrey got along well with Joe Bettencourt. Elizabeth was, well, not to my taste."

"So, here, the city, and AVI. How much time did the two of you spend at each place?"

"Ugg." She released one hand and tugged the other, headed for the study's door. "You are persistent to the point of distraction."

"Well?"

"Mostly the city. We'd spend summers here. During winter's cold, a Virgin Islands respite. And we did not always travel together. Now enough. Come with me."

A right turn out the study door, another wide hallway—white again—and seventy feet later we stopped at a wide door. During our little stroll, she'd used her free hand and unbuttoned more of the blouse, evidenced by lace-lifted décolletage when she turned and addressed me at the mystery entrance.

"I recently acquired a new duvet for my bed. Would you like to see my duvet, Jack?" She took both hands again and pulled herself closer. She smelled of jasmine body wash and Chanel.

The stovetop cranked up and the flame hissed. And I tried, *tried* to maintain a grip on the mission.

"I do have a concern, Melinda."

"What might that be?" She pressed against me.

"A serious concern your blouse is defective," I said, false worry and real humor plastered thick. "The buttons keep coming undone."

We both laughed. Hers trailed off much faster than mine.

"Shall we cross the threshold?" she asked, releasing a hand and grasping the brass doorknob.

A large chunk of me said "Hell yes," and I didn't hesitate admitting it. Few, if any, straight males wouldn't embrace the same emotion. A no-strings offer from a gorgeous woman. An enticing woman filled with fun and class and a slice of what's-behind-the-door mystery. But a smaller chunk, weighty, constituted a firm anchor in my makeup. I'd never gone for the quick liaisons, the frantic clutching and spent relief. I was an emotional sucker, with emotional ties part and parcel of the whole deal. Yeah, I could have fallen— big time—for Melinda Whitmore. But a Case and Melinda relationship didn't have a chance in hell, and Melinda would have been the first to press the acknowledgement.

"Can't. Mercy, I want to. You are nothing short of fine beyond description. Hot fodder for long drive musings. And I may regret it the rest of my life. But I can't."

Her voice lowered, eyes soft. "An emotional component?"

"'Fraid so."

She dropped the cat on a hot tin roof demeanor and returned to soft and pleasant and appealing on another, less physical level.

"You are quite the package, Mr. Tilly."

She kissed my cheek and released my hands. I stared at the floor and ran fingers through my hair. A barrel-full of desire still tugged and pulled, incredulous at my stupidity. Melinda lifted me from the swirling drain.

"I really should begin preparations for the Bryce-Coddington event. Would you let yourself out?"

A groaned sigh and a returned kiss on the cheek. A regretful smile and a nod as I turned. No point unbalancing the clean exit she offered. Oh man.

Sally eyeballed me in the front entrance hall with a no-nonsense stare and pursed lips.

"A quick question or two, Sally. Would you mind?"

A single raised eyebrow was her only response.

"So I understand you found Mr. Whitmore."

"I did. And immediately called 911."

"Anything catch your eye about the scene? Anything unusual?"

"Other than Mr. Whitmore dead in the pool?" She crossed her arms. "Does that constitute unusual, Mr. Tilly?"

"A terrible scene, I'm sure. But did anything seem strange? Out of place?"

"Nothing. His pool slippers and robe were at the edge of the back porch, above the steps. His cell phone on a nearby table. A towel draped across a poolside lounge chair."

The towel placement was weird. With the light rain, you wouldn't place your towel where it would get wet. You'd set it alongside your robe and slippers on the porch. But I didn't know Geoffrey Whitmore, and maybe he didn't consider such things.

"Any security alarms for the house?"

"Yes. But they are turned off when the Whitmores are in residence."

"Security cameras?"

"No. Are we finished Mr. Tilly?"

Yeah, finished. I didn't possess great wherewithal for solving crimes. No training in that area, and no idea if a crime was committed. Besides, Sally would have gone over this with the cops.

"Thanks, Sally. I'll be on my way after a walk around the per... property." The perimeter. The operational area. Chill, Jack Tilly. I wrote off the ops jargon slip as the rattled aftermath of Melinda's duvet-viewing offer.

Sally returned a tight nod and remained immobile while I exited through the front door. A glorious day, and an opportunity to enjoy the landscaping and stretch my legs. Help clear the Melinda Whitmore regret music sounding as a Gregorian chant inside my head. The single vocal line low, haunting. The chant's three words stretched, restricted scale. Case. You. Idiot. Rinse, repeat.

Focus, Lee. Get real, get serious. Pettis. And according to the dread pirate Tig—a guy named Jordan. So I'd Google a Jordan Pettis from California. New money as per the gorgeous woman I'd just turned down. Jordan Pettis. A name, maybe. And two dead rich guys with maps of Costa

Rica. One with stick pins, the other hand-drawn red ink. A clear tie there. But no assurance murder was another tie. I held no assumption Geoffrey Whitmore was whacked as well.

So I walked the perimeter and considered far-fetched possibilities. No dog, a sliver of moon hidden behind summer shower clouds, and no one else around the night he died. It was possible a professional hitter took the situational opportunity for a stroll to the swimming pool while Whitmore did laps, stripped and eased into the pool on the dark rainy night, and pulled the old guy under.

Done right, a hitter could tug the guy from below, with no indicators or signs of struggle. No body marks, abrasions, bruises. The autopsy report would state drowning. Then exit the property. The light rain would mask any wet footprints on the concrete around the pool. Still, a bit of a stretch.

Each landscape island held a theme, a different tone and texture. Pretty stunning stuff and manicured to an extreme. A collection of fine gardeners traveled with the riding lawn mower fleet. I paced the outer property line, delineated with intermittent tall boxwood hedges and small stretches of low brick and wrought iron fencing. A little-used gravel two-track road ran along the east side of the property between the Whitmore estate and their neighbor's similar layout. A vehicle maintenance path, seldom used.

A delivery truck rumbled down the road past the entrances for this series of Hampton estates. Someone's kids or grandkids called from farther down the beach. A trio of gulls passed overhead, their flight silent and synced. I considered removing the light sport coat, but the Glock precluded such action. Residents would freak at the sight of an armed man wandering around.

Tracks, or rather footprints in the mulch led from a set of boxwoods and onto the lawn. Closer inspection showed a few small, broken branches where someone squeezed through. Seven steps farther, footprints back through the hedge. I followed them, brushed aside the flexible foliage, and stood on the gravel two-track. Someone drove down this maintenance road and worked through the hedge, returned, and exited a short distance from the entry point. Signs pointed to a dark nighttime move—ingress and egress close but not exact. Tire tracks were discernible on the two gravel strips, weeds growing between them. An expected thing for a maintenance road. And landscape workers had worked the place recently. But I just didn't see them pushing through the boxwoods, causing damage, albeit minor. They took too much pride in their craft. Weird. But weak soup and speculation and a big fat what if.

I circled toward the front, survey complete. A bird-like glass tapping stopped my slide into the rental car. Melinda, fingernails rapping on a window and followed with a sequential finger wave and could-have-been smile. I returned a heartfelt grin and a regretful head shake. Oh man. She'd be remembered.

The front gates swung open, and I eased to the intersection with the quiet hardtop meandering among this section of Hampton estates. I considered the importance of showing up—both here and the Bahamas. On the ground stuff. Nothing beat on the ground. If I hadn't visited Abaco and the Hamptons, Central American connectivity wouldn't have happened.

A wrap-up blind trail remained. A path toward completing this job. I'd research into the maybe-he-exists Jordan Pettis. Then a final Clubhouse trip and collect whatever pearls of insight Jules offered me—a price attached. Between the Clubhouse and personal excavation of informational dirt perhaps uncover a Central America business connection. I knew Bettencourt was murdered. There was no solid evidence Geoffrey Whitmore received the same treatment. I'd present facts, connectivity, and let the Zurich gnomes sort it out. Soon a Global Resolutions report would be written, encrypted, and submitted on the deep web. And back to Ditch life, job over. Sweet.

Chapter 9

The map guy occupying the nondescript sedan had moved. He'd parked farther down the shoulder of the quiet road near the Whitmore's estate entrance. The map still spread across the steering wheel. Not good.

A Mercedes convertible approached from the right and zipped past map guy. I turned and followed it, an eye glued to the rear view mirror. Map guy rolled off the shoulder and followed me. Not one little bit good.

So I punched it, accelerator floored, and swung the wheel hard. A tire-screeching one-eighty. And came to a dead stop, facing the following sedan. He slammed the brakes, stopped, and stared.

A pro. Not special forces or clandestine spook or undercover law enforcement. A hitter. It was in the eyes. Soulless. I represented a piece of meat, his target. He made no attempt to avert his eyes or present any countenance other than sighting his prey. On the Serengeti, his tail would have twitched.

But as a professional hitter his style, his modus operandi, was the close kill. A silenced pistol to the back of the head stuff. Seedy bar restrooms, quiet and empty except for his prey. Or sidling up to car windows, a quick bullet to the occupant's head. Clean. Professional. His usual approach now off the table, the hitter had a decision to make. Would he cruise past my vehicle, driver to driver, and attempt a kill shot? I'd soon remove that option.

One thing rang clear—Geoffrey Whitmore had been whacked. And a big money player saw me as a loose end that required clipping. A description of Jack Tilly had been forwarded to this little conspiracy's mastermind. A description, or cell phone photo, provided from an Abaco Island source. And a hit man hired from the NYC area. Melinda Whitmore's estate was the wait point.

I turned off the car, windows down. Insects buzzed along the roadside ditch, the sun bright and warm. A hundred feet separated us. He displayed no emotion. Just remorseless, hollow eyes. Doing his job, considering options. The Glock rested in my right hand.

Whoever ramrodded this operation knew I wasn't Jack Tilly, insurance examiner. A fake name and occupation provided limited cover. A bit of research and anyone could call BS on my temporary persona. And now the guy in charge wanted me cleaned. Taken out. But the head honcho knew who

I wasn't, and the failure to understand who I *was* meant bad news for this murder-for-hire dude. As well as for the mastermind, if I ever ran into him. So welcome to the world of Case Lee, former Delta operator. Buckle up, you SOBs. It's a rough ride.

I popped from the vehicle and sidestepped past the open door, Glock on display. Marker laid—I was ready to party. The move afforded a confirmation of his intent and an assessment of his weaponry. His rapid right shoulder movement told me everything. A quick shoulder lift to open the between-seat console, a dip as he dug the pistol out, and an upper arm movement indicated it now rested across his lap, ready for action.

So there we stood, two modern day gunslingers, awaiting the next move. Absurd on its face, but split-second death a moment and movement away. The road stood quiet, distant ocean waves broke along the shore. The sun beat down, shimmered the air in the distance. A fat dragonfly buzzed between us, halted in mid-air, and took off, hunting.

Confirmation of his intent and weapon accomplished, I eased back into the car seat. Our eyes remained locked. We'd do this on my terms, out of sight. The option of losing him flashed and faded. Speed away and maneuver through pedestrian-packed tourist villages. Hope he didn't pick up my trail farther down the road. Run. That wasn't happening.

He was a far cry from the Nassau amateurs. I remained eye-locked with a stone cold killer. A murderer. Whether he personally drowned Whitmore didn't matter. He was involved. And now I'd situate us in a place, an isolated location, where no remorse and absolute finality ruled. I'd kill him.

The question remained whether he'd accept the challenge. I backed into an estate entrance and turned toward my original direction. Headed down the quiet road and checked the rear-view mirror. He followed. Challenge accepted. He wouldn't cut and run. Murder was his job. He'd formulate a plan to work close and take me out. Not to worry, asshole. I'd take care of the plan.

We entered the Big Strange. Rolled into a nearby village at a sedate fifteen miles an hour, flowed with traffic, the setting Kafkaesque. The hitter remained on my tail or one car back as we navigated through streetlights, stop signs, and pedestrian traffic. Tourists wandered past fresh produce stands, art shops, and coffee houses. Sidewalk cafes where children laughed and parents called and chattered. A riot of flower colors dripped from hanging baskets.

A glorious Hamptons summer day. With the lone blemish a two car funeral procession. The second vehicle as the hearse, its occupant with a near-term expiration date. We passed through another village and another. The short stretches between the cluster of antique shops and coffee houses were filled with traffic. Thirty miles per hour along the stretches, a crawl through the villages. Rear view mirror glances returned a man in his late forties, dark hair greased straight back. Windbreaker, casual dress shirt. And cold unblinking eyes, an absolute focus on his job.

I doubted if this guy ever found himself with this situation during his murderous career. His victim both aware and challenging and taking his sweet-ass time toward the killing floor. I'd never know.

I took a less-traveled hardtop toward the center of Long Island. The surroundings became more rural with scattered maple and oak and scrub junipers as well as a few farms. The hitter could have made a move, but clearly sensed this little procession would end soon. He stayed thirty yards back, traffic now light.

An old junkyard showed on the right. A line of Sweetgum and Juniper trees offered a visual barrier for the collected junk. An abandoned wood plank shack—a once-upon-a-time office—now leaned, rusted nails holding it together. The paint long since weather-washed away, it stood inside the tree line. A little-used gravel road led past it and into the collection of rusted hulks scattered around a five acre piece of property. Perfect.

With a conscious move, I flicked on my blinker. Here's where we turn, bub. Let's dance. The tire song changed from an asphalt hum to the crunch of gravel. I goosed it past the shack as tires kicked brown dust and pulled a hard left past a cluster of rusted auto bodies. The hitter eased down the gravel entrance, saw my dust trail, and pulled a hard right. He disappeared among the junk and scrub brush and weeds opposite my position. The curtain rose.

I popped the trunk and leapt from the vehicle. His vehicle noise ensured he didn't hear my trunk open. Too bad for him, as it signaled he'd brought a pistol to a rifle fight. The sound of his vehicle shutting down carried across the two hundred yard distance separating us.

The Colt M4A1 rifle snatched from the trunk, I dashed right, toward the shack, and slid into a weedy space between a rusted collection of auto bodies, old water heaters, and cracked fiberglass camper tops. And waited.

He'd assume I'd work my way deeper into the junkyard since designating this place. So he'd spend his time stalking the wrong direction. The Colt was equipped with a suppressor and a 2X magnification red dot scope. The suppressor reduced the weapon's sound signature from the sharp crack of a rifle to a stout hand clap. No one from any distance could discern the sound as the result of a trigger squeeze.

I hunted. Eye to the scope, safety off, finger resting against the trigger. The two-power magnification sufficient to send a 5.56mm bullet into a golf-ball sized object at a hundred yards. The hitter's head wouldn't present a challenge.

A professional hit man, an urban killer, against former Delta Force. Across an outdoor obstacle-laden environment. Advantage, Case. Big time. Glimpses of him appeared between junk piles. Gray khakis, black walking shoes. Portions of his body moved past thin open cracks among the piled junk. He held his weapon with one hand, chest high. A position better suited for urban up-close hits. He moved slow, steady, never assuming a defensive posture. Whatever he guessed as my background, he now counted on years of successful assassinations as a leverage point. He knew how to kill. And no doubt owned acute awareness of quiet city streets and parked cars and dark alleys. His turf. Not now—we faced off among trees and brush and random junk piles.

The scattered trees and tall shrubs held birds. They called and fluttered, going about their birdy business. Except when he crept past. Pockets of moving silence as the critters ceased calls and rustles, waited for the intruder's passing. Plus his windbreaker and pants scraped brush—small but distinct sounds. Even when lost from sight, I knew exactly where he moved.

I knelt among the junk, hidden by weeds and long-abandoned metal. The rifle rested on the horizontal bar of an old A-frame hoist, now collapsed and rusted. The guy would present soon enough, clueless, his life's terminal point imminent.

Ten minutes passed, then twenty. He circled the junkyard, worked toward my parked sedan. He stepped from behind a piled collection of old washing machines, weeds growing through the collapsed and disintegrated sheet metal. And offered a perfect full-second exposure. A clean head shot.

Couldn't do it. No moral qualms drove this multiple murderer's short reprieve. I wanted him to talk. Reveal something, anything which could clarify who ran this murderous mess from Abaco to Long Island. So I continued waiting as he moved closer, focused on the kill. He'd accepted a contract and intended delivery in full.

Seven paces away, he stepped past head-high junk and surveyed the five acre jumble, his back to me. Perhaps he thought I hid like a rabbit, frozen with fear. Or figured I'd hoofed it away through the brush and trees, losing him. I'd never know.

"Freeze, asshole."

He spun left, dropped to a knee. The pistol whipped toward my hidden voice. His last move on this earth. The rifle's muted crack sounded his death. Birds flapped and fluttered, a distant truck ground gears.

Damn. Dead men tell no tales. I retrieved the ejected cartridge casing—nothing left behind—and donned latex gloves. Extracted his wallet and anything else that might help identify him. A New Jersey driver's license. I memorized the name and rifled through the wallet for more. Two credit cards—one with the same name as the driver's license, the other under a different name. His "only for business" card. I pocketed that one. No cell phone, but I soon discovered it on his car seat. The screen was password protected. No worries. Back at the *Ace* I owned a device that connected with the charger port and drew out a phone's entrails, allowing the oracle an easy read. The vehicle held no other identifying documents.

Dragged his sorry ass into the weeds and junk and left the pistol alongside the body. A body discovered in a day, week, or month. The Colt back in the trunk, the Glock on the passenger seat, I pulled alongside the old collapsing shed at the entrance and shut the car down. Listened without engine noise interference. There was no traffic, dead quiet. I started the car and pulled onto the still road, headed for home.

Eight hours back to Chesapeake and the *Ace of Spades*. I held no great satisfaction, no elation, no sense of a job well done. Too dirty, the whole affair. A pathetic rich guy wallowing in hedonism, killed with a hard-core professional's poison. Administered through one of the play boys or girls or servants.

A Hamptons rich guy drowned, murdered. Managed and triggered by the same person who'd taken out Bettencourt. No doubts. Plus three dead hitters left for others to find. And a bunch of Abaco kids abandoned, used, their future unclear. Their predicament bothered me as much as cleaning the hitters. Can't save the world and all, Case. But still.

So I'd poke around on the internet and snoop for a Jordan Pettis connection. Check in with Jules. Write the report for my Swiss clients, and couch activities with nebulous terms. *Met extreme resistance collecting tissue sample.*

Challenged by aggressive unknown party on Long Island. The report filed, as always, on the deep web, 256-bit encrypted. Where sniffers and electronic hound dogs wouldn't pick up a trail. While ugly events and death and used young people floated as flotsam in my wake. Helluva way to live.

Chapter 10

Bo called after I turned off the interstate and began the coastal road route. A physical relief with the absence of high-speed crowded freeways and I rolled my head, rotated my shoulders, and opened a window. The tight two handed wheel grip relaxed and warm salt air whirled.

"Hi ho," said my blood brother. "How be my favorite goober?"

A mile-wide smile accompanied joy and positivity and possibilities. I adopted an immediate mental atmosphere change and rode the Bo connectivity express.

"You don't call, you don't write. Clearly the special bond we once had is now lost forever."

A Bo belly laugh and quick retort. "And yet messages, my brother, were sent your way. Ongoing and consistent."

"Were not talking standard communication formats are we?"

Bo often alleged the efficacy of mental messages or universal personal pipes or mere chance. Cosmic chance, serendipity. Although he vacillated on the chance vs design concept, arguing metaphysical uncertainty as the appropriate approach. Bo being Bo—a full time job with a worldview I reveled in. Yin to my frumpy yang.

"Standard communication? As standard and, perhaps, as real as our surroundings."

"How is Oz?"

A poor assumption. Bo tooled across Australia last we'd seen each other. But this call could originate from any locale. Including a trailing vehicle a mile behind me. Bo Dickerson was that good. A tracker extraordinaire, with the mystical ability to slip unnoticed and appear among the bad guys at the perfect moment. Our Delta Force team spearhead. First-in. With a wildness and fearlessness and remarkable sense of time and place. The best, and most peculiar, warrior we ever met.

"How *was* Oz," said Bo. "I drifted back and waltzed among the dripping conifers and wrestled a bear and abided in spiritual love with the bear's mate."

Portland, Oregon. Bo returned stateside and now spent time with Catch—the bear—and his partner Willa. Catch—Juan Antonio Diego Hernandez, another member of our Delta team. Catch lay low in the Pacific

Northwest where he tried conducting a normal life. Normal for Catch. His name was unattached to a driver's license, credit cards, or utility bills. And he lived with a remarkable woman. But while Catch preferred living open and large, his pedal-to-the-metal life approach remained muted. The bounty.

"How are Catch and Willa?"

Bo was back. Outstanding. And another opportunity for elaboration on the benefits of the *Ace of Spades* lifestyle. I'd often offered the *Ace* option if he found himself without a settled spot in the world.

"Robust and ornery and beautiful and inspirational."

"Give them my love."

"I already have my Georgia peach. Yet a subject beckons. A request from this gentle soul."

His tone and projection contained a dash of hesitancy.

"You already know the answer." I'd die for my blood brother and best friend. Whatever he requested would get done, pronto.

"I require your time. It's a large request. Perhaps the largest."

"All the time in the world."

"Including time aboard your watery steed?"

The *Ace*. Bo would head this way and spend time with me cruising the Ditch. It didn't get any better.

"I'll go nab your skinny butt and haul you here if that's what it takes."

"There's no nabbing necessary."

"Then come. Post haste."

"Not a bad name for a folk-rock band. No Nabbing Necessary," he said.

"Or conjure yourself up alongside this coastal highway. Jump in this fine vehicle. We'll sing songs of love and battle and brotherhood. You choose."

"So as not to rattle you, how about tomorrow morn' via a more standard conveyance? A flight from Portland."

"Grand and glorious. Come. Come and settle with me."

"Might you provide a destination? I discern rushing wind, which precludes the sedate *Ace*. You're driving, so a runway of sorts should reside nearby."

"Norfolk. I'll meet you with bells on."

"Meet me with wisdom and insight, brother."

A semi-concerning statement. Perhaps Bo muddled through an existential crisis or a bout of depression. It happens. He lived full-tilt boogie and never presented himself with less than wild definitive perspectives with the strangest combination of gentleness and warrior attitude. But everyone hits road bumps. Bo and the *Ace* and the Ditch would afford time and contemplation and heartfelt rapport, a potent salve. We signed off after I emphasized, twice, a text message with his arrival details was much preferable over cosmic communications.

Everything changed. The drive till now had been filled with doubts and uncertainties. Mental pinball with worry the object, paddled with angst and concerns toward the job I wrapped up and doubts about my abilities.

I made a healthy living as a contractor with Global Resolutions. It made for regular employment—and consistent work was a requirement based on a sense of responsibility and an element of pride. The lion's share of the money went to Mom and CC. And I was good at what I did. Until now. When hired for more dangerous jobs, a well-honed sense of environment, proactive movements, and trained reactions held me in good stead and high demand. The Delta Force background played well among elements of global intrigue and revolution and geopolitical maneuvers. But this job required different skills, and I reflected on what could have gone better.

More Abaco interviews. Enquiries with staff and more of those kids. A more thorough rifling through of Bettencourt's desk seeking Central America clues, information. Asked for his cell phone and taken it. Captured, not killed, one of the Nassau hitters and coerced answers by hook or crook. Asked Sally more questions at the Whitmore estate. Coulda, shoulda.

I held pride as someone who over-delivered. Couldn't say that about this one. I committed to improvement. Learn to focus on the gumshoe aspects of these gigs. Anticipate where the killing might appear and avoid it. Sidestep, maneuver, and find answers.

Bo's arrival plopped a blood brother on board the *Ace*. We'd hang out, talk through issues, laugh, live. And hammer out those doubts and worries and address whatever was sideswiping him. It was all good and needed and anticipation at this arrival ratcheted up.

Entering the outskirts of Chesapeake, late, I parked behind an abandoned warehouse a quarter mile from the *Ace*. Rucksack across my back, Glock holstered, the Colt rifle locked and loaded, I maneuvered through the dark and gritty industrial setting. Remaining shadow-bound was the moment's directive. I paused at regular intervals and listened and watched. Entered the dock area through a ripped hole in the old Hurricane fence and waited fifteen minutes. Eyeballing the docks and the *Ace*, I sought any movement large or small. Other than the dark dashes of a few wharf rats, quiet.

I boarded my home and performed the usual routine—a quick check of the onboard tripwires and movement cameras. Then inspected the engine room, bedroom, and wheelhouse with left hand wielding a small flashlight and the Glock filling the other. All clear. Tension eased, normalcy returned. An iced Grey Goose joined me in the wheelhouse. A quiet night on the Elizabeth River, the night traffic minimal. The *Ace* and surrounding boats shifted through a languid dance, gentle tugs at the tie-up lines within each boat slip.

Sleep wouldn't come for several hours, so I produced the junkyard hitter's cell phone and credit card. Plugged the phone into the extraction device and let the software perform its magic. Laptop software checked the hitter's business credit card through online backdoor access. Nothing unusual on the card—clustered purchases spaced six to eight weeks apart. The frequency of his murder contracts. The last group of purchases were in the Hamptons. Room, food, drinks. He'd waited for me, having been instructed I'd arrive.

The cell phone tool listed recent incoming and outgoing calls with associated limitations. All the calls were either restricted or unknown. No trails, no leads. Nada. One disturbing aspect was revealed when the tool peeled back layers of inbound restrictions on several inbound calls the day after I left Abaco. My tool could dig and capture details to a certain level and no more. With the post-Abaco calls, the no more consisted of 256 bit encryption technologies. A brick wall. Same as my phone.

I fixed another drink and conducted a concerted search for a Jordan Pettis. Lots of folks shared the name. A Tuscaloosa banker, Reno insurance adjuster, a Beaumont welder. Searches associating a Jordan Pettis with Bettencourt or Whitmore or Central America drew a blank. Another nothing, nada. I was one remarkable sleuth.

My satellite phone rang again, the call tone a wooden tick-tock. A call from the soon-terminated exchange for a Mr. Jack Tilly. It was strange timing this late at night.

"Mr. Tilly. It is Elena. You gave me card."

Eastern European accent and young. Kid-like. The young lady on Abaco who had approached me and Tig asking if I needed anything.

"Hi, Elena. How are you?"

I was glad she'd called. A touchpoint for a tribe of lost kids and unsettled business.

"It is good. All is good. I am leaving."

"Probably a good thing. Tell me where you're going."

"Barbados. Sister there. I have work."

"What kind of work, Elena?" I wasn't sure I wanted the answer and sat up straight.

"Hotel maid. With sister."

A half smile and cocked head toward the heavens. A whispered "Thank you."

"That's excellent. Excellent. I'm glad you let me know."

A pause as her thoughts gathered. "I call for another reason. I think you are a nice man. So maybe I can help."

"Okay." No clue where this line of conversation headed.

"Tig left. On boat."

"Okay. Tig left. Is he coming back?"

"I do not know. But he packed many clothes, many things."

"What kind of boat?"

"Big boat."

"Whose boat?"

"A man. One man."

So Tig jumped on board a man's boat and left Bettencourt's dreamland. And odds sky high a man with ties to the Nassau hitters and the Long Island pro. I should have questioned Tig more, much more. Stupid.

"What did the man look like?"

She didn't hesitate. "Tmcruz."

"I don't understand."

"Movie star. Tmcruz."

I chewed that for a moment, rifling through images of celebrities. My awareness reservoir in that arena was both shallow and brackish. Silence brought another attempt from Elena.

"Tm. Okay?"

"Tm. Tom? Is that right?"

"Yes, Tm. Cruz."

"Tom Cruise? The man who picked up Tig looked like Tom Cruise?"

"Yes. And now Tig is gone."

Tig floated with the fish if this sponsor desired tying up every conceivable loose end.

"Okay. Are you safe?"

"Safe. Good. And travel tomorrow to sister. You are a nice man."

We signed off with Godspeed and a quick prayer of protection and guidance for young Elena. All right. A good end for a strange day that included a dead hitter left among junkyard weeds. But the phone call relieved one gut knot created when I walked away and left those kids to fend for themselves.

Sleep now came easy. Bo tomorrow, joyous and needed. Nothing but dead-ends with further job digging, so I'd do a wrap with Jules and submit the report with salient, valued information. Elena was saved, rescued. And maybe, just maybe, other young people at Bettencourt's place followed the same path. A solid stop point for the day. The *Ace* cradled me, the Glock my bedmate. I dreamt of violent struggles against unseen enemies, deep within warm blue-green water, the surface light far away and unreachable.

Chapter 11

Wild red hair, a scraggly beard, wide grin, and eyes filled with mirth—it wasn't a challenge picking Tulsa, Oklahoma's own Bo Dickerson from among the crowd exiting the Norfolk Airport's security area. The hug was tight and lasting. He smelled of eucalyptus and ginger.

"How's the bod?" I asked. Bo incurred serious bullet wounds last we'd met. Courtesy of Jemaah Islamiyah terrorists.

"Fine as kind. And you, old son?" My head received a gentle knuckle rap. "Body good and mind better?"

I'd also caught bullets during the firefight. Those, along with an upper chest arrow wound, healed at their own pace. The occasional manifestations barked at odd and unforeseen moments—throbs, the random sharp bite. The mental health portion of Bo's enquiry wouldn't be dwelt on at the moment. Plenty of time for that. More important was *his* overall equilibrium.

"Robust and sterling. All aspects," I said. "Let's get your stuff."

He carried one rucksack, the other checked as baggage. The entirety of his worldly possessions. We waited at baggage claim and stood separate from the other travelers. Close, heads bowed, low and gentle tones. Our private world.

"You worried me," I said. "Tone and texture of your phone call. You down?"

"You have a keen ear, my brother. A bit down. Just a bit and nothing earthshattering. Maybe all that's required is a home base for a while."

"You got it. From now until old age. You know that."

He returned a wry smile and scratched his scalp. Then lips pursed, he squeezed my upper arm. "I'm spinning in the blues, my brother. I'll reveal what I believe to be source, the driver of this malaise, once we're situated. But spring no alarms nor gather any troops. It's a Bo issue, and one not worthy of any great concern."

"No worries. Spin with me till it stops." I meant it. And relief flowed at the indicators this was Bo's way of handling a touch of depression. Bo hoisted all the sails with the cosmic winds, and the occasional running aground on rocky shoals was to be expected. There was no crisis indicated and whatever the issue, we could talk it out.

"I've been seeking signs and answers and don't know if it's the right tactic. And maybe, just maybe, active seeking hinders the universal flow."

"I'd suggest a reset. Leverage the *Ace's* slow rumble as Ditch life flows past. Take your time and reset the situation."

Silence. A relaxed, tension-relieving silence filled with acceptance and non-judgment and palpable love. All good and needed and as solid as a continent.

Luggage rolled past. His eyes brightened. "And that's why you draw me, brother. A potent dose of rational stability. A perspective both mundane and holding little imagination, but the universe requires this in small doses. To support the likes of me."

"Helluva compliment, outback boy. Mundane and lacking imagination."

"Playing to your strengths."

"Bite me."

We both laughed low chuckles, squeezed arms and shoulders, and snagged his rucksack. Back on stable ground.

"You have a plan no doubt," Bo said as we left the airport.

"Get situated on board. I've got a Clubhouse appointment this afternoon. Then we leave. Ditch time."

Bo stroked uneven chin growth. "Jules."

"Yeah. Jules."

Bo pursed his lips, an unwanted trail sniffed. "This is a potent marker placed smack-dab before me. It could be significant."

He meant my afternoon Clubhouse visit. A potent marker. He smelled an exploration opportunity. An opportunity to check out this happenstance. A Jules visit prior to our departure. Nothing potent about it, Bo. And a bad idea for you to attend.

"Mundane stuff. As you well noted. Back in an hour."

"You've told tales, bucko. Tales of her."

I'd mentioned Jules more than a few times with Bo. And Catch and Marcus.

"I've got to visit her and wrap up a job. Rehash a few items. Nothing new. I thought we'd get into North Carolina tonight and anchor."

Instant regret. The Uber driver, a nice enough woman, was now privy to our travel plans. And privy to someone named Jules. Bounty paranoia blossomed. Two million bucks occupied the Ford's back seat.

"But later, Bo. Later. Tell me about Oz."

He did, the conversational shift recognized with a wink. The ensuing twenty minutes covered the tale of a man tooling across the outback on a BMW motorcycle with sidecar as dust filled the air. A good tale, but without anchors or purpose or epiphanies. The driver dropped us a quarter-mile distance from the *Ace*. I handed Bo a small .45 Kimber pistol as we started the walk. An appreciative nod returned and the weapon slid into his jeans' front pocket.

"I sense reticence, my brother. The Clubhouse oracle and me," Bo said. We strolled past decrepit buildings and warehouses. I toted one of his rucksacks.

"It's a poor fit between you two. Pretty simple. Besides, she asked about you and Catch. A recruitment endeavor. Hardly your cup of tea."

"The fit isn't our choice. And perhaps I've taken a shine to tea. Organic."

"Okay." A wide smile and head shake. Bo's cosmic interplay logic bubbled toward the surface.

"I do see the timing as a marker. A signal of sorts."

"Okay."

"As for recruitment, perhaps she requires a consultant. A trusted advisor."

"Don't think she'd cotton to the concept, bud."

"Such concerns aside, a wave of energy washes. What it portends, a mystery. The confab, set. We will move forward and meet our fate."

We slowed and sidled alongside a warehouse filled with broken glass and hunks of rusted metal. The *Ace* lay below us, tied. We held five minute reconnoiter while the discussion continued.

"She points a shotgun when you enter."

"A tribal custom from the clandestine world. Spooks, as you too often say."

"And makes you empty your pockets. Which better have little other than money."

"We all have personal affectations and quirks. Does she have any passions?"

"She likes licorice."

One person walked the pier, dragging a hose toward a weekend sailboat.

"Fine. I'll make an offering, then allow goodwill free reign."

"It's not a sound idea, Bo."

"Let's allow the cosmos to make such a decision, my brother. Now, shall we enter the domain of the *Queen Mary?*"

With that, he strolled down the small rise, headed for the *Ace*. I followed. The aft cabin was his, a storage spot. He'd sleep on the foredeck, hammock strung near the throne. The atmosphere was right and tight. Bo on board. We'd cruise late today. Ditch life.

I sent a Clubhouse message, deep web. *Today's appointment. With red-headed stranger?*

Jules was irascible, and exhibited a strong dislike for changes in Clubhouse schedules. She might even cancel the meeting. But the encrypted response arrived within a quarter hour.

Bring him.

All righty then. We'd traipse toward the Clubhouse in a few hours. Bo settled, sandwiches were made, two cold beers opened. Bo asked about the current engagement, as always, interested. He absorbed the tale and peppered the high-level framework I'd delivered with questions.

"The texture of Abaco? The mansion?"

"Sad. Soiled."

"And those kids?"

"Heard from one of them. A sister in the Caymans landed her a job. Hotel maid."

"A flint strike on positive tinder. The others may also fare well."

"How's the sandwich?"

"The tomato is sublime. Which one?"

He lifted a chin toward an array of black plastic pots aligned along the railing for full sun exposure. Each contained an heirloom tomato plant.

"Black Krim."

"An admirable pastime, your small-scale agriculture." He took another bite, chewed. "The red dot hitter in Nassau. Did you consider capture?"

"Yeah. After the fact. During the fact required a split-second shot."

"The trailing boat as you exited the scene casts possibilities."

"I'll never know who or why."

"Don't speak with such surety on the matter, goober. Answers may yet reveal."

I rehashed, again, the final act of this engagement. A Clubhouse visit and then adios. Bo brushed aside the assertion.

"For a plodder, you lack patience. Allow for a ripening process." He lifted his chin again toward the tomatoes and smiled large.

"End of the gig, Bo. No ripening."

"That was a cool move in the junkyard. You exhibited restraint. Allowed the hitter sufficient rope. I'll assume the finale quick and violent, without discourse."

"I yelled freeze. He didn't."

"A poor choice on his part. You have skirted over the palatial Hampton estate owner. Melinda, was it?"

"Fine, fine woman. Another time, another place."

"Maybe it *was* the time and place. You fought it."

"I don't move among the opposite sex with the insouciance you do."

Bo attracted women. Period. The guy didn't try—quite the opposite. He avoided overt signals. I'd never evidenced any such efforts. He focused on the person. Passions, joys, tribulations. A weird mix of joyful acceptance and camouflaged bad boy. Whatever the mix, they drifted his way, enveloping.

"You might stop focusing on the movement," he said. "Adopt acceptance."

"Standby while I get a pen and paper. Capture these pearls of wisdom."

We both laughed, wiped breadcrumbs off ourselves, finished the beers. The day turned warm and sticky. The overhead tarp provided needed shade. His beer bottle rapped the foredeck with announcement-like vigor.

"I should follow my own advice, laddie."

"Do tell." Man I missed him.

"The subject of partners. It was driven home when hanging with Catch and Willa."

I lacked a grip on this. My brother never exhibited issues meeting women. Hell, they sought him out.

"You don't have issues with female companionship. A mystery to me given the mess you are."

"This is deeper and of greater import than companionship."

"Okay."

"A partner and soul-sharing mate and lover. A fellow traveler sharing the same path. *That's* the fulcrum of this dilemma."

"You're having a personal crisis over a lack of a mate?"

"Shared experiences tied with solid love. But a bit of firmament is required on my part. I think. Hence the spin."

He twisted in the hammock and rooted around inside his on-deck rucksack. Produced a small clay pipe and smaller container of pot.

"You'll catch a buzz before a Clubhouse visit?"

"I feels appropriate."

Oh man. Bo and Jules. My unease at the meeting cranked up.

"Let's get back to firmament," I said.

"A partner requires a semblance of stability. A nest. I had one not long ago."

Bo's old houseboat illegally anchored deep within the Dismal Swamp, south of where we sat. Burnt to the waterline during a firefight with bounty hunters and a brother gone bad.

"You've got the old farmhouse."

Across the highway from the Dismal, Bo owned a seen-much-better-days shack and a rickety barn where an old pickup sat parked. He hadn't visited the place in a year, and never lived there. He preferred Dismal Swamp deep immersion.

"That shack holds bad vibes," he said, exhaling smoke through his nose. "Poor atmosphere."

"Just so I'm straight, in my plodding manner, you have an existential hole. Hopefully caulked and filled with a loving partner. Well, I could join you in that quest."

To some degree I was relieved. A slip-slide into the blues, a bit of depression over past deeds and activities and extreme violence required areas of solace, I feared, well beyond my abilities. All I had to offer—often sufficient—was the healing power of time, wrapped in non-judgmental love.

"You have family," he said, voice low and wistful.

Bo had no siblings, and both parents were buried back in Oklahoma. And he was right. Mom and CC were part of my world. It meant more than a lot.

"Point taken. So, still plodding along, you first require a place. A nest."

"Maybe. It's unclear what the universe spins for me at the moment. Maybe a place. Maybe a partner first, then a place." He took a hit and exhaled toward the overhead tarp. "How are you on deciphering smoke signals, kemosabe?"

"Damn poor," I said, chuckling.

The mental machete, at this moment, was inadequate to slice through such thick and longing vegetation. A path best cleared over time. So I endeavored assurances that time aplenty awaited.

"But know this, my brother. The *Ace*, and yours truly, are here for however long it takes. Even if it means another throne and lots of gray hair. Although it's unclear whether that mop of yours turns gray."

"Time."

"Roger that. All the time in the world."

A tiny change displayed, near impossible capturing. Bo performed a mental exhale, unhooked from worry, and truly relaxed. And it filled my heart to the brim with relief and joy. At least, maybe, I could do some things half-right.

Chapter 12

I reviewed Clubhouse rules and protocols as we walked, keeping it succinct—edicts and stipulations weren't Bo's strong suite. Chesapeake's old industrial section segued into an equally old and rundown retail area. Liquor stores, auto body shops, small appliance repair. Bo steered us toward a chain drugstore.

"Supplies, old son," he said.

"So nothing but cash allowed. Cash and index cards with hand written information. What supplies?"

"Our pistachio stock. Is the larder well stocked?"

"No. And we leave our sidearms with the Filipinos behind the dry cleaner counter. And your cell phone if you brought it."

"How about body wash?"

"Got soap. You listening to the rules? Jules is prickly about such things."

"Botanical body wash is crucial. How are we set with body butter?"

We walked lockstep, Bo's eyes scanning, mine locked on his profile.

"Did I just hear one of the most fearless Delta Force warriors ask about body butter?"

"And a spiral notebook. I may start journaling. Scatter breadcrumbs. A tool, perhaps. With a black cover for added gravitas."

"Did you bring your cell phone?"

"I'm running clean. Pistola. Cash. Open mind."

The drugstore outfitted Bo with the necessities plus a small tin box of specialty licorice. His offering. We waited a moment outside the dry cleaner and ensured there were no customers. I pushed aside how weird this felt. Bo and Jules. A mixture for the ages and discomfort was my prime emotion. But they both wanted this. I would focus on closure. Complete the Caribbean job. The other two could do their dance. If incompatible, no loss. And no hard feelings. Maybe.

The door handle bell rang, expressionless Filipino faces greeted us. The air was hot and steamy—the dry cleaner used no air conditioning. Two handguns placed on the counter, both covered with dropped-off laundry and backed with deadpan expressions. Bo's sack of supplies were covered up as well. He kept the licorice tin. Through the obscure side door. The first stair step, as always, creaked.

"Happens every time, every step," I said. "Can't avoid it."

Delta members, current and former, weren't fond of creaking stairs. They announced arrivals. Bo brushed past. The first two steps gave their wooden protest. The third less so. And the remainder dead quiet as he climbed. No clue how he did it. But he always did it—part and parcel of the remarkable ability to approach his objective with spooky silence.

"That pisses me off a little," I said, hands on hips and staring upward. A small window at the landing provided the sole light for the flight of stairs. A sunshine square backlit wild red hair as he cast a Cheshire cat grin. I joined him. Each step made noise. Two knocks and the remote controlled lock mechanism of the steel door clanged. We were expected.

"Honored guests," Jules said, squinting her one eye along the shotgun's double barrels. "Enter! Enter and present yourselves."

Pockets emptied, we both performed a slow turn. I hated this part, but Bo smiled and spun on the tiptoe of one foot. Pirouettes completed, I closed the door. The AC hummed, the room cool. Jules rested the shotgun after a gesture with the weapon's business-end toward the two chairs.

"Sit. Sit, dears."

We did. Bo glanced at the Cirque Du Soleil poster. "*Tout le spectacle.*"

I spoke Spanish, Portuguese, and Arabic. Not French. Bo did.

"*Ils sont remarquables*," Jules said. Clearly she did as well.

He placed the tin of special licorice at the desktop edge. Using his index finger, he eased it toward Jules.

"Mine?" she asked, her eye twinkling.

"I hope so," Bo said. "Unless my associate snatches it away. I like the blade. A statement?"

He referenced the desktop-embedded KA-BAR knife.

"A declaration, perhaps. May I?" she asked and pointed a bony sealant-covered finger at the tin.

"I would be hurt if you didn't."

He smiled. She cackled. The tin was opened, a select piece of black candy inspected, sniffed, and dropped home. Leaning back, eye closed, she sucked and chewed and hummed the *La Marseillaise*. We remained silent until her chair squeaked forward. She rested elbows on the desk, clasped hands, chin on hands. Welcome to the freakin' Clubhouse.

"Mr. Dickerson. How marvelous. It is a joy to finally make your acquaintance, and to salute your taste in confectionary gifts."

I'd never mentioned Bo's name when discussing the past with Jules. But she knew. Of course she knew.

"Case directed my path. I'm a follower in this regard."

"And little else I would venture."

They both smiled. All righty. Bo and Jules. An auspicious start.

"So, to business," I said. "Back from Long Island. Would you like an information dump?"

"That would be grand, dear. May I assume Mr. Dickerson has been informed?"

"And has provided cosmic insights," I said, smiling at my partner.

"A valued perspective," Jules said. "One I'd be most interested hearing."

Full recruitment mode. A potential new client. A gatherer of information. I wasn't too sure the victim was buying it.

During my operational review, she pulled a cigar from her desk drawer and spun the sealed tip against the embedded knife. Fishing around her work-shirt pockets she produced a kitchen match and fired it along one of the chair's arms. The unruly shocks of white-spiked tips remained, the look still a tad disturbing. Bo sat, legs extended, hands across his belly. He listened, a benign pleasantness painted over his countenance. He declined contribution to the tale. Jules's abacus remained static. That wouldn't last for long.

"The only loose end, or dead end, is the mysterious Jordan Pettis," I said, ending the summation.

"Neither mysterious nor loose nor, as of today, expired," Jules said. She cocked her head. "Middle name."

"Middle name?"

"William Jordan Pettis. Your search attempts *would* fail using such overly focused parameters. Our Mr. Pettis uses his first name for public endeavors and formal business settings. His middle solely for personal connections. Particularly when raising funds. A 'Please call me Jordan' gambit."

"Okay." That hurt. I should have searched Pettis and tagged an assortment of qualifiers such as business ventures or overseas investments. Stupid.

"A member of the venture capital class. Sand Hill Road, California."

Melinda Whitmore's words flashed back. California. New rich.

"How does he tie?" I asked.

65

"Here is where it becomes most interesting. Are you comfortable, Mr. Dickerson? I want to ensure my guests are accommodated."

"All good, thanks. And we should give a pass on the middle name misstep."

"Not exactly a misstep," I said and glanced at my brother sprawled across the hard wooden chair. Yeah, it was. But I'd gotten defensive. A simple Bo and Jules meet-and-greet, gather Clubhouse information, wrap the job. The train wasn't headed that direction.

"Oh, I have Mr. Dickerson. Be most assured. Passed over with tender mercies. For such things are outside his bailiwick."

"But a good man. Brave and true."

"Of this, I have no doubt."

"Although linear by nature," Bo said.

"And a needed place for such people amongst our ilk. Truly."

"Could we get back to Jordan Pettis?" I asked.

"But as I understand the situation, layers are involved," Bo said, bypassing my question.

"Exactly!" Jules tapped the desktop for emphasis.

"Layers and dimensions and flows of influence," Bo said, nodding.

"Back to Pettis, people."

"Most astute, Mr. Dickerson," Jules said, ignoring me. "Most astute. Layers and flows and relationships."

"I smell big players," Bo said. "Global. Shadowed."

He didn't mean multi-national corporations. No, he alluded to spooks and clandestine operations and a world at the other end of my ten foot pole.

"You can both slam the breaks on that line of thought," I said.

Jules cast a knowing smile toward Bo. He reciprocated. Under normal situations, both acts would have irritated the fire out of me. But this setting fell well outside normal's realm. A fly buzzed near the spider's web, and whatever plans Jules might have for Bo, she first would ensure capture. Unbeknownst to Jules, this fly flitted well beyond constraints—webbed or otherwise.

"Those types of players don't send amateurs," I continued. "Nassau was amateur city in the murder-for-hire department."

"Layers," Bo said.

Jules chuckled. "We make our resident Braveheart uncomfortable, Mr. Dickerson. Let us plow ahead, straight line."

"Linear," Bo replied.

"Precisely. Now, dear," she said, addressing me, puffing smoke and tilting her forehead my way. "A bit of backstory. A tale which will cement your perception of business affairs gone awry."

"Okay."

"And a treat for you." She opened a drawer, the wood on wood rasping, and produced an index card. Slid it across the desktop. It contained the name Jordan Pettis and his cell phone number. I memorized it—index cards were allowed viewing at the Clubhouse, but never an exit. Hotel California. I slid it back to her. It disappeared back into the drawer, and Jules began her dissertation.

"You are familiar with the Panama Canal?"

"Not a schoolkid, Jules. And you two can stop the Case Lee critique."

Bo gripped my arm and said, "Levity, my brother. Chill. You're my hero in oh so many ways. Don't forget that."

"And mine," Jules added. "A stalwart individual, undaunted. There is much to admire there. Lower your hackles, Odysseus."

They'd had their amusement, riffed off my personal tendencies. Enough.

"Then slap the reins on the mule, Jules. Plow ahead," I said.

Her chair protested as she leaned back and contemplated the ceiling. "Talk. Talk and chatter and little action regarding a competitive Canal alternative. A dry canal, if you will. Highways, rail lines. Unload containers from the Pacific, reload on the Atlantic side. Overland pipelines for crude oil transportation. It is proposed one might perform the transfer functions faster and with less of an economic bite than traversing the Panama Canal."

"Okay."

"Costa Rica is the clear option for such endeavors. A stable government, peaceful residents."

Both Bettencourt's and Whitmore's maps detailed the route. I never connected the route with a Canal alternative. Man, I had to up my game.

"Highly lucrative if successful," she continued. "A financial disaster if it were to fail. Hence the lack of action toward realization."

"And Pettis pulled together funding? A California venture capitalist?"

"A commercial peculiarity within the sea to shining sea landscape." She puffed the cigar and paused, tossing the Jules version of an appealing smile toward Bo. Welcome, said the spider to the fly. Then she returned focus my way.

"The west coast, it would seem, dominates bits and bytes and social media and entertainment. As you well know."

I nodded as response.

"Massive infrastructure endeavors, on the other hand, have an old money appeal. Expectations of quiet financial returns for decades. Economic positions solidified through political and inherited influence. Power wielded over a lifetime or three. Such funding sources tend to reside on the east coast. Quite a dichotomy between the two."

"So our Mr. Pettis dipped the bucket into the deep well of old money," I said. "Put together a deal, for lack of a better term."

"A deal which would compete with the Panama Canal. A dry canal."

"So whose ox gets gored? The big Panama Canal player?"

She cocked her head, shifted her eye from me to Bo and back again.

"Why, our large Asian friend. In a major and concerted and very, very serious manner."

I stared back, unblinking. She inspected the cigar's lit end.

"The Chinese, dear. The Chinese."

Chapter 13

Not what I wanted to hear. The Chinese did business at this scale as an arm of their government. Serious stuff. I glanced toward Bo. He shrugged, above the fray. Well, I sure wasn't above it given two attempts at taking me out. And if the initiator of those little efforts nested with the Chinese government, bad news all around. The Russians were already plenty pissed at me and wanted my head on a stake. And now the Chinese after my butt. Just freakin' great.

"So let me clarify this. You're saying the Chinese thought it a wise idea using Jack Tilly, insurance adjuster, as target practice. In Nassau. And Long Island."

"You take this far too personally," Jules said. "Your tenure in the game is sufficient for a more detached perspective."

"Yeah, well, two murder attempts personalizes perspective."

She fished another kitchen match from her front pocket. The cigar had died out. "If it is any consolation—and it should be," she paused, struck the match, and puffed the cigar to life, "they would not directly engage with such activities."

"Layers," Bo said.

"Precisely, Mr. Dickerson."

The AC hummed. I shifted position, crossed my arms, and sat back. The revealed road was Spookville bound. Time for a detour.

"This is going the wrong direction. I'll buy the Costa Rica dry canal thing. The maps with both Bettencourt and Whitmore. Fine. Toss in Jordan Pettis, dealmaker. Fine. But forget the Chinese. You're discounting other possibilities."

"Hmm." Jules smoked and waited.

"Another competitor for the Costa Rica play. A direct competitor."

"A possibility, of course."

"And the whole mansion of debauchery thing. There's a Bettencourt trust fund in the Bahamas. Who knows where the fund manager plays in this?"

"And Mr. Pettis?" she asked. "How would he play into the paradise island mix?"

Not well. Not well at all. Straws grasped, although the direct competitor angle held water.

"Let's stick with motivation, Jules. Motivation to whack an insurance adjuster from Omaha. Two attempts."

"I must have another." She laid the cigar on the desk, the lit end suspended over the edge. "May I indulge myself?" she asked Bo. Her finger tapped the licorice tin top.

"Why celebrate deprivation?" Bo asked. He tilted his head, the benign smile still pasted.

She plucked another candy and sucked it, eye closed. I shifted again, and the chair protested.

"A bridge, Monsieur Lee." Her eye opened hooded and focused my way. She continued working the licorice. "One we must cross."

"Not too sure about that."

"Perhaps a dash or two of added impetus, dear. Allow me."

I did. Jules detailed China's Panama Canal involvement. To counter competition, China invested billions in port facilities on both sides, Atlantic and Pacific. And they invested billions in the Canal itself. Increased carrying capacities, enlarged the system of dams and locks. Big money. But their goods, which filled US shelves, were valued at half a trillion dollars per year. Serious business, indeed. About as serious as it gets.

But competition for the Canal's services did exist. Several large shippers already headed west from China, loaded with Chinese goods, and used the Suez Canal. Through the Mediterranean, across the Atlantic, and unload on the US east coast. An added couple of days travel, but doing so they also bypassed the hefty Panama Canal transit fee—as much as half a million bucks. No small chunk of change.

"Why not mandate their ships use the canal?" I asked. "No Costa Rica dry canal, no Suez Canal, no competition."

"Because, dear boy, they do not own the most shipping vessels. Far, far from it. And those large shippers—French, Danes, Japanese, Swiss, South Korean—will utilize the fastest, cheapest route from point A to point B."

A disconnect wide and deep remained. Take a leap of faith and assume China's hand in the demise of Bettencourt and Whitmore. But going after an insurance adjuster? Too discordant, a bridge too far.

"So back to that bridge," I said. "I'm not hearing anything definitive. Could be, might be. And the thread between China and an insurance adjuster is too thin to see."

"A legitimate view," Jules said. She inspected the cigar's end and blew on it. A few sucking puffs ensured it remained lit.

"So let's whittle this thing down. The basics," I said.

"Do not disregard the shavings," Jules said.

"Nuances," Bo said, his lone conversational contribution.

"Subtleties," Jules concurred.

"Yeah, well, let's flush nuances and subtleties for the moment. Concentrate on yours truly as target practice for the Chinese government. Not buying it."

"Again, brave Ulysses. Not them. No. A third party. A third party assigned the job of stopping a competitive project. A layer of separation. And nothing personal about it."

"You don't know that."

"I do, dear. Experience drives such perception. And the third party sent less than qualified individuals to dispatch you in Nassau. Having learned, the same third party upped the ante, or professionalism, on Long Island. It makes perfect sense."

"Fine. But they—whoever the hell they are—still don't know who Jack Tilly of the Providence Insurance company is. I want to keep it that way."

"As well you should. But the layer in question, if one considers the Long Island miscreant, may well have a view of you beyond the insurance impersonation."

She intimated I was made. A happenstance I was unwilling to accept. It opened way, way too many doors.

"Long odds, Jules."

"Perhaps."

"I'll grant you someone on Abaco could have taken a photo of me. Passed it to their boss. Which set up the Long Island hitter. Okay. Got it. But plucking Case Lee from a cell phone photo requires deep resources. Clandestine resources."

She puffed her cigar. Her expression neither adamant nor resolute. The Jules version of empathy. I gave a sigh, a head shake. It was possible I'd brushed against clandestine operatives. So what?

"Doesn't matter. The job is over. Except for one last thing. I'll contact Pettis. He's on the hit list."

"Then do so, dear. And disappear down your watery trail."

"So my client's report will tie Bettencourt and Whitmore and this Pettis guy together. Commercial endeavor. A dry canal through Costa Rica. One investor dead from poisoning. The other dead under suspicious circumstances. Plenty of unknowns, but that's okay."

"Okay indeed," she said. "Tempering such an outlook with the one big item."

Enough. I turned toward Bo. "You ready?"

"Ready." He smiled.

Jules shifted focus toward Bo. "What a delight conversing with you, Mr. Dickerson. We shall exchange contact information. Our Sir Galahad shall provide you the rules of communication."

"Cool." Bo beamed.

"And perhaps our next little tête-à-tête shall involve the future. A future together. Welcome to the Clubhouse."

One large disconnect remained. The abacus, untouched. I'd provided Jules valued information, and she'd provisioned me. The balance for this discussion accepted, whichever side of the ledger it fell. But, very unlike her, the device remained unused. I lifted a chin toward it, raised an eyebrow. She waved a dismissive hand.

"Your introduction of Mr. Dickerson constitutes sufficient payment. Let's not soil this grand and glorious acquaintance with such considerations."

I turned toward Bo. "Let's hit the Ditch, bud."

"Let's do it. And you, Madame," Bo said as he stood and delivered a slight bow. "You have been a surprise and a joy. The appropriate whale identified, the harpoon sharpened for our hero. Bravo and a tad intimidating, and I like your hair."

Jules palmed the tips of a few bright white spikes, smiling. She may have blushed. Mercy.

She captured Bo's phone number and asked me to provide him her contact information. Downstairs we collected our weapons and Bo's groceries. We maintained a quick pace toward the docks as I held a strong hankering to get underway. Our quick dance with the land of shadows was over and it was now adios time.

"You got pissed at me," Bo said.

"A little irritated. I didn't appreciate the dissection. Particularly when you have Jules as a scalpel-wielding ally."

"It wasn't that."

"Do tell, mister savoir faire."

"The Clubhouse is your private domain. I represented an interloper. It was understandable you'd get protective."

"Protective about Jules?"

"She loves you," Bo said. "I know why."

"Don't think she loves anyone or anything. She's Jules. Period."

"No, my brother. No. She dons a knobbly mask but underneath, love. You represent brightness and truth. A rarity in her world. You are lucky, and should consider reciprocating."

"I'll think about it. You good now? I mean, with meeting her?"

"Better than good. Insights, observations. A new channel opened. Now let us sally forth, my Georgia peach. Sally forth and adopt a more languid pace and place in the universe."

We did. I released the *Ace* and cruised down the Elizabeth River, the diesel's low rumble fine and steady underfoot. A solid and pleasant late afternoon as the sun lowered inside a clear sky. Friendly waves were cast toward the few workboats plying the river—the kick-off for a relaxed several days traveling. A fine evening lay ahead while a Charleston visit with Mom and CC sat on the horizon. Then the danger klaxon sounded, loud and shrill.

Chapter 14

They had staked the Clubhouse. An educated guess on their part, playing pre-guided odds. Whoever wanted this investigation into Bettencourt, Whitmore, and Pettis cleaned held inside information. The Clubhouse location—an open secret—was known among clandestine players world-wide. Hence the shotgun greeting. Jules was a nondenominational procurer and dispenser of information. With a heavy thumb pressed on the US homeland concerns side of the scale. But she was well known. And when Bo and I exited and jabbered while strolling toward the *Ace*, they trailed us. Followed on foot and now followed as we cruised. I'd let my guard down. A stupid mistake, no excuses.

"Hey, Bo. Take the wheel for a minute."

He occupied the throne and surveyed his cosmic kingdom as we tooled down the Elizabeth River at the *Ace's* cruising speed of twelve knots.

"No worries. Did you fix the turn signal? I may want to make a few course corrections."

"Keep her straight and steady for the moment. Potential target. Trailing."

Step one—define danger as the target. Place the bullseye on them, not us. Bo joined me in the wheelhouse.

"How rude," he said. "And just when a fine day was ending."

Zeiss binoculars helped identify a sport fishing boat. Their large outboard engine matched our speed. Cranked up, their vessel would fly. It maintained a discrete quarter-mile distance. A few other boats occupied this stretch of the Elizabeth, moving both directions, but they each presented common activities and attributes. This trailing boat didn't.

"A bit late for a fishing trip," I said, handing Bo the binoculars. "And no rods evident."

Sport fishing boats in this area were equipped with fishing rod holders. Four or six rods, pointed skyward, a typical configuration when headed toward the fishing grounds.

"Four dudes," Bo said.

We turned east—a cut-through toward the North Landing River.

"And they aren't planning an overnight stay." Their boat wasn't designed or built for night cruising. A sport fishing boat was built to get the occupants into fishy waters and back home.

They took the east cut-through as well and maintained their distance.

"Four dudes modeling khaki fatigues. Perhaps a photo shoot awaits," Bo said. His voice inflection lacked any pretense of humor. This was more than potential danger. It was an affront, a rude incursion on our sedate trip down the Ditch.

"Gimme five minutes. I'll gather a few tools."

I dropped below deck and readied two Colt 901 assault rifles, swapping red dot scopes for Elcan Specter scopes wired for night vision. The sun would set within an hour. I attached noise suppressors to the barrels of both weapons. If hitters, they'd strike as soon as we entered lonely turf. That wouldn't be long. Once we entered the North Landing River, Currituck Sound lay a short hop south. A spillage area filled with marshes, swamps, sloughs, and isolated tree-filled hummocks of dry land. I wrapped a blanket around the rifles and toted them up the steps and into the wheelhouse. No point showing our hole cards.

The entire exercise accepted there was a chance their boat represented no danger. A logical explanation for their activities clear and evident for those not imbued with bounty-fueled paranoia. But Bo and I had faced bounty hunters in the recent past. And my well-founded suspicions were mixed with awareness that the Caribbean job could also manifest this type of activity. Killers. Killers sent to stamp a period at the end of the Case Lee sentence.

"Swapped scopes," I said and uncovered the weapons alongside Bo. "Night vision."

"Good on ye, goober. You do have a fine nose for nefarious activities. Our buddies display a keen interest regarding our progress. They view us through binoculars." He lowered the binoculars and glanced my way. "Any other handy tools downstairs?"

Cold resignation that these were bad guys ratcheted up. "Yeah. But I wanted these ready. There's a quiet stretch of river coming soon. They may goose it and make a play."

"If so, welcome to their final curtain call." Bo grinned, eyes glittered. The warrior began shedding his husk.

"You want full whisper on the handgun?"

I'd attach silencers to two H&K .45 semi-automatic pistols. My question was whether Bo wanted sub-sonic ammo. Regular high-velocity ammo—my preference—spit a muted sound signature. Sub-sonic ammo emitted only a light pop and the near-silent mechanical slide of the weapon's autoload mechanism. An up close and personal configuration. The way Bo worked.

"If you would be so kind," he said. "And I've got my own knife."

Bo preferred the Bundeswehr combat knife. Another working-close tool. I stuck with a KA-BAR knife, since my personal preference was killing the bastards long before knife-range.

Collected pistols and associated battle gear were toted into the wheelhouse where we'd change clothes, visible to the following boat. Fatigues, lace-up boots, webbed vest. A statement. One not needed if they were benign travelers, and a potential dissuader if they held ill-intent.

Shadows lengthened and the sun approached the horizon. We turned onto the North Landing River, headed for Currituck Sound. A few short miles and then the estuarial area where swamp and marsh and sloughs presented an uninhabited patchwork of wilderness.

"Bounty hunters or gentlemen associated with your current endeavors?" Bo asked as he laced a boot. "Or do they hate us because we're beautiful?"

"No telling. Suspect the current contract."

"Snared us at the Clubhouse?"

"Better than even money."

It stunk of spooks. An Abaco playhouse member might have clicked a cell phone photo of me. Then passed it on to the head honcho. Possible. Which meant the Caribbean conspiracy mastermind would have clandestine ties with knowledge of the Clubhouse. It played into Jules's murky assertions.

Or plain vanilla bounty hunters, fed through clandestine operators who already possessed photos. A collective play for quick cash.

Or the Russians. Still mightily pissed and with a strong tendency—second only to the Sicilian Mafia—toward exacting revenge.

Or four guys out for a boat ride as nightfall approached. Where there were no towns and no riverside burgs within twenty miles.

Block it out, Case. Deal with the situation. Mull over who sent them later and get real. These guys weren't selling personalized bowling shirts.

The act of gear prep unlocked the kill switch protective cover. These weren't two-bit killers taking a hit job. Another level, an escalation. A firefight. Unlike my former teammates—Bo, Catch, Marcus—who owned the ability to flow from workaday life into full-tilt battle violence, I required commitment time. Marcus, our team leader, termed it my clinical assessment. Whatever the attribute, I kept the requisite mindset, the ferocity, tucked well away. Pulled from deep hiding when called for and shaken to remove wrinkles. Done with something different than hesitancy—a reticent knowing, an acceptance. An acceptance the killing would start soon, so time to throw the switch. My teammates long ago internalized my personal preparation and accepted it without comment. They did so for a simple and single reason. Once the switch was thrown, I delivered with the best of them.

The boat traffic thinned and sunset loomed. The *Ace* entered an area of expansive marsh, swamp, and trees. A set-aside nature preserve. We slid past a large sign stipulating, *Notice: The Preserve is now closed due to increased illegal activity and DCR's lack of funding.* Yeah, well, illegal activities would soon escalate exponentially.

"This damp and primal turf holds promise," Bo said, assessing potential battle grounds.

"I know this area. An offshoot of the river turns right at the southern end of the preserve."

"Let's take it. And see who wants to join our picnic, Boo-Boo."

We did. Pines and scrub brush filled the preserve's center, the ground a few feet higher than the surrounding marsh and sloughs and swamp. If they followed, then game on.

"Your kind of turf, Bo." His former home within the Dismal Swamp held such surroundings.

"It's all my kind of turf. Tighten your jockstrap. The party starts soon."

Dusk settled, night edged. As we curved up the river's narrow arm a deep slough appeared on the right. We turned and eased our way in. Egrets roosted among the scattered trees and the v-wakes of fish rushed past the *Ace*, escaping our intrusion. The slough made a slight curve and dead-ended. We nudged onto a muddy bank. End of the line.

Engine killed, we listened. The idle rumble of a high-powered outboard followed our trail up the river arm and came to a full stop at the entrance to our slough. Out of sight, silent, three hundred yards away. They'd stopped and either anchored or pulled onto the shore.

"Two by two," Bo whispered. "Headed toward the ark." He handed me bug dope—mosquitoes swarmed full force, buzzing around our heads and arms.

His battle assessment—two would take one side of the slough, two on the other. The four would work our way, toward the *Ace*, and take care of business. Collect their fee and maybe the bounty. Well, the collection plate started at the end of my rifle barrel, boys. So kiss your butts goodbye.

Battle commenced, silent stalks, no quarter given or expected. I threw the switch and became all fight.

"Stealth and vigor, my brother," Bo whispered as he slid over the side. Wild eyes crackled with energy, his face tight. "We shall meet anon."

Bo pointed toward the preserve's hummock of high ground a hundred yards in the distance and signaled that I should take it. My nod of agreement committed Bo to the slough's opposite side where marsh grass, knee-deep water, and thick mud reigned. Where two of them stalked our way. Welcome to Bo's playground.

I slid over the side and hunkered. Paused and rubbed marsh mud across my face, neck, and back of hands. Then I moved fast. Long wet strides, hunched over, no splashes. The elevated patch of trees and brush were my destination and hunting blind. Night draped, moonlight shone. Each silent step brought the smell of decayed vegetation and brackish water. The enemy would assume we'd hold a defensive posture and make their way toward the *Ace*. They'd fall short of their goal.

Hand and knees into the brush, I worked my way toward a collection of pines, low scrub thick at their base. Finding a home and belly-crawling to the edge of the brush, I held the rifle's night scope at the ready.

The forty second crawl afforded final entry of contrition and remorse— short, fleeting, and dismissed. I didn't ask for this, didn't want this, and wished it didn't have to happen. But it did. They were here to kill me. Me and Bo. The insanity of the act stood tall. And any guilt over their soon-to-be deaths departed as whispered wings of night flight, passing. Previous battles and encounters flashed—death the common platform. Motivations varied, time passed, my personal outlook more disillusioned. Rusty hinges protested, but the Case Lee castle door slammed shut on such thoughts. Time to live, or die.

Bad news across the landscape. No movement. None. Either these guys remained with their fiberglass fishing boat and reconnoitered the situation or they were former operators, hunting. Retired Special Forces and take your pick of origin. British, French, Israeli, Russian, Czech. Or US. Nationality bore no meaning. What did matter was these guys, if coming, moved low and slow and silent. I shouldered the rifle and relied on the night scope. Naked eyeballs failed to identify hostile actors.

Although marsh grass obscured the view, the *Ace's* upper deck railing and wheelhouse were visible. The scene held elements of a Homer Winslow painting—marsh water reflected the quarter moon and starlight. A small animal, rabbit or possum or weasel, scuttled nearby my position. Mosquitoes droned.

I spotted one. He belly-squirmed near the slough's bank, headed for the *Ace*. He performed an incursion, a violation not tolerated. I'd take him first. A game trail provided an opportunity. The attacker continued sliding along the slough's bank, made his way toward my boat, and offered minimal glimpses through the thick grass. That is, until he crawled a hundred fifty yards away across a twelve-inch wide path beaten down by assorted critters. Too late for a head shot, his body was already a quarter way across the line of sight. Crosshairs fixed on his exposed side, lungs and heart shot attainable. Trigger squeezed, a low rifle crack, and he flinched, attempted a crawl, and died. No exaltation, and no remorse. A clinical dispatch that kicked off the battle. Three left.

Whether they moved among the vegetation and stagnant water toward me or were split with one or two on the other side of the slough as Bo assumed remained unknown. A bullet whipped above my head and popped foliage, followed by a suppressed rifle crack. Bogey number two. He'd keyed on the brief glint of my muzzle flash. Two more rapid shots hit close—too close—and his muzzle flash shifted in the night. A classic setup—fire and maneuver. He'd try and keep me pinned while his cohorts worked their way into a kill shot position.

Screw that noise. Belly-flat, I scooted backward and sought temporary sanctuary deep into the brush, under the copse of trees. A collection point and opportunity to reposition. I stomach crawled forward again to my right and established another fire position. The shooter continued popping rounds into my former location. His comrades, unseen, headed my way as I scoped, searched. The first among us to be seen, died.

The fire toward my former position stopped. The shooter changed tactics. Or met Bo. I bet my life on the latter. Meaning all four adversaries attacked from my side of the slough. Bo, grasping the reality, swam the slough and hunted at their backs. Adios, dude shooting at me. No noise accompanied the cessation of fire, so Bo used either his knife or the silenced .45 pistol. Two down. Two left.

A breeze picked up. It helped keep the mosquitoes at bay, but hindered sighting the enemy. Marsh grass waved and camouflaged non-natural vegetative movement. A fish splashed, unseen but close, the sound carrying. Every sense maxed, breath steady. Two operators hunted me, stalked my position. I hunted them, static, searching. And Bo as a marsh ghost at their backs.

Chapter 15

Time doesn't stand still. It compresses. Twenty minutes of intense searching passed as five. Sounds, sights, smells accentuated. A hyper-focus on movement, irregular shapes, splashes, animals of the night disturbed.

Nothing. Nada. These guys were good—operators, without doubt. Flat against the ground, my movements were minimal. Slight shifts of the weapon, scoping waving grass and moving water and moonlight shadows. Another compressed fifteen minutes passed, the tension meter pegged.

One of them made a mistake. It cost him his life. Fifty yards away, as chest-high grass moved with the breeze and standing water amongst the vegetation rippled, a larger ripple presented. Slight, barely discernible. A ripple pushed, forcing its way through the small breeze-induced water movement. I focused there and scoped a small patch of swampy marsh. Waited.

The barrel of his shouldered weapon peeked through the marsh grass first, its progress in inches. Slow, cautious. Then a hand, gripping the weapon's forestock. The world blocked out and acute concentration reigned. His head appeared. I didn't hesitate and squeezed the trigger. His body splash sent small waves through the immediate section of marsh.

One left, assuming Bo took out the shooter who fired at my previous position. I scooted backward, flat against the ground then forward again and assumed another firing position, thirty feet to the right of where I'd last squeezed the trigger. And waited, searched.

The breeze moved pine needles overhead, their aroma mixed with marshland. Time condensed again. I was dead still, filled with awareness a bullet could drive into my innards any second. A loon called, another answered. No sign of Bo. Or the fourth shooter. Bo might have taken him down, done his invisible stalking thing. A possibility. But I wasn't counting on it and was prepared to remain, scoping, hunting, until daybreak. Anticipatory movement meant a bullet, death. I'd wait. If one remained, he knew my general area. He'd come.

Thirty minutes, an hour. My movement of the rifle was deliberate, miniscule. Both eyes open—one sited through the scope, sussed detail. The other captured a wider field of dark vision, movement-focused.

Bad, bad news arrived. I smelled him. The breeze crossed from right to left, and he'd approached from the right. Crawled, inch by inch. And now, with his weapon aimed my general direction, stopped and sought. The aroma of pine needles, decayed marsh grass, and the sweat of human exertion. Close, close. I ceased all movement. My cheek rested against the rifle's stock. A slow, slow head twist of an inch or two. Eyes strained toward my right and sought his position. A vague shape hugged the ground through the lower limbs of scrub brush. A darker area, nebulous, unmoving. Could have been a log. A log that appeared in the last thirty minutes. Seven paces away and pointed my direction. Pointed toward my side profile. My movement meant death. Any movement. A quick snapshot to the right mandated I first shift my weapon his direction. And he'd cut loose with high velocity lead prior to me firing a shot. Son of a bitch.

No motion from either of us. I'd identified him. The reverse wasn't true. Otherwise I'd be dead by now. So he remained still, quiet, and hunted me. He may have reciprocated—stared straight at me, another dark log-like shape, wondering if I was a recent addition to the landscape. Mosquitoes hovered between gentle gusts of breeze. Wing flaps slapped water as a pair of ducks hustled away from a perceived predator. Seven paces. Twenty feet.

I considered my options but damn few presented. Waiting him out gave the best odds. He'd move again, crawl again, hunt forward. Toward me. But a crawl required assistance from shoulders, arms. And each shift, each progression, took his weapon's aim off my location. The rifle barrel pointed either to my right or left as he crawled. It offered the lone opportunity to strike. It would be close. My weapon would swing a wider arc before firing a snapshot. Odds in his favor, but no other option presented. He was headed toward me, inch by inch. I rested, shallow breaths, head faced right, and pressed against my weapon's stock. His move.

A light pop and metallic snick of finality. A silenced .45 with subsonic ammo cycling a round. Bo. My adversary displayed the slightest of movement. The log-like shape relaxed, lowered even more into the ground. Dead.

"Goodnight, Irene." Spoken, not whispered, less than ten feet from the dark shape. Oh, man. Relief flood gates opened.

How he did it, with both myself and my adversary so intent, so focused, would remain a mystery. Our Delta teammates had experienced his ability across a wide swath of settings and locales. Bo's cloak of invisibility. No freakin' clue how he pulled it off, but he sure did, and it couldn't come at a more opportune time.

"You take care of another one?" I asked, voice low.

I didn't want a conversation among the pines without knowledge the battle—this stealthy silent battle—was over.

"Did indeed." His shadowed figure loomed over his latest victim. The Bundeswehr knife appeared, shining in the moon and star light. He leaned over and removed a body part. Likely an ear. He'd make use of it as a weird Bo totem.

I rolled onto my back. The adrenaline pump eased off. My mouth's metallic taste evidenced how jacked my body was the last hour. Oh man. Bo appeared above me, backlit with moonlight through the trees. He squatted, holding the knife.

"Operators," he said. "Good ones."

"Not that damn good."

He wiped the knife against his soaked fatigues and sheathed it. He'd swam the slough and crawled through marsh and now hovered next to me drenched.

"Felt a twinge or three. From New Guinea. Wonder if the universe is signaling?"

Bo's injuries during our last adventure were the worst of our bunch. If I'd been shot up as much as him, I'd sure have felt more than a twinge or three hunting through the swampy marsh.

"Maybe it's signaling we should shunt aside this peculiar way of life," I said.

"Peculiar?"

I lifted my head off the ground and stared into his shadowed face. He'd cocked his head, questioning.

"You don't find this peculiar? Right now? Four dead bodies sprinkled about an isolated marsh? A freakin' battle before supper?"

"What are we eating?"

My head rested back on the pine needles and dirt. It was over. Thank God.

"What did you collect, Bo?"

I required recovery time. Allow body and mind to return, embrace, a state of normalcy. Pull back on the throttle. Bo wasn't hindered with such requisites.

"Ears."

"Necklace?"

"Haven't decided. I'll allow them to dry for a day or two. I feel like steak."

"I feel like another permanent bloody benchmark was pounded into the ground. And I look back and see a long trail of those."

He stood and rolled his shoulders. An owl hooted above us, having perched and watched the killing floor below. Mosquitoes came and went with the breeze. The smell of the nearby dead man's blood carried over us.

"Coronado and the staked plain."

His statement referenced the conquistador explorer. Which would segue into one of Bo's life tales. I could rise and check dead bodies for ID, but didn't feel like moving. Stars were flung by the bushelfull overhead. Post-battle drain ruled. My heartbeat stood normal, but the backwash of adrenaline still coursed.

"Okay. Staked plain."

"The Texas-New Mexico border lands. The Llano Estacado. Where Coronado sought the city of gold. The terrain featureless. It was said he set tall stakes as he moved. Back-sighted on those and ensured he kept a straight line. Never found gold. Maybe he should have stopped having those left-behind stakes guide him."

Pine needles pricked the back of my neck and I scratched a spot along my thigh that called for it an hour ago.

"You're making a helluva point. Which means I've slipped off the deep end. Or unknowingly received a head shot."

"Tonight was a single point on our path. Future points need not align with this one."

I extended a hand and he pulled me upright. The profile of the *Ace*—dim, with stark geometric lines surrounded by the softer curves of nature—shone sufficient to anchor me. I gripped the back of Bo's neck and shared a forehead bump.

"Thanks. He had me," I said.

"Perhaps you had him. Don't dismiss the possibility. Schrodinger's cat."

"Screw the cat, my brother. You took care of business."

He patted my side. "So shall we finish this business, cast off, and eat?" His white teeth gleamed, the smile so genuine and so, so needed.

We finished this business. Each body searched. No ID, no identifiers. They carried MK17 assault rifles with night vision scopes —standard stuff. Man was I lucky. The guy Bo shot twenty feet away from me likely relied on naked vision, focused on movement within the brushy area. Use of his scope may have identified my shape. I'd never know. Thirty minutes later we boarded their boat. We wore gloves—no fingerprints. The vessel contained no papers, registrations, nothing. They ran this ops incognito. Operators.

We backed off the mud bank and eased away from the preserve. Entered Currituck Sound, headed south. Currituck—a thirty mile long and five mile wide estuarial bay—held a few tug/barge combinations and fewer pleasure boats as the evening progressed. I fixed a double shot of Grey Goose on ice. Bo grabbed a beer. We shared the wheelhouse.

"Pay Case a visit," Bo said. "Relax. Get it together. I'd forgotten you don't live a boring life, El Conquistador."

"Could use some boring."

"A substantial body count for a Colonel Mustard in the library gig. Seven?"

"Two of those are yours."

"Five, then. I mention expired inhabitants of this earth only to ward off your angst-filled reflection BS. A preventative assault."

"Good of you."

"Yes it is. And those weren't bounty hunters. They wanted your Jack Tilly butt in a sling. Layers and timing, bucko."

"The Caribbean job kicked it off. I'll buy that. But the bounty might have been the sugar frosting. Added incentive."

"Which plunges recent events into a different category. Driven by clandestine ops," Bo said.

"Yeah. I get it."

The damn bounty. Catch, Bo, and I came close in New Guinea. A Russian. We sniffed, circled, and captured someone who knew the funding source. But he was killed before answers emerged.

Besides the Russians and the CIA, bounty knowledge nested among the unknowns. The Chinese may have owned awareness. Or not. Hard to say.

"Well, get this goober boy. You can make a clean break. You're off the grid again. Change course. Stop looking back at those stakes."

"I'm tired, Bo. My own private swirl. Let's let the clock tick for a while."

We did. The night was night warm and clear, the *Ace* rumbled, life washed past. We crossed into North Carolina waters and an hour later turned east. Found anchorage among the marsh islands of the Currituck National Wildlife Refuge, part of the long barrier island separating the bay from the Atlantic.

I retrieved steaks from the fridge, fired the upper deck grill, and opened a bottle of Virginia wine. Bo lit a bowl of weed and hung in his hammock.

"So, just spitballing here," he said, voice low and filled with humor. "But a niche market may have arrived at your doorstep. A business opportunity."

"Do tell." The steaks sizzled while the dim lights of far distant burgs were the sole reminder we weren't alone on this planet. The aftermath of killing began shedding its weight.

"Young folks appear enamored with adventure activities. Well, crank it up a notch."

"I know where this is going."

"I can see the social media ads. Thinking of hiking the Andes? Why not take it to the next level?"

"Come take the ride of your life on board the *Ace of Spades*," I said, grinning. "Get your adventurous tail shot at."

"Yes, the Russians will be after your adventure-seeking ass. But that's not all! The Chinese have joined the chase. Attempts on your life from multiple sources!"

"And it all starts with a visit to the Clubhouse. Where the business end of a double barrel shotgun greets you at the door."

"And as an added bonus," he said. "We'll visit a variety of exotic spots and ensure a professional killer or three joins the fray."

"Weaponry and bullet-proof gear not included," I said, laughing. Release flowed and equilibrium reset. Silly, foolish stuff—but it fueled the relief valve.

"Your mileage may vary." Bo chuckled along with me.

I was home, nestled. Bo added much needed companionship. And we'd made it. Made it through another dark slice of life. One hidden from all but a very few on this good earth. Events unknown, unmarked, tucked away in the inky shadows as the grand clock ticked on. I cast quick glance well past the stars to express gratitude and make a request. "Thanks. Sincerely. From both of us. But could use a little help navigating forward."

Chapter 16

Dawn. A new day and greeted with open arms. Coffee time. I padded onto the foredeck, avoiding excessive noise in case Bo slept. His hammock hung empty. Well, he'd always been a pre-dawn riser. Coffee water heated as I stretched, working out the kinks. I heard my red-headed brother before sighting him. He belted out an old Rolling Stones song from around a shoreline curve of head-high marsh grass. He appeared, splashing along, a driftwood-made spear—no more than a sharpened stick—raised and pointed my direction as a mock threat. Then tossed into the marsh. His other hand gripped the gills of a large redfish. Breakfast.

"The menu stipulated croaker," I said. "What kind of B&B you running here, mister?"

A blank canvas, another day, and started fresh. A personal commitment not to back-sight those bloody stakes. All good.

"Fresh out of croaker, my Georgia mullet. Catch as catch can." I handed him a filet knife and avoided his use of the Bundeswehr—a weapon recently used for other activities. Two ears were strung on a looped length of cord at the front rail, gaining full sun exposure for quicker drying. Bo squatted near the *Ace*'s bow and with a deft hand produced two fat filets.

"You want anything with that?" I fired another burner and placed a cast iron skillet over the flame. Poured a bit of olive oil and rummaged for spices.

"Coffee."

"Can do easy."

We cruised, ate with our fingers, and relished the act of being. The day turned hot, the wind light as we headed south. A wave and smile toward passing vessels—tugs, pleasure boats, cruisers. The low rumble of the *Ace*'s diesel felt through bare feet.

Bo plugged his version of music into the sound system. Low verbal hums, deep kettle drums, and random short high frequency electronic slashes. It washed over the foredeck and into the wheelhouse.

"Just an FYI," I said through the wheelhouse's open windows. "This so-called music has limited appeal. A limited time-frame appeal."

Bo lay in his hammock, feet pointed toward the bow. At each electronic screech across the drummed and hummed backtrack, he'd raise both arms

89

and gesture outward. A push-away. "Limited being the operative word. Dig deep, Mr. Lee."

"Or dig out some earplugs below deck."

Four or five hours until Albemarle Sound. A five mile crossing and re-enter the hemmed-in Intracoastal Waterway. The Ditch. No place I'd rather be.

"So what's the plan, Stan?" Bo asked.

His general enquiry about where this sojourn might head. My response offered an opportunity to turn off the music.

"Four hundred miles between us and Charleston. A three or four day trip. Take in our private slice of the Ditch."

"And visit your mom and CC?"

"Yep."

"Cool."

And that was that. Bo world—take it as it comes.

"Gotta make a phone call," I said. "And file a report. That's the extent of this day's plans. Other than to keep heading south."

"The mysterious yet much beloved Mr. Pettis?"

"One and the same." I'd try him through my Jack Tilly temporary phone exchange. It would appear as an Omaha number for Pettis. "He's in Cali and may still slumber with sweet dreams. Those will halt in short order after he hears from me."

"Roust him with the dulcet tones of your voice. Fill me in post-contact. I'm here to help. But there may be a learning curve with this sleuthing stuff."

"You'll require a trench coat. At least look the part."

"Bo Dickerson. Man of mystique."

"You mean mystery."

"No, goober." He swung his legs from the hammock and beat a rhythm against his rock-hard stomach. "Mysteries abound. It is one's *approach* to them that matters."

"And what type of sleuthing gigs would interest you? I can place a good word with the Zurich gnomes." Man, I missed hanging with him. They broke and buried the Bo mold.

"Time and space issues. Navigating the universe."

"Serious stuff. You have experience?"

"Beaucoup. I'm awash in it."

"The Swiss should be duly impressed."

The breeze stiffened and the *Ace* plowed its rolling gait forward. Another pot of coffee brewed and the final step of the Caribbean job was initiated. I dialed Jordan Pettis.

"Who's this?" Demanding and accusatory and delivered with buckets of attitude.

"Mr. Pettis. My name is Jack Tilly. Providence Insurance Company."

He hung up. I tried again. No answer. So be it. As a final effort, I texted. *Hey, dumbass. This is about Bettencourt and Whitmore and you staying alive.*

Ten seconds later my phone rang. He didn't wait for me to speak.

"Insurance company my ass. And I thought you people never contacted the client."

I didn't have the foggiest notion what he meant.

"You want to run that by again, Pettis?"

"I. Am. Your. Client. And those Zurich people said I'd never hear from you. Well *that's* worked really well."

Oh man. Pettis contacted Global Resolutions for the Caribbean job. With Case Lee the appointed finder of answers.

"Didn't know you were my client, so cool your jets. This is a courtesy call about the deaths of Bettencourt and Whitmore."

"Tell me."

Bo cranked push-ups under the foredeck tarp. I eased west toward Albemarle Sound. A pod of dolphins angled toward the *Ace*, the sun dancing off their backs as they surfaced.

"You there?" he asked.

"Not for long. Bottom line, Mr. Congeniality—you'll want to keep your head low. Hitters might be after you."

"Hitters?"

"Killers. And their ranks swell the longer I talk with you."

"Hey! Chill! I'm stressed, all right? Tilly, right? Jack Tilly? You ever been the target for bad guys, Tilly?"

"Once or twice. Read the report after I submit it later today. You paid for it. But understand you're in a precarious situation."

"No shit, Sherlock. I contacted the Bay Area FBI after Bettencourt and Whitmore died and told them the same thing. They blew me off. Blew me off!"

"I'm stunned. Read the report."

"Wait! Wait! We need to talk."

"No we don't."

"Look, look. I could use someone like you. I'm hiding on this stupid island behind locked doors. I'll pay."

"Don't do bodyguard work. Good luck, Pettis."

I hung up. He called back. When I didn't answer, he began texting. What a jerk.

Turned out he sat in the American Virgin Islands. Even I could figure that's where he met Whitmore. And pitched his Costa Rica deal. Whitmore knew Bettencourt, and brought him into the fold as another investor. Chain complete. But the text messages also came with offers of further employment. He knew when he'd contacted Global Resolutions they'd hire someone like me. Someone with special skills. Fine. But I wasn't playing nanny for this venture capital jerk.

Bo piloted while I completed my report. I mentioned the conversation with Pettis—full disclosure. Sent it encrypted through the deep web. Zurich would acknowledge receipt and fatten my Swiss bank account. Done and done.

Chapter 17

"So here's what I don't get," I said. "You've always clicked with women. So what's the issue?"

We sat in the lone bar of a tiny burg along the Ditch. I'd refueled and bought a few food items. This stretch of the Ditch was hemmed with Spanish moss-laden oaks. Bright green aquatic vegetation bobbed across the surface as a wealth of insects started their nighttime cacophony. The bar's screened windows and doors kept them at bay. My poison was Grey Goose on the rocks. Bo drank a beer. A dozen folks sat with us along the bar or at tables. A few younger couples, several retirees, and three large guys liquored up at a corner table. Intermittent waves of their loud laughter filled the place. And a barkeep who paid close attention to the televised ball game droning above the bar. No killers, no bounty hunters. The docked *Ace* was visible through a screen window.

"Issue connotes a problem," Bo said. "I would contend that's the wrong category."

"Okay."

"Let's look at this swirl we call life. And have a gander at you."

"Okay."

Bo peeled off the beer bottle label, wadded it between two fingers, and dropped it on the bar top.

"Among the billions of stars and planets and through a weird time continuum, you and Rae connected."

My murdered wife, Rae Ellen Bonham.

"Like a nuclear collider," he continued. "Two atoms among billions connect. Explode."

"We fell in love, Bo."

"Exactly! A collision improbable and far-fetched. But it happened. A soul mate collision. High odds lay there, my brother. Astronomical odds."

"Yeah. I get it. And this isn't about Rae. Or me."

He lifted off the barstool and with a sad smile bumped heads. A gentle gesture, message understood. Let's leave Rae's memory alone. Bo gestured toward the barkeep, who'd delivered another nearby patron a long-neck bottle of beer. The barkeep smiled, approached and asked if we'd like another.

"My simple friend would. Yes, please," Bo said. "As for this magnificent creature perched before you, something pink."

"Pink?"

"And frothy."

The guy blinked, cogitated, and clearly struggled to fulfill Bo's request.

"Got a bottle of Campari. Been sittin' on the shelf since I bought the place ten years ago."

"I like it. A hidden gem. Perhaps a totem. A fine start, sir. Fine start," Bo said.

Bo didn't converse on drink selection with a frivolous attitude. He exuded respect toward the barkeep, a serious discussion with a man who'd taken his request seriously. A pink drink. Frothy.

The barkeep turned and surveyed his domain behind the bar. Then addressed Bo. "Could add club soda. It would make it pinkish. Bubbly-like."

"Whipped cream?" Bo asked. "It would both facilitate the appropriate color and add texture."

"Not a lot of call for whipped cream here."

"Hmm." They locked eyes, a decision awaited. "Yes. Yes, if you would please. Campari and club soda." Bo's nod sealed the deal.

As the barkeep assembled his drink, Bo continued. "A connection with a specific woman is a different domain. I'm talking soul mate collision. A melding with someone who gets me."

A challenge large and evident—find someone, anyone, who *got* Bo Dickerson. A barn door wide open for a joke, a quip. But I didn't go there. My blood brother was serious and resolute.

"If it's any consolation, I considered my soul mate a one in a million shot." Rae. One in a million, for sure. "So maybe it's a matter of time."

"*That's* the dimension I struggle with. Time."

"You're not exactly getting old, Bo."

"But I require an old soul. An old soul partner."

The ball game droned as another young couple wandered in and ordered beers.

"For whatever it's worth," I said. "Hang with me until you at least half-figure it out." I straightened two fingers and began poking his side with vigor. He squirmed, dodged, and cracked a smile. "And maybe part of this is a desire to settle. You've always liked your own bit of turf."

The three large and drunk men shoved off from their table. One staggered before he gained a semblance of steady.

"The skew toward geographic placement of said turf would appear minimal," Bo said. "It's a battle with the odds. Odds of the atomic collision."

"Could be. But I'm a blind pilot, bud. You seek life partner advice from a man who lives alone on a boat."

The barkeep placed our drinks and removed a resting twenty from the bar top.

"And maybe *seeking* is a hindrance. An unwise active effort while the universe demands languid randomness. I don't know."

The three men headed our direction. Bo sipped his drink, smacked, assessed. The barkeep held a finger pressed against the mechanical till's entry button, watching. Bo looked up and nodded approval. The till rang.

"We heard you boys like pink drinks," one of the men said. The three crowded around our corner spot at the bar, our backs near the wall.

"Pink *and* frothy," I said. "But right now we'll settle for semi-red and bubbly."

Bo raised his drink and shined a benign smile. "Why don't you fine gentlemen join us?" he asked.

The three looked to intimidate. Perhaps deliver us a thumping. Man, were they barking up the wrong tree.

"We don't drink pink. And pretty sure we don't appreciate people who do."

"Spice of life, bud. Maybe you should try it," I said.

"Maybe you should get the hell out of here," another said.

"Wait!" Bo said. "Wait. We require music."

He scooted between two of the men, headed for the jukebox. They watched him leave our little crowd and turned toward me. Tightened their circle. Bullies. Man, I hated bullies. And they forgot about Bo. Big mistake.

A coin dropped, a button pushed. Patsy Cline's rendition of *Crazy* started. Mercy, she could sing that song.

"Where you ladies from?" another asked, delivered with a drunken snarl.

"From a place where dreams die and nightmares hold court." I raised the Grey Goose as a salute.

Bo did his stealth approach thing. He appeared between the two on my right, at their backs. A slide—rapid and smooth, silk-like. Each of his hands found purchase along jawlines. The head holds numerous pressure points.

Painful points. Know the right ones through training and practice and an immobilizing force can be applied.

The effect was immediate. Both of Bo's new acquaintances froze, eyes popping wide. Harsh breaths through nostrils. They stood stock-still, frozen. Bo sang along with Patsy. First toward the man within his left grip. He rested his chin on the larger man's shoulder. Crooned a line or two. Then the right-side guy, who balanced on tip-toes as Bo increased the pressure. Bo sang into his ear.

I addressed the third member of their party. "Now, you may note my compadre and his strange ways." The guy stared wide-eyed and slack-jawed at his two friends, paralyzed, eyes panicked. I continued.

"There are those who'd say he's, well, not quite right."

"No shit," the man said. He turned toward me, dumbstruck and confused and unsure of next steps.

Bo added a gentle sway as he sang. And ensured his two victims joined the motion.

"So it's probably best if you listen up and pay close attention to me."

The guy shot another glance at the little vignette as Bo sang and the three moved back and forth. Bo's bookends maintained a zombie-like countenance. My guy returned focus to me and nodded an affirmative.

"Between the two of us, he's the *nice* one. Sabe?"

He took another glance as his buddies. One of their right arms twitched at his side.

"Yeah. Sabe. Let's shut this whole thing down. We're outta here."

"No, I don't think so. You and your two friends will join us for a drink. A semi-red and bubbly drink. Right?"

"I suppose." The guy stood beyond confused and shook his head. Drunken wheels turned and grasped at familiar firmament.

"Bo, these fine gentlemen will join us for a drink."

He stopped his song and dance, and released his grip. "Bully! Say, you fellas ever read Thomas Hobbes?"

The two men rubbed jaws and worked their necks while maintaining a wide-eyed view of their immediate environment. One rubbed his arm. The barkeep wandered over, unsure himself of what he'd witnessed.

"Sir, we'll require five more of those drinks," I said. "We've made new friends."

The barkeep locked eyes with the men, regular customers, and sought confirmation. They responded with short contrite nods. The three stared at us with the greatest of wariness.

"That's one sure-fire way to sober up," one said, working his jaw. "Man, oh man."

"We were speaking of partners, gentlemen," I said and downed the remnants of my Grey Goose. "Life partners. You fellas know anything along those lines?"

"A challenging question," Bo said. He slid past his two dance partners and occupied the barstool again, facing outward. "It could be unknowable. So let's work with the feel and texture of harmonic joining."

"It ain't hard."

It came as a surprise from the man who'd missed the dance call. "Treat her like you'd wanna be treated." He shifted focus toward Bo. "And that's one hell of a technique. It frazzles a man. No thank you."

One of the victims nodded and worked his jaw again. "You some kind of ninja cage fighter or something?"

Bo presented an angelic appearance. "Heavy on the something," I said.

The barkeep arrayed five glasses along the bar, each with a few ice cubes. A presentation passed as formal along the Ditch as he poured the Campari and added club soda.

"A sound philosophy," Bo said, lips pursed as he addressed the man who'd offered his partner perspective. "Golden rule sound. But let's discuss the precursor. The connection. The match-up."

"You mean finding the right woman?" one of them asked.

"Again, let's minimize strictures on the action. Find, maybe. Bump into. Perhaps collide."

Bo, with great ceremony, offered each of the men a fresh semi-red bubbling drink. They accepted. And sipped and grimaced while they alternated glances between each other and the two of us.

"So what I'm hearin' you say is it's best to rely on pure chance. You ain't gonna work at it." The first-time speaker sipped his drink again. "And no offense, mister. None." He nodded my way. "But this tastes like mule piss."

"An ancient aphrodisiac," Bo said. "Or not. I always get confused about those."

"A man's gotta work at it," another said. "Gotta work at finding the right woman. And I'd *rather* drink mule piss. No offense again." He stared at the floor and shuffled his feet.

I sipped mine. They had a point.

"What if a man simply accepts," Bo said, arms stretched wide. "*Receives.*"

"Well and good, fella. But if you don't mind me saying, a man's gotta try. Make an attempt." He checked our reaction, ensured we weren't offended. "I'm here to tell you, the whole collision thing works best with two moving bodies."

"Nice. A nice insight," Bo said. "Moving bodies. A collision. A soul mate, wise and understanding and true."

The three looked among themselves. One shrugged, sniffed the glass of Campari, and said, "Sure, fella. Sure. Not about to argue with *you*." He locked eyes with me. "We good now?"

"We will be when you finish those drinks," I said. Perhaps overkill with the press-the-point-home part. But still. They'd approached as large bullies, bent on intimidation.

The three contemplated their drinks. Each glanced my way, a hard stare returned. They choked them down and set the glasses on the bar.

"We gotta go." He grimaced and straightened his well-worn Tar Heels ball cap. "This beats all. You fellas will be remembered."

"Au revoir, my dear friends," Bo said. "Bonne soirée."

"Yeah. I guess. See you fellas around."

They slid out the screen door. Two looked back and shook their heads. The barkeep wandered over. I paid for the round of drinks.

"You think those might become popular?" he asked. "Should I buy another bottle of the stuff?"

"I wouldn't. What you've got left should cover the next ten years. Let's scoot, Bo."

We did. Our thin plan included spending the night at this burg's small dock. I had an urge—after our little Campari party—to move down the line. Engine fired, I kept the *Ace* at a sedate five knots, the Ditch dark and quiet.

"It may be a matter of exposure." I spoke through the wheelhouse's open window. Bo sat sideways on the hammock and pushed off the deck and swung. "Meet and greet and mingle."

"Thin gruel."

"Yeah. But it could beat flinging cosmic thoughts about."

"Love. Love deep and abiding. You had it with Rae."

The Ditch widened and a small bay appeared on the left. I steered us into it. The more open area afforded the light breeze room to work, keeping the mosquitoes at bay. I killed the engine, moved past Bo, and dropped the bow anchor.

"And there lies *my* one big question." The anchor eased down and bit mud. The breeze tugged the *Ace* against it. "What if we each get one shot, one chance, and Rae was mine."

No house or town lights visible, the Milky Way paint-brushed overhead. A loon called. Bo arranged his mosquito net.

"Doesn't work that way, my brother. The universe doesn't say one go at it then you're through. Nope." He settled for the night. One of the hammock's ropes called a gentle squeak as it swayed. "I'll fire thoughts for you *and* me. Good thoughts, solid and accepting."

"You do it, Bo." I padded downstairs, closed the hatch, and settled for the night. Tried closing the door on thoughts of Rae Ellen Bonham. And failed, miserable and yearning.

Chapter 18

Money and Bo's gut feel and an irritating burr about unfinished business drove the decision. Jordan Pettis. The text messages from him stopped. Which coincided with a first-ever delay in acknowledgement and payment from Global Resolutions. A pre-dawn email check confirmed my suspected background activities.

Job well done. Payment made. The client desires an extension with an additional deliverable.

Sent from my Swiss client, with a payment for the initial contract and a scope outline for the contract extension. Jordan Pettis held nothing back. A ride on his personal jet, plus return trip. St. Thomas, US Virgin Islands. I name the pick-up and return point. The contract extension's scope—meet and talk. Period. He'd work me when I got there, try and play me. Jack Tilly, active muscle for the rich venture capitalist. That wasn't happening. But the money. Oh man. Pettis ponied up, big time. And the allure for a quick trip bucket-full of benjamins shined bright. I was only human after all. So I kept the Jack Tilly of Omaha electronic phone exchange active.

Underway, we approached the Nueces River, the town of New Bern, NC upstream. Bo stood on the top rail at the bow, knees bent, sipping coffee. The *Ace* rolled with the gentle waves and Bo trained his sea legs.

"Pretty amazing," I called from the wheelhouse, laptop open.

"My mad balancing skills or your coffee? If you meant the latter, we shall debate."

"Pettis. Throwing big money at me for a St. Thomas trip. Have a talk. Then return."

Bo remained silent, finished his cup, and spun a leap onto the deck.

"A strange signal," he said and plopped into his hammock, facing the wheelhouse. "St. Thomas. Virgin Islands?"

"Yep. Hand-holding with the rich and famous. And he'll try and enlist me as a card-carrying member of the Jordan Pettis protection league."

"Still, an action. Movement and vibrations."

"You want to go?"

An earnest question. A piece of me lacked closure. Other jobs ended with definitives. Here's the deal, client. Not always a neat bow, but details and confirmed paths. The "who done it" answered. But maybe I required a personal expectations reset. These sleuthing jobs might often end this way. Still, the Caribbean job left a small itch, and I scratched.

"Allow me a minute or three," Bo said. "This requires thought."

While Bo cogitated, I sent Global Resolutions a reply with a few contractual scope definitions. One meeting. Period. A two hour limit. A fifty percent price increase. I'd travel with a partner. And, as always, all expenses covered. I dived the deep web and shot it off.

"I asked for a fifty percent increase. That's your money."

He wafted a dismissive hand. None of our Delta brothers—myself, Catch, Marcus—knew how Bo supported himself. But he never lacked funds and never mentioned it. Cosmic bucks, I supposed.

"The timing. I struggle with the timing," Bo said.

"No mystery. His ass is in danger."

"Not Pettis. Why would we flounce over to St. Thomas? Now? What message am I missing? *That's* the mystery."

"Okay, bud." I couldn't help but grin.

Frantic bait fish skimmed the surface as predator fish worked underneath. The risen sun backlit the barrier islands, the towns of Ocracoke and Hatteras far distant. The response came within ten minutes. *Client agrees with scope and price.* Pettis sweated his expensive britches off in St. Thomas and wanted me there pronto. Protection for hire.

"Hell, let's go," I said. "We'll park the *Ace* in New Bern. An hour away. Have the jet pick us up in Raleigh."

A prompt, a decision, based on closure and money. I could live with that. Bo sealed the deal.

"Yes. Motion. Let the universe drive. Kinetic energy. Move." He leapt from the hammock and yelled a Tarzan yell. "Done and done. Who will turn my ears? The drying process is critical."

I called Mom and let her know an ETA at Charleston. I figured two days in St. Thomas plus three days Ditch travel to Charleston.

"Well and good, my son," she said. "As always we look forward to it."

"How's CC and Tinker Juarez?"

My mentally challenged sister and the family dog. CC anchored me. Provided wonderment I—and most everyone else—wandered past.

"Fine and happy. CC gave Tinker his spring clip. It's turning warm."

It was turning hot. Charleston, old and sultry, steamed during summer.

"How's Mary Lola Wilson's beau?"

Mom had taken back her maiden name after cancer took dad. Along with the move from Savannah to Charleston it added a layer of protection for her and CC against people who sought leverage. Leverage against me. Bounty hunters.

Mom started dating a nice man, Peter Brooks, retired insurance agent. A good man who encouraged me to try the insurance business. I wouldn't be comparing Jack Tilly notes with him.

"He's fine." She slurped coffee and loaded Mom advice. "We'll have a nice supper when you arrive. And I've made a decision."

"Do tell."

"I'm going to cease and desist the matchmaker role."

Mom arranged dates for me at every visit. Nice ladies but, to Mary Lola's chagrin, we never clicked.

"Okay."

Another slurp. "I've prayed over it. And decided it will happen when it happens."

"A sound approach."

"Which doesn't let you off the hook regarding effort. You must make an effort, son of mine."

"Bo and I hold similar discussions."

"Is that wild creature with you? Put him on the line."

She slurped coffee again and loaded a Bo barrage. She'd met Bo once and worked hard with him. At the end they arrived at a mutual concurrence. With regard toward marital potential, he was a mess.

Bo took the phone and wandered toward the bow. Their discussion lasted over ten minutes. I headed up the Neuse River toward New Bern—a regular stop with a dock owner who would water my tomatoes. I'd decline mentioning the proper management of battle-removed ears.

Bo handed the phone back and strolled away, lips pursed after tossing, "She is wise," over his shoulder.

"Bo needs help," Mom said.

"Yeah. One of those momentary life spin cycles."

"Don't brush this off, Case Lee. You're no master of interpersonal relationships."

"Bit harsh," I said and grinned. Mom was in high gear.

"Bit true. Don't fill his head with your version of an appropriate life path. The poor thing requires better than that. He and I need a sit-down."

"No argument here."

"Good. We'll see you both a few days from now. With bells on. And be careful, oldest child. I worry. And I love you. And can't wait to see you."

"Love you too." The best mom in the world, bar none.

Three and a half hours later we boarded a Gulfstream at Raleigh-Durham airport. We each carried a rucksack and small duffel bag. The first carried personal necessities. The duffel bags—qualified as a tourist over-the-shoulder tote—carried armament. HK416 assault rifles with eleven inch barrels, no suppressors. Big bang. Extra ammo magazines. And Glock .40 pistols. Again, big bang, although I packed pistol suppressors in case the situation called for it. I had little expectation of pulling either weapon, but someone likely wanted Pettis dead. We could find ourselves between him and the hitter. The duffel bags ensured the hitter lost.

Such thoughts prompted a Clubhouse message. A recent added twist with my Jules relationship. I now considered the odds of death during a job. And the party who would let Mom know. Low odds for this job, but headed for New Guinea with the last engagement Jules appeared the prominent choice. Her spider web tendrils stretched across the globe and little escaped her. Should my demise take place, I could count on her to deliver Mom the message. And, maybe, solace. A sea change for my relationship with the Clubhouse, but Jules claimed I held a special place. Bo contended she held love in her heart for me. Maybe. And I owed her news about the trailing hostile contingent that started at her place of business. She'd want to know and to deal with it. I sent her a message.

We were followed from your locale. Four. Serious business. Off for St. Thomas. Both of us.

She'd understand and tune her radar my direction. As well as backtrack the killers who'd come after us. The Clubhouse wouldn't tolerate such behavior, and woe be the recipient of her ire.

She responded quick. Too quick. Very much unlike her.

Forces converge. Be aware.

Typical. So typical. Cryptic and nebulous and left hanging. But something stirred and I'd keep the awareness dial turned up.

Pettis traveled in style. A steward on board asked if we required anything. We both declined and both napped. Three hours later we circled St.

Thomas. Ten by three miles, surrounded with paradise-like Caribbean waters. Aqua water glistened, white sand beaches called, and palm trees galore waved in the breeze. The town of Charlotte Amalie overlooked a photo-worthy bay. About as inviting as you could want. This would be my and Bo's first trip there.

As a US territory, there were no St. Thomas customs as we arrived from the mainland. A Martha Stewart good thing as they might have more than a few questions about the contents of our tourist duffel bags. Pettis arranged a vehicle and driver who met us. A text message from the man himself arrived as we climbed into the vehicle.

Meet you in the hotel bar later.

Fine. The setting for our one and only caucus. A sense of satisfaction with this contract extension settled. A pleasant, short plane ride and meet the jittery Pettis. Stay the night. Maybe Bo and I would make a snorkel trip tomorrow a.m. Then a Raleigh return trip on board a private jet. While the cash register sang. Sweet.

Then I spotted him. It was the incongruity. A look and feel about the guy, here in paradise central, rang instant awareness. A gut jump signaled strong and sure confirmation. We cruised past the small commercial air terminal before a turn toward Charlotte Amalie. He stood and leaned against an exterior wall as tourists filed past. A short ponytail, full beard. Ball cap, bright tourist-shop T-shirt, jeans, running shoes. Sunglasses and a tourist guide opened. And at his feet, a smallish duffel bag. An operator. One of us. You could try and hide it, but when you'd been there done that, it stood out. The vibe, the benign cover and taut underlay. Behind those dark shades, eyes scanned and no doubt about it.

"You see that?" I asked Bo as we passed.

"Delta-do, for sure. Don't know him. After our time."

"Oh man."

"Perhaps languid is off the menu, goober." Bo unzipped his duffel and—hand inside the bag—chambered a round into the HK assault rifle. The driver heard, comprehended the sound, and stopped his running monologue about St. Thomas.

An event, a crisis, an attack—take your pick. Something was going down. Forces converged, indeed. Delta didn't show for preventative missions. They showed and engaged and stomped on the proceedings. We scanned figures and faces throughout the drive. Focused on body set, attitude, walking styles. And tourist duffel bags. Spotted one more. His overall vibe edged full-on dangerous, separate from the wandering tourists. But the training to blend in so thorough, tourists never noticed.

Danish colonial architecture filled Charlotte Amalie. I wished I could have enjoyed it more, but all bets toward a relaxed visit were off the table. The driver stopped at a historic old estate converted into a fine hotel. Home for the night.

The unofficial greeter stood away from the main entrance, near an oversized landscape container that housed a bright orange hibiscus plant. Another operator. No beard, but unkempt hair and a two-day stubble. A vacationer, set on relaxation. With another duffel at this feet and a patterned untucked and loose shirt over jeans. The shirt ballooned with the breeze. Underneath, dollars to donuts, a tucked pistol. He wouldn't waste the two seconds pulling the duffel's assault rifle.

"You gotta be kidding me," I said. "This is too surreal. And the timing too coincidental."

"Real as real can be, my brother."

Bo and I thanked the driver and wandered over. Caribbean salt air blew, palm fronds swayed, and bougainvilleas lit the layers of landscape. The operator eyeballed us as a half-grin grew. Recognition of Bo and me. We couldn't return the favor, although he held a familiarity. We'd passed each other before.

"Nice day," I said and lowered my shades.

He returned the gesture. "Didn't realize they allowed geezers back in the game." Said with a full smile.

"Bite me. Case Lee. Bo Dickerson. Here on a private gig."

Nods all around. "So what's shaking?" I asked.

"Shake, rattle, and roll. So says the other side."

The other side. The CIA. Delta often worked as the hammer for their pointed-out nail.

"Is it real?" The CIA had sent us chasing a perceived imminent threat, non-existent, more than a few times.

He shrugged a noncommittal response, valid. Who knew until it hit the fan?

"Terrorist attack?" I asked.

"So sayeth the spooks."

"Head spook got a name?" This Delta operator might not reveal more. Bo and I represented inactive duty, retired. We worked a low-key commercial engagement. He was here to perform a much more intense job.

"Stinnett."

Didn't know the guy. Nothing unusual there.

"What's the AO?" I asked. Area of Operations.

"Tourist central."

The hotels, eateries, and streets of Charlotte Amalie. And the airport. A terrorist attack. Delta wouldn't show unless it was imminent. Or a false flag.

"Need help?" I lifted my duffel, an indicator.

He slid the shades back up his nose and turned his head, scanning.

"We're good. You guys did your time. Stick with private ops. But keep low for a day or so. I'll spread the word you two are around."

Tight nods and the operator again adopted full vigilance. Appearance-wise, another tourist chilling alongside the hotel.

We checked in at the front desk. "It strikes mighty discordant," I said.

"The timing," Bo said. "Strange in anyone's book."

"I'm not fitting the pieces. We're here to hold a rich guy's hand."

A strange buzz, a tie to recent events, but separate, distinct. The Caribbean job was an outlier, a kissing cousin, but still related. Pure coincidence wouldn't play. I'd been involved in a contracted event, a happening. And somewhere I'd inadvertently dragged a finger through a layered cake's frosting, leaving a small trail. Had to be. Faith in pure coincidence got a person killed. Yeah, something might go down that required a Delta team. A major event. And somewhere in the background, in the shadows, a slender tentacle reached out and had me by the ankle. Too strange, too weird.

"Pieces, parts, and flow," Bo said. "More things in heaven and earth."

I lacked his distance and third-party perspective. I was wrapped in this, somehow. Bo wasn't.

"Thanks, Shakespeare." I was pulled, hard, toward the immediate. Firmer ground. "We gonna engage if and when this happens? A terrorist attack?"

"We're the good guys, Batman. Capes optional," Bo said, accompanied with a wild grin.

We agreed to meet in the bar ten minutes later. I dropped my rucksack in the expansive room, the view incredible. Below, the bay was filled with pleasure boats and two cruise ships. We both carried the duffels into the bar, handy tools just in case, occupied a corner table, and waited for Pettis.

She approached with a saunter that hollered no BS allowed and a demeanor that cried "try it, buster." A stunning woman—jet black hair, nut-brown skin, high cheekbones. Khakis and knit shirt, a too-large light material jacket. She stood alongside us and flashed a badge.

"Special Agent Johnson. FBI. I know you two gentlemen won't mind if I join you. Let's chat about Jordan Pettis."

Chapter 19

As she sat, Bo—slumped and stretched out, head rested against the chair's back—asked with a smile, "May I see your badge? But please don't hand it over if it violates your object space. Or threatens bad karma." He tilted his head. "I mean, with me touching it and all."

A half-smile returned. "A little karma change might do me good."

She handed him the leather-bound badge and ID card and addressed me.

"You're Tilly?"

Pettis. The SOB set this up, pulled in the FBI, and expected the world to circle the wagons and protect his sorry butt. While Delta roamed the streets, prepared for an attack of some kind. An event Special Agent Johnson would know about. The CIA had no jurisdiction on US soil, so they would, at a minimum, inform the Feds about impending assaults. The CIA, Delta Force—big stuff for a sleepy FBI assignment in St. Thomas.

"Yeah. Jack Tilly. Out of curiosity, how big is the FBI's presence on this tourist island?"

Did Pettis have enough stroke for an FBI agent to fly into St. Thomas?

"The field office is San Juan, Puerto Rico. Next door. They term this station a resident office. A one person show."

"Nice assignment," I said.

"Not really." She glanced at Bo who held her badge overhead and viewed it from different angles.

"Julie Johnson. Alliteration at play," Bo said.

"To the extreme. I go by JJ." This time she smiled full, teeth bright white.

Oh man. She'd dropped every indicator of officiousness. At least with Bo. I couldn't fathom how he did it.

"And I'm Bo. Bo Dickerson." He returned the badge. "And about that not really thing. How does working this island make you feel?"

She was torn between getting down to business mode and talking with Bo. She chose the latter.

"Isolated. Confined." She sat back, hands across her midriff and inspected Bo. He always looked a mess to me. Clearly not for Special Agent

Johnson. "I was raised in Flagstaff, Arizona. A lot of space to move around in."

"You have Native American blood. It is striking stuff, truly." He spoke with a soft gentleness, affirming.

She rolled her eyes and smiled. "Part Apache, with Hispanic and white and who-knows tossed in. Classic American mutt."

"So what I'm hearing is you prefer wider spaces."

"That's part of it. Plus the lack of FBI business. And a lack of social activity."

Enough. These two could hit on each other later.

"What can we do for you Special Agent Johnson?" I asked.

She turned toward me. "Fair enough. Let's wrap up this wild goose chase with Pettis. Right now, there are much more pressing things for consideration."

Yeah, like some sort of freakin' attack requiring Delta operators.

"So let's keep this short and sweet and focus on Mr. Jordan Pettis," she continued. "And by the way, there is no Jack Tilly of the Providence Insurance Company."

Short and sweet was right. I'd left a string of bodies behind, three on US soil. Five if you tossed in Bo's kills. Best to avoid a lengthy wander down that alley.

"Let's keep it Jack Tilly for now. I work private investigator jobs. Pettis contacted my client. I investigated Joseph Bettencourt's death in the Bahamas. And the death of Geoffrey Whitmore of Long Island. There's connectivity, tenuous connectivity, to Pettis. A large business deal."

A waiter arrived and took our orders. Diet Pepsi for her and ice tea for me. And a too-long back-and-forth with the waiter about a fruit drink from Mr. Cosmic Vibrations.

The FBI waited until the waiter left. "Your client is Swiss, as I understand it," Johnson said. "And you contend Bettencourt was poisoned. Whitmore, maybe, drowned. What else?"

That SOB Pettis. He'd shared my private report with an FBI agent. What a freakin' idiot.

"Ask Pettis. You read the suspected ties with an overland route through Costa Rica. A big infrastructure deal that would compete with the Panama Canal."

Sufficient information, benign enough.

"Peculiar happenings," Bo said.

"Yes they are. Peculiar," she said. "Do you want to explain the 'met with extreme prejudice on Long Island' part of your report, Mr. Tilly?"

"I meant our immediate environs," Bo said. "Here and now. Peculiar and fraught with ill-intent."

Well done, Bo. Pointed the cannon elsewhere. She locked eyes with Bo, quizzical.

"What are you talking about, Mr. Dickerson? Bo."

"You have special guests on paradise island. Special guests with special skills. Prepared to ride the whirlwind."

The blender behind the bar pulsed Bo's drink. Johnson remained silent, although she cast hard stares toward us both. Warm salt air blew through the bar's open windows. She adjusted her jacket and placed forearms on the table.

"Who are you people? And don't feed me crap about private investigators." She sat back straight. "Are you two here for Pettis or something else or both? Because the something else constitutes my main concern at the moment."

"It rolls and tumbles, doesn't it?" Bo flashed teeth as our drinks arrived. "Would you like to try this, JJ? I sense a magical blend."

I couldn't believe it. He slid the concoction toward her, and she sipped from the straw. A bit of lipstick remained on the straw.

"The tamarind adds a nice touch," she said and placed the tall glass within Bo's reach. "I don't like job-related mysteries, Bo. *Especially* the here and now type. I'd appreciate it if you'd fill me in."

Playing him or true connectivity? Man, I was sitting with Alice in Wonderland.

"Our former selves," Bo said and took his own sip. "The tamarind *is* nice. Can you have a former self? A question for the ages."

I glanced out the open window. Tourists wandered, vegetation moved with the breeze. Laughter drifted from the sidewalk.

"Tell me," she said. "No kidding. I really do dislike immediate unknowns."

I wasn't part of the discussion. Which was fine. Questions from an FBI agent about US turf activities lay low on my wish list. And discussions of our past mapped just fine to Bo's wheelhouse.

"My associate and I, as decrepit as we might appear, were special ops. The force which cannot be named." He smiled wide. Delta didn't officially exist. The world's worst-kept secret among, well, everyone. The military, clandestine services, books, movies—you name it. But the façade remained, and helped. Added mystique.

"You're both former Delta? And showed up now?"

Great point, Special Agent Johnson. Where was the tie? Did Pettis have connectivity with the Company? Did the Company have a hand in requesting our appearance on St. Thomas? Jeez, this was weird.

"I believe at Mr. Pettis's request. A simple meeting regarding business dealings. He'll have to elaborate," Bo said. "You know, salt therapy is considered beneficial for the skin. You're living proof of that, JJ."

She touched her cheek and, I swore, blushed a bit. Oh man. Well, at least we'd left the world of Long Island extreme prejudice.

"I actually think it may be drying. The constant salt breeze."

"I have some eucalyptus-infused shea butter you might try."

A man wearing khakis and a polo shirt approached. Topsiders, no socks, and a Patek Philippe watch. He paused, looked at the three of us, pulled a chair, and sat. I welcomed the interruption.

"Good, good. You've all met. Which one of you two is Tilly?"

Jordan Pettis had arrived. I wondered if Special Agent Johnson would arrest me if I punched out the dumbass.

"I'm Tilly. And this is important, Pettis, so listen. If you ever again reveal a private report or private conversation of mine with any third party I'll nail your ass to a wall. Literally."

"Hey. I paid for it."

"Then I'll set you on fire. I mean it. You get that, asshole?"

Dead silence. I was beyond pissed—this guy had shattered the Case Lee engagement rules. He'd revealed my work to a Fed. And God knew who else.

"Part of your marketing strategy, Tilly?" Johnson asked, chuckling. "Is this how you drum up future business?"

"Chill, Special Agent. You two continue discussing skin care. This is between me and my clown of a client."

Pettis, wide-eyed, scooted his chair toward Johnson. Protection.

"Look, look. I'm in danger. We can all agree to that. I was setting the stage, Tilly. That's all. Lay it out there so the FBI might actually *do* something." He pointed toward Bo. "And who are you?"

"Another man of mystery," Bo said. He sat back, crossed his hands across his belly, and addressed Special Agent Johnson. "About that something else you mentioned. If it happens, please be careful. The lightning moment, a fuse lit—it's always filled with full-blown peril, JJ. Toward all parties. My associate and I speak from vast experience."

"What are you two talking about?" Pettis asked. "What about me?" The waiter approached Pettis and was promptly waved away. "Let's focus, people. I'm in danger."

"Maybe," I said and joined Bo and Johnson with hard assessments of the world as seen outside our bar window.

A dark mindset threaded thoughts. Ties and relationships, unknown, threw questions. A terrorist attack, maybe. On edge, the stage wobbly, nothing solid. Bo scooted his chair for a better outside view. Johnson checked her phone—a nervous move as no calls or texts had sounded. The possibility of a false call to action loomed. In the past our Delta team stood around more than a few times when the spooks misread the tea leaves. So I'd take care of Pettis and remove him from the immediate, then focus on the backdrop of potential imminent danger.

"You paid for this meeting. Here's my advice," I said, turning toward my client. Pettis checked his expensive watch. "You got a pressing appointment, bub?"

Half-petulant, he paid attention. "Go public," I continued. "Announce your Costa Rica endeavors are off and will never happen. Back to bits and byte, Pettis. Stick with what you know."

"What? I'm working on more LPs right now. The train has left the station, once again."

"LPs?"

"Limited. Partners. Investors for the project."

"Let them be disappointed. Pull out."

"You're not getting it, Tilly. There's a lot of buzz with the possibility of an early IPO once capital expenditures start rolling. It's shaping up to be a ripe, ripe deal."

I stared at the idiot.

"Someone or some organization doesn't want you doing this deal. And will orchestrate your death to see it stopped. How's that for buzz?"

"Oh yeah? Here's what I *do* get. This is exactly why you're here. You and Johnson. What's the matter with you people?" He pointed a finger my way. "I *paid* you." The pointing digit swung toward the FBI. "And it's your *job*. So find who's after me and stop it." He sat back, satisfied with himself. "Have I left any gray areas or do I need to get a crayon and draw it out?"

Johnson pulled away from her outdoors scan and checked the phone again. No alerts, so she locked eyes with Pettis.

"Let me draw it out for *you*," she said. "Bettencourt's death, the poisoning, had extenuating motivations. A Bahamian sex palace and Bahamian trust fund. And Whitmore died a natural death as per the local cops."

"But there's the obvious ties," Pettis said. "The clear associations. Think in terms of the scale of this project."

"Plus, the FBI doesn't chase conspiracy theories," Johnson said. "So here's my advice. Do what Mr. Tilly advises. Go chase another dream, another magic opportunity. Go public with your intent to drop the deal."

Pettis's face grew bright red. He wasn't getting his way, clearly an unusual situation. He loaded up for another salvo. Bo plugged the barrel.

"Death isn't something to fear, Jordan." He leaned across the table, washed with sincerity. "Embrace it. Added spice for life's gumbo. Every day's an adventure. Consider it a gift!"

Pettis scanned the table's occupants, shook his head, and stood. He started with the FBI.

"I know people. Important people. They will hear about Special Agent Johnson's lack of diligence."

Johnson shrugged, broke his stare, and returned to eyeballing outside activities. Pettis addressed me.

"My plane leaves in the morning. Be on it."

"Happy to oblige. And don't think about stiffing me on the contract, Pettis. Or the gumbo gets spicy as hell."

Cheesy, yeah. But it worked. His eyes widened again as he absorbed the threat.

"Did you hear him?" he said toward the back of Johnson's head. "Did you hear his remark? That's *twice* he's implied violence against me."

She remained glued on street activities but did raise a hand and deliver a dismissive rodeo queen wave toward the VC.

"And you!" he called toward Bo. "What's the whole point of *you*?"

"From a metaphysical perspective? Great question."

Johnson chuckled. Pettis blinked once, then lifted and pounded the chair onto the floor. Revved for another diatribe but realized he addressed a group who weren't open for further discussion. He stomped out as well as Topsiders allowed.

"Gumbo?" Johnson asked, chuckling again. "Added spice? I've gotta hand it to you, Bo."

They talked, connected. I listened and thought and puzzled. Another round of non-alcohol drinks were ordered. Shadows lengthened, dusk fell. I overheard talk of bloodlines, island life adjustments, life's passions and wonders and worldviews. While I pondered if I'd fallen into another Spookville passion play.

Heaven knew I'd populated peculiar scenes in my time. This one ranked. We knew Johnson was involved in the preparation, the anxiety, of a terrorist attack. She knew we knew. And wasn't sure if we were part of the government's response setting. Neither of us would discuss it, keeping doors shut. A shadow game of feigned construct, marbled with maybe. But at least Long Island events were shoved into the background, and I sure wasn't mentioning those again. Bo and Johnson continued light banter as the falling darkness masked strong possibilities of mayhem and death. Charlotte Amalie, a tranquil and charming Caribbean town, settled for the night.

Then the killing started.

Chapter 20

A pistol boomed. Double tap. Two shots fired in rapid succession. An ingrained special ops technique, delivered outside our window. Bar patrons screamed, yelled, and threw wild-eyed glances. Many hit the floor, seeking protection. Bo and I snatched our duffels from beneath the table. Special Agent Johnson leapt up, pulled her pistol, crouched, and covered the bar's entrance.

More shots echoed down the street accompanied with frantic screams. The moment held every evidence of a full-blown terrorist attack. Innocents slaughtered, the terrorists in force. We tossed our bags tossed on the table with a thud and unzipped. As we produced weapons, an eye-lock with my blood brother. Brief, intense, knowing. Bo's eyes were bright, feral. Into the breach with no hesitation. Lock and load and take out the bad guys.

"Freeze!"

Johnson's semi-automatic pistol aimed our way, flung from me to Bo and back again. Understandable. She couldn't be expected to grasp our adopted role. And she'd gone from zero to ninety on the adrenaline scale. A dangerous moment.

"We're the good guys," I said, weaponry extraction halted and voice calm, along with a sincere stare. "Your side, JJ. Whatever is going down, we're on your side."

"Why the weapons?" Her pistol still aimed our way. Hesitancy, but not acceptance. Couldn't blame her.

"Former Delta, remember?" Bo asked, calm and soothing. More shots outside. Automatic gunfire, a returned double tap. The noise was sharp, explosive. JJ flinched at the intense reports and glanced out the window. More yells and screams inside the bar, everyone now on the floor. "We come prepared," Bo continued. A sufficient answer. "Part of the deal and a well-trodden path, JJ. Let us go do our thing."

A second's hesitancy, situation assessed, decision made, and her pistol swung back toward the bar's entrance. We slid pistols into jeans pockets and stuffed extra HK rifle ammo magazines into waistbands, the assault rifles produced. I chambered a round and head signaled Bo. Let's hit it.

"Wait!" JJ remained crouched. "I'm coming."

Bad idea. Firefights weren't the FBI's domain. They'd been trained, sure, but the odds of a special agent engaged with storms of two-way flying lead remained remote throughout their careers.

"Cover this area," I said and headed for the door. "Protect these people." A nod her direction, affirming and confident. Provide her a mission.

More gunfire outside, shrieks and shouts and cries of pain. We exited the bar and halted at the hotel's entrance doorsill. We stood uninformed, operationally blind. The nature and extent of the enemy unknown. It didn't matter.

"Friendlies! Friendlies coming out!" I cried.

The Delta operator was positioned somewhere close, and even though we'd met the cold appearance of two armed men during an adrenaline-washed melee invited instant killing fire. A half-second for the message to register and we stepped into the battle. The Delta operator stood plastered against an overhang column, his eyes our way. A tight nod both directions. Two dead bodies lay near the short hotel drive. Their blood tracked downhill. Both with automatic weapons dropped nearby. AK47s. The preferred automatic weapon of terrorists worldwide. Their appearance—Caribbean. It made no sense, but sorting came later.

Echoes of more automatic fire rolled uphill toward us from downtown Charlotte Amalie, a tourist nightlife hot-spot. The rapid cracks of terrorist weaponry were interspersed with short controlled bursts of return fire. Delta, downtown. Screams drifted our way as well, the sound of terror and disbelief. And death.

"Headed downtown," I called. A brief nod of acknowledgement from the Delta operator. He'd pulled his assault rifle after the initial pistol salvo and now sought targets. A parked taxi stood near, the driver huddled under the front bumper. Bo and I dashed his direction.

"Keys in it?"

The driver, eyes wide and filled with disbelief, replied, "Ya, mon," and dived into adjoining landscape plants as two well-armed men entered his taxi. I drove. The engine started and I slammed into gear when a back door flew open. JJ flung herself inside.

Bo twisted around and addressed her. "Bad idea."

"Drive." She was resolute. The FBI badge now hung from a lanyard around her neck, pistol pointed through the open back window.

"We're headed into the middle of it," I said into the rear view mirror. "For God's sake get out."

She wouldn't budge and said, "Move!"

I did. I floored the taxi and flew downhill, headed toward the sound of gunfire. Locals and tourists huddled and hid in doorways and alongside parked cars. They ducked as we sped past, our weapons visible. Several turns later, tires screeching, we captured several bright muzzle flashes and entered the small downtown area.

A burned rubber stop and we bailed, running to press against an old colonial house. Overhead, a porch with wrought iron railing. A series of close-pressed houses and porches, reminiscent of New Orleans's French Quarter. Gunfire echoed from around the corner.

Bo dashed across the narrow street and plastered against a house wall. JJ took two steps his way, hesitated, and fell in behind me. Somehow she grasped, sensed, Bo's battle approach—singular and wild and headlong. True enough.

"Watch our six," I said and nodded toward Bo. We both progressed along the street, toward the intersection and sounds of automatic AK shots.

"What?" Her voice was tight, loud.

"Our backs. Watch our backs."

A dozen rapid strides and gunfire popped overhead. Rapid rattling shots fired toward Bo from the balcony above me echoed across the enclosed street. Hyper-tuned, full throttle, I watched several bullets punch brick dust near Bo. Throwing my HK into full auto and cutting loose straight overhead, I drove round after round through the wooden porch floor, spraying lead. Bo's rifle spoke from across the street. Three seconds of ultra-violent firefight, then quiet. The shooter moaned once from above. A final burst from my HK ended that noise. We continued toward the street intersection. More automatic gunfire, more panicked screams and shouts.

I halted and pressed against the corner brick wall. Flicked my weapon's selector switch back to single shot mode and aimed the HK around the corner toward the sound of the latest gunfire. Shot a quick glance Bo's way. He dashed across the street, exposed himself, and found cover against an outdoor pillar. Sharp cries and muffled pleas came from an unidentified bistro. More gunfire sounded farther away, and more from a different direction. Darkness, scattered streetlights, a sprinkling of lit-up signs above the entrances to bars and bistros. And the blue lights flashed from a stopped

Virgin Islands cop car a half-block away. The killed police officer's upper body was draped out the open door.

This was a massive coordinated terrorist attack with dozens of bad guys armed with automatic weapons. Delta would have assigned no more than eight or ten operators for a "maybe." Shots crackled uphill in the area of more tourist hotels. My mind worked frantic addition. One operator at the airport. One at our hotel. Figure another one or two among the other tourist hotels. Three or four downtown. That was it, with, at best, one or two additional operators. My God. And this was Charlotte Amalie, St. Thomas Island. Insanity. Horrific insanity.

A dark figure sprinted across the street nearest Bo, spraying lead his general direction. He disappeared into another bistro before Bo could get a shot. My brother and I exchanged a quick look and quicker nod. Bo went after him.

Single shots sounded half-way down the short block where I aimed. They echoed from inside a restaurant, a neon sign casting light over the entrance. The sound of explosive singular blasts arrived along with howls of terror and pain. The earmarks of terrorists murdering individuals, one at a time. I bolted toward the entrance, JJ on my heels. At that moment, an armed man turned the corner at the end of the block, full speed and weapon raised. An operator. He slammed the brakes. JJ and I ran toward him, armed people in the darkness. My hand flew up, palm open, while I continued a mad dash.

"Good guy! Good guy!"

The operator lowered his weapon and sprinted, continuing his advance. We both headed toward the bistro from opposite directions. He arrived first and didn't hesitate. He slammed through the entrance, sought targets, weapon firing. I followed two strides behind.

Carnage and death and screams and pleas for mercy. Three shooters. Two headed for the floor as the first-in Delta operator took them out. I plowed three chest shots into the third. The operator and I scanned the dim room, weapons shouldered, ears ringing. We hunted for any remaining killers.

"Clear," he said.

"Clear," I echoed back.

Triage of the wounded pulled hard. But as always, first remove threats. Among the immediate survivors were capable people, if they could keep it together and help the wounded.

"What's the situation?" I asked and moved toward the door. JJ stood at the entrance, spread-leg stance, pistol now pointed toward the floor. Her head moved with short sharp snaps, taking it in. Eyes wide, jaw clenched.

"Thirty to forty bogeys we reckon." He had a radio earpiece and would have communication with the team leader. "Where's your partner?"

He'd been told of Bo and me. "Down the street, hot after one. How many operators?" Rapid fire discussion, time ticked.

"Ten."

A serious deficit. Less than a dozen Delta deployed. They anticipated a large attack. But not this large. We stepped outside, prepared for the next round. Eyes scanned, intent, while our brief conversation ended.

"Where's the weak spot?"

This terrorist attack stood well outside the norm. There were unavoidable vulnerabilities with this scale of assault. Had to be.

"Cruise ship. Got a solo there."

One Delta Force member to handle an attack within an enclosed multi-divided space. A space containing two thousand passengers. The other cruise ship had departed the bay. This one would have prepared for its departure—loaded with passengers—when the attack began. Too much for one operator, too much opportunity for carnage.

"On it," I said. "Don't shoot my partner."

Both our heads snapped toward Bo's area as automatic gunfire erupted. Fire from multiple sources. The operator sprinted Bo's direction and tossed, "Good luck, I'll pass the word," over his shoulder. He'd alert his team, via radio, we were headed toward Havensight Pier where the cruise ships docked. A ten minute sedate drive around the bay on a normal day. We didn't have ten minutes and it damn sure wasn't a normal day.

I turned toward JJ. She'd already dashed away and jumped on a nearby Honda scooter. Started it and zipped toward me.

"Get on!"

Gotta go, gotta move. And the scooter offered movement, transportation. With our butts exposed to passing fire. Beggars, choosers, gotta go.

"Turn off the headlight."

"It's night."

"Turn off the headlight until we leave town. Makes us a target."

She did. I perched behind her, and she juiced the throttle. I was near thrown off the back. Intermittent street lights, bistro and café signs, a better than quarter moon. Sufficient for navigation and return fire. Two blocks forward a figure dashed around a corner. He carried a rifle. An operator. Style of movement, physical carriage—easy to identify. We didn't hold the same advantage. He aimed our way. Two people on a scooter, the back passenger holding an assault rifle.

I screamed "Friendly!" and hoped it carried over the scooter's strained engine. The operator remained locked on us. I removed my left hand from the weapon's forestock and reached around JJ. Snatching her bright plastic-enclosed FBI badge, I held it toward the operator. Jerked JJ's head in the process. The scooter swerved, and she regained control.

The badge's reflection or preparedness on his part or blind luck—but a slight lowering of his weapon. He continued a dash toward gunfire behind us. Oh man. Too close.

No traffic, normal activities frozen while this hellish scene played out. Three blocks later shots cracked at us from the right. Bright hot muzzle blasts. The popping sound carried over the whine of the scooter's engine. A terrorist, coming or going from a well-lit café. And our direction brought us closer. He wouldn't miss at close range.

The scooter slowed—big time bad news, making us an easier target. "Goose it!" I said and swung the HK over JJ's head to take aim. Before I could, our contingent boomed back with voice and weapon.

"Stop yelling!"

JJ had taken her hand off the right side of the handlebar, and the throttle, to pull her semiautomatic pistol. She cut loose with multiple shots. The terrorist reacted to her first hit and sprayed bullets across the asphalt at his feet. The distance closed as the shooter staggered, recovered. Our gunfire filled the air. He spun with another JJ shot. I ended the firefight as two assault rifle bullets ripped through him. Dead before he hit the ground.

"And stop jerking my badge lanyard!"

"No choice. And good shooting. Now kick this thing in the ass."

She did. As we left downtown and its streetlights I asked her to turn the scooter's headlight back on. My mistake. At the edge of Charlotte Amalie, a mile and a half from the cruise ship dock, more muzzle blasts came our way from deep darkness. We weren't hit, so it wasn't an operator. If it had been, game over. I flicked the weapon's selection switch to full automatic and laid half a magazine of return fire into the cluster of continuous muzzle flashes as we zipped past. They ceased blinking.

Gotta go, gotta fly. JJ knew what she was doing. The Honda would hit fifty mph with the two of us on it, and she used every bit of speed. Gravel stretches, potholes—she plowed through with assured aplomb. Headed for combat. My assessment of Julie Johnson ratcheted up a solid notch or three.

Minutes passed, the pier approached. The scooter's small engine screamed and drowned out other noise. JJ's ponytail whipped across my chest. Across Long Bay I could discern activity—dim figures abandoned ship. They jumped into the water on the vessel's bay side. Bad, bad news.

Chapter 21

We entered the dock area and flew past wet, fleeing passengers. Wild-eyed and frantic—people who'd jumped ship and swam to safety. They ran away from the dock area and disappeared into darkness. The cruise ship was lit as a beacon. Bright deck lights, cabin windows glowed, reflections off calm bay waters. But my gut said the interior resembled a charnel house.

JJ slammed the brakes, killed the engine, and we went into a controlled sideways slide. Momentum slowed, we both jumped off, and the scooter slid another ten feet. It bounced off the rear bumper of a parked vehicle. The scooter's slide brought unwanted attention. Sparks flew as the scooter met concrete, and the rear bumper collision ensured our position known. Couldn't blame JJ—I'd have done the same thing. But bullets whined past our heads and skipped off concrete at our feet. And explained why passengers hadn't departed via the gangway.

We dashed behind a group of parked vehicles and caught sight of a dead body sprawled at the foot of the gangway. Beyond the gangway shooter, echoed explosive reports from an onboard firefight. The Delta operator, engaged with the enemy.

"What's the plan?" JJ asked, pistol drawn and peering over the vehicle's hood. Her voice was tight, committed.

"You stay here. Herd escapees away from the ship. Engage shooters if they come your way."

The shots toward us stopped once we'd left the area of the downed scooter. The terrorist lost his target in the night and now sought our position.

JJ slapped a hand across my forearm, gripping hard. "What are you going to do?" she asked, her voice a tight explosive whisper.

"Run toward the sound of battle. Attack."

It was what Delta did. I ejected the assault rifle's half-empty magazine and slammed a fresh one home. Muffled screams and cries poured from the ship's interior. JJ wouldn't release her grip. Sufficient moonlight provided a view of her face.

"No." Puffed cheeks, an emphatic exhale, and tight head shake. "No. I'm going in. With you."

No time. No time for arguments or discussions. Gotta move, gotta go. Inside, every second, passengers were slaughtered.

"Look. I need your help for this maneuver. You got an extra pistol magazine?"

She nodded.

"Use it. Now."

While she exchanged her used ammo mag for a fresh one, I said, "Give me seven seconds. Count them off. Then rise up and pop a few shots toward the shooter's position. Draw his fire. Got it?"

"Yeah, yeah, got it. Then what?"

"I head up the gangway to take the shooter. So draw his fire and stay here, do what I asked." I shot a quick fist bump against her thigh. "Stay low, be safe, shoot to kill."

I made a quick dash past several parked vehicles and crouched at a front bumper. JJ fired several rounds, the pistol's blasts, huge and sharp, rolled across the nearby bay. The shooter keyed on her shots and ripped bullets toward her position. I took off, hitting the bottom of the gangway at a sprint, seeking the shooter. He hid behind a life-boat and fired through a seam in the boat's rigging. Protected by the craft and surrounding equipment.

The gangway held railings and canvas sides. The killer keyed on my pounding footsteps as the gangway rattled. Hot fire poured my way, and holes ripped through canvas siding as I ascended. Near the top, he adjusted his position for a better shot. Big mistake. I slowed where gangway met boat deck and leapt over two more dead bodies. He stepped from behind the life-boat. And died. Two rapid successive chest shots. His AK dropped, clattered. The deck lights illuminated another man who could have passed for a Caribbean islander. It made no sense, none. New footfalls thumped the gangway, behind me, coming my way. I whipped around and sighted, prepared to squeeze a terminal shot. It was JJ. Running toward me.

"What the hell are you doing?"

She skidded on the deck's pooled blood, crouched with pistol ready. She lowered a hand and checked for a pulse on one of the splayed victims. "Headed toward the sound of battle."

No time, gotta move. Screams and gunfire continued from the ship's interior. If JJ committed to joining the battle, so be it. A quick eye-lock, a questioning look shot her way.

"I've got your six," she said. "Move!"

126

I did, JJ close behind. We ran toward a nearby interior opening. Hand on hatch handle, I addressed her a final time before we entered the killing floor.

"One other good guy on board. Delta. Anyone else with a weapon goes down. No warnings, no arrests. Shoot the bastards."

A tight nod of acknowledgement and we stepped into the breach. Five freakin' levels on the ship. We sought stairs and firefights. The scale of this entire terrorist attack boggled the mind. It was huge. At least forty men, maybe more. Perhaps a half-dozen on the cruise ship alone. It was a coordinated, well-armed attack and hell-bent on carnage.

Shouts and screams and commands came from one flight up. The rattle of enclosed automatic gunfire deafened. I sensed it represented a warning, a do-what-I-say signifier. The yelled commands were simple. "Get out! Get out of your rooms! Now!" A Caribbean accent. Insane.

A quick glance toward JJ, a head point toward the steep ship's stairs. I dashed, JJ on my heels, two stairs at a time. Hit the stairs landing and turned for the final flight of steps. I kept low and saw heads. Dozens of passenger heads bobbed, panicked, as I climbed. There were more screamed commands.

"Go to the dining area! Now!" Followed with the rip of a half-dozen bullet blasts.

I crested the stairway. The hall was filled with passengers, all ages and sizes. Abject terror across faces, eyes frantic with fear. Piercing cries, wails.

"Move!" The command came from a tall man in their midst. His AK was displayed, ready for another rip of automatic gunfire as an attention-getter or to kill. Doors flung open, people streamed, stumbled, toward large double doors leading to the ship's interior. No clean shot. My target was surrounded, covered, with sobbing and screaming passengers. Absolute mayhem.

"Hit the ground! Everyone down!" I called and waited for a split-second opening. The weapon's site sought the terrorist's head as he sought the source of the yelled order. Opportunities flashed, too quick, as people milled, yelled, and cried with confusion.

JJ's pistol boomed twice in succession, a full second pause, and a third time. I couldn't look, couldn't take my aim off a possible shot. But the cacophonous pistol blasts resounded within the enclosed space and prompted more passengers to drop and hit the floor. My terrorist slammed an elbow into an elderly passenger's head, clearing his aim. His aim toward me. Too late, asshole. A head shot ended this life. Blood and brain matter flew, more screams and yells.

"Back in your cabins!" I called. A quick glance behind me. A terrorist lay sprawled on the lower set of stairs. He'd approached from another area of the ship to help with the round-up. JJ's shots put an end to his plan. "Back in your cabins! Lock the doors!"

People scrambled, crawled, and clawed their way into cabins on both sides of the hallway. Cries and shrieks continued. Blood from the terrorist spread across the parquet floor. Automatic gunfire from multiple sources rang above us. The next deck up. Answered with tight two-shot taps. A Delta brother, alone.

Two choices. Head for the massive dining area and assess the situation. Or sprint toward the firefight above us. An easy choice.

A foot on the second step upward and a back-check on JJ. A seconds-long respite, loins girded, before the next battle. She was on fire, a hyper-adrenaline state. She maintained a two-handed pistol grip, internalizing the scene. Passengers continued mad dashes into rooms as doors slammed on sobs and wailing.

"You all right?" I asked.

"Fine." She absorbed the scene of carnage and death and terror, then glanced down the stairs at her expired target and back at me. "What's your name? Your real name."

Legit and not unexpected. We were engaged in a life or death firefight with multiple innocents dead. More to come, guaranteed. Sealed in combat, a strong pull for a personal tie.

"Case Lee."

A head dip of acknowledgement and a hard exhale. An emphatic hand wave toward the few stragglers—shocked, rattled—who still hadn't ducked into a room. "Get in the rooms," she said, and ejected her pistol's magazine, checking the bullet supply. "I'm low."

Gotta move, gotta go. Firing continued overhead. I jerked the pistol from my waistband and tossed it her way. "Firefight up one deck."

She caught my weapon, holstered her almost-empty one, and gave a last glance toward her pistol's handiwork lying dead below her. "Let's do this, Case Lee."

We did. Another upstairs dash, stopping before cresting to captured the immediate situation. At the end of the hall was a corner room, the lone Delta's Alamo. He returned fire along both hallways to his left and right. Action on his left was beyond our sight, but before us three terrorists leveraged the protection of doorways on both sides of the hall. They rained short bursts toward the corner room. The faux-wood paneling around the operator exploded with impacts. The gun blasts reverberated and deafened.

Enough of this crap. I knelt two steps below the floor level and played a brief lethal game of whack-a-mole. As each target exposed themselves through their sanctuary doorways, two lightning bullets ripped into them. Over and done.

The corner operator realized that one assault direction was terminated and, with half the hail of fire removed, focused on the hallway to his left. Two quick shots, two second pause, two more shots. Repeated several times. Threat eliminated.

I sprinted his way, one palm toward him. A tight nod returned. JJ on my heels. My ears rang, tinny, a high frequency buzz. The operator stepped from the room's entrance. He'd been hit. Blood poured down the side of his face. The left leg of his jeans clung, soaked with blood. A thigh wound.

"Reeves."

"Lee."

He nodded toward JJ, recognition. They'd met.

"Situation?" I asked and pulled a pocket knife.

"Think it's focused on the dining area, now. Cleared most activity elsewhere." He'd taken on all of them, worked his way through the vessel. Attacked and pushed and swept decks with absolute efficiency. Numbers caught up with him, overwhelmed, and forced him into a corner.

"Gotta patch you, bud," I said and sliced off a section of his tourist shirt, a bright print of surfacing dolphins. The floor was littered with empty bullet casings. The ear ringing diminished.

"Head's not bad. Leg stings a bit." He wiped blood from one eye. The wound continued to leak. Crimson trails slid down a cheek.

I checked the head wound. A furrow plowed through the scalp. Close, close call. Head wounds bleed bad, but he'd survive it. The leg was another story. A single shot fired from the deck below, muted. As were the horrific howls that followed.

"Let's go," he said, and began movement toward the nearest set of stairs. His wounded leg dragged.

"Gimme one." One minute or less. I cut the jeans near the entrance hole. Clean entry and exit. Not a mortal wound. Debilitating, with howling pain. For normal people.

"Heard you and your partner were around," Reeves said. His radio earpiece dripped scalp wound blood. "Cavalry arrives soon. The town is locked down."

The other Delta operators would arrive in minutes. Charlotte Amalie and its immediate environs were covered, terrorists eliminated. I took no umbrage at his reference to the soon-to-arrive operators as the cavalry, setting JJ and me aside. Reeves and his fellow operators trained seventy hours a week. Physical, mental, tactical. I'd left their world a while ago.

"We can't wait."

"Understood," he said. "You'll have to take lead."

I worked fast. Two quick wraps with the shirt section around his leg, tied tight. It would stanch the bleeding. He grunted when I jerked the knot closed.

"Who are these people?" I asked.

"ISIS."

"They're Caribbean."

He returned a quick shrug and minor grimace as he fought back pain.

"I'll explain later, Case," JJ said. "So what's the plan? We have to do something."

"They're herding passengers toward a large dining room. Three to six bogeys there," Reeves said.

"Number of innocents?" Gotta move, but this situation morphed in the blink of an eye from an assault on terrorist forces to a hostage situation.

"Several hundred, best guess."

The Delta Force methodology for hostage situations—concurrent head shots for the hostage takers. No negotiations, no mercy. Position for the shots, execute. Tough to pull off with two of us. And JJ's pistol lacked the required accuracy to help with blowing away three or more terrorists across a large dining area.

Firing stopped. Whimpers and cries, low, from hallways. And a louder voice yelled, one deck below. It pronounced, preached, spewed jihadi gibberish. Had to be the dining area. I cocked my head and listened. JJ held up a finger. Reeves's jawline tightened at the booming voice. Then it began. A single shot. Wails drifted from the below deck. Another single shot. Screams and cries rose.

No time, gotta move. I turned and dashed. Reeves would follow, but lag behind. JJ likely on my heels, but I didn't check. Gotta go, gotta fly. Get to the dining hall. And kill the bastards.

Chapter 22

I flew. Three stairs at a time. Pulled and loaded a fresh ammo magazine in the process. Through a door at the bottom of the flight. Another single shot and another. Screams rose, more cries, prayers. I dashed toward the sound. Another door opened on a lounge area. Fifty feet ahead and behind double swinging doors the shrieks and howls and pleas rose. Another shot. JJ pressed against my back, peeking inside with me.

Four of them. The preaching terrorist delivered a single shot to the back of a prostrate passenger's head. He continued his proclamations. An execution shot from another. Howls and pleas crescendoed. Death stalked within their midst and touched one at a time. A sharp crack and another back-of-the-head murder. Enough.

"Stay here, JJ."

Before another shot fired and before Reeves could position, I stepped through the swinging door. Took quick aim and drove a bullet into the side of the closest one's head. I swung on the next. He took a half-second and flicked his AK to full automatic fire. It cost him his life as I delivered a double tap to his chest. I moved, stalked, aimed toward the next.

The third one also switched the selector lever on the AK to full automatic and now ripped shots at me. I blocked it all out—the angry high-whine of bullets zipping past me, the cries of passengers. I kept absolute focus as pumping blood rushed in my ears. Aim, squeeze twice. Double tap. Seek the next target.

Fire continued toward me from the fourth and farthest one. I stopped my movement, acquired the target. He might hit me first as his AK spat a chain of hot lead. But the bastard was going down. At his back, across the cavernous room, a swinging door blew open. Reese's weapon spoke twice and the final terrorist collapsed. As he fell and the AK clattered to the floor I put one through his head. To be sure.

Reese and I scanned the immediate area, weapons shouldered. How he arrived there so fast, wounded, was beyond amazing.

"Clear," Reese said.

"Clear."

And a third "clear" behind me. JJ.

The passenger's pleas and wails reduced volume. They were replaced with frantic murmurs, low crying, sobs. Heartbreaking looks as wild eyes questioned. I held no answers.

"We're the good guys," Reese called across the room. "It's okay. Everyone stay low until we've cleared the ship."

It was over. No gunshots, the ship now filled with eerie lamentations, echoing. I lowered my weapon.

"Case." JJ stood behind me. Both hands gripped the pistol. Concern and horror and a hard jaw-set painted her face. "We have to help the wounded."

"No wounded here. Dead or alive." Brutal truth.

She absorbed that reality. "Then other parts of the ship. We have to triage what we can."

The door behind her swung open. Three more operators—the cavalry—poured through, fingers on triggers. I lifted a chin their direction. They spread out.

"Yeah. Yeah, good idea. Let's go," I said to JJ, then addressed a nearby operator. "We'll go help the wounded."

"Wait five. Confirming this vessel secure." The other operators would scour every inch of the ship, weapons ready.

"Roger that. You see my friend downtown? Former Delta, wild red hair?"

"Not me. Heard you two were around. Check with the others." He focused on communications coming through his earpiece and wandered off.

"Unreal," JJ said. She remained near me. Her body language said the adrenaline pump throttled back. "So, so unreal."

"You okay?"

She scanned the room. The murdered passengers' blood formed irregular patterns across the floor. Survivors sat, some stood, most cried and hugged with wild eyes toward the horrific scene surrounding them.

"I'll never be the same."

I could only nod back. Each warrior internalized carnage, dealt with it in their own way. I couldn't shake the unreal element. Caribbean terrorists. ISIS. The largest attack on US soil since 9/11. Crazy. Absolute insanity. Answers lacked form, definition. Soul-ripping stuff, and now wasn't time for contemplation. But the ache, the heart-rending pain for those who suffered and lost loved ones stacked the emotional deck and wouldn't leave. I was unsure if I wanted it to. A marker sure and real—evil among us.

Bo. Last I'd seen him he'd dashed toward a bistro filled with gunfire. I left the dining area to capture a cell signal. Through three sets of doors and onto the deck's outdoor area. Below, vehicles poured into the parking area. Emergency personnel, volunteers, tourists who might lend a hand. The flip side of the coin. Good folks who stepped up and delivered compassion with the same acuity the terrorists delivered death. Oh man. The big universal "why" surfaced again and remained present, a backdrop painted large.

My phone showed three texts and three missed calls from Jordan Pettis. All within the last thirty minutes. I called Bo. Nothing. Texted him. It irritated the fire out of me. He'd answer in his own sweet and peculiar time. If he was okay. I worried, and couldn't help it. My blood brother.

I checked the Pettis text messages. Pleas for my arrival at his place. An address in the first message, more urgent pleas in the two subsequent ones. As I checked the final text message the phone rang. Pettis. He weighed insignificant given my surroundings. I considered letting the call drop to voice mail but answered with the goal of putting a period at the end of our relationship.

"Okay, Pettis. What is it?"

"Listen, listen. I'm begging you." Terror and hysteria drove his words. "You there? You there, Tilly?"

"Yeah. Here."

"Listen. I have this *needle* in my neck! You've got to come. I'm a dead man, Tilly. *Dead* man! Unless you come. This guy means business. You there? Are you listening?"

Another puzzle piece, small and vague and brittle. Tied, maybe, to larger events. A link, nebulous, related to the carnage on St. Thomas. I considered hanging up. Cold, I knew, but compared to the flood of terror around me, it was a bloody drop in the bucket. My head wouldn't wrap around this venture capitalist's situation. Not in my current environment. He had a needle or knife or icepick against his neck. So he said. No empathy or urgency on my part. Not with wanton slaughter spread wide the last hour.

"Tilly? You there?"

Another voice, indistinguishable, near Pettis.

"This guy says your name is Case Lee. Whatever it is, you have to come! This guy will *kill* me if you don't come."

Deal sealed. The mastermind of the Bettencourt and Whitmore deaths stood near Pettis. A man who orchestrated attempts on my life. Three times.

Connectivity to current events were unclear, but one fact shouted. The SOB knew my name. And what else he knew was a question I'd get answers to.

"On my way, Pettis. Hang in there."

Chapter 23

I found JJ and retrieved my pistol. I'd head for Pettis's place with a full complement of firepower.

"When the dust clears, let's meet at the hotel. In the morning," I said.

"Where are you going?" She handed over the pistol amid the passengers and grim Delta operators.

"Business. See you in the morning."

She asked another question, delivered toward my back. "What business?"

I wasn't opening any doors for more mystery, more questions. But she deserved acknowledgement and thanks.

I halted, turned, and said, "Well done, JJ. Through this whole thing. Well done, you. And thanks for covering my back. The stairway shooter would have punched my ticket."

A tight lipped half-smile returned. "Thanks. But something tells me you could have handled the stairway. Do you need backup where you're going?"

"I'm good. See you in the morning. Let's try and make sense of this."

The scooter was still operational. My cell phone GPS tracked the route to Pettis's house, and I puttered away. No speeding. With everyone on edge, calm and steady offered the best insurance against errant aftermath fire headed my way.

My route took me through downtown. Many areas appeared normal—shadowed Danish colonial architecture, spaced streetlights. A few people milled or huddled in doorways, many with hand to face, horrified. But some downtown sections appeared post-apocalyptic. St. Thomas emergency services and medical care were woefully inadequate for this. No knock on them—who knew this would happen? Linen tablecloths pulled from restaurants and draped over dead bodies. I assumed both terrorists and innocents. Cover the dead. I prayed Bo wasn't among them.

People hustled along streets and entered shot-up bistros. They were there to help triage the wounded. The scene held dozens of people on their knees alongside draped bodies, sobbing. They knelt in liquid patches, pooled blood black in the night. Ambulance lights flashed red, mixed with blue from a cop car. Dead and wounded mixed with sidewalk sandwich boards advertising food and drink specials. I rolled past at the speed of a fast walk.

Absorbed the scene without a sense of the macabre, but a desire to understand, get a grip. Nothing stuck. It was insanity. Senseless gory insanity.

I turned right and headed up the hill toward Pettis's house, a half-mile away. Surprised to find it wasn't a mansion, but a substantial old colonial two-story sandwiched between others. I parked several houses away and walked along the narrow space separating his house from a neighbor's. Checked his windows for a sign of him. Nothing. Circled the back and scoped rooms on the other side. Again, nothing. Pettis and the conspiracy boss were upstairs. The guy who orchestrated Bettencourt and Whitmore's death. The guy who sent four operators after Bo and me, starting at the Clubhouse. The guy who knew my real name. This would get interesting.

I checked for downspouts or other upper floor access, but it was solid brick with no grips or hand holds. So I worked the problem. Sought a sincere chat with the chief while avoiding a Mexican stand-off, albeit one with less than deep concern for the man in the middle, Pettis. There were better ways to accomplish this mission's goals and find answers. And maybe save Pettis.

The first neighbor's house I'd scooted past displayed multiple room lights. People were home. The other next door neighbor's place stood dark. Easing into their backyard, I listened. No sounds and no vehicles parked front or back. Odds were high the place stood empty. The back door was locked, unlike a nearby kitchen window. I swung the casement window outward and again waited. The Caribbean breeze rustled nearby palm fronds, and muted keening from downtown came and went with the wind. I climbed through the window and waited for eyes to adjust. It was darker inside than out.

A high-ceiling kitchen with dark cabinetry. It smelled of allspice, cinnamon, and nutmeg. Still no evidence of occupants. The narrow and steep back staircase creaked twice as I climbed. I focused on rooms to my left. Rooms that faced Pettis's place. Chose a mid-house door. Bingo. A bedroom with a large window. And straight across, a view into the venture capitalist's office. And a view of a slender man's back behind the desk chair. The man stood with legs spread, lowering his profile. He held a semi-automatic pistol pointed toward the room's door. And gripped the left arm of someone sitting in the chair. Pettis. The venture capitalist provided a human shield for the guy with the gun. They waited for Case Lee's grand entrance through the doorway. Fat chance.

Their window was closed. Good. It masked the sound of forced rusty hinges as my window opened sufficient for me to kneel and aim the HK rifle. And their closed window afforded a barrier against my voice carrying across the short divide.

I laid the phone on the window sill near my cheek which nestled against the stock of the HK. Kept it off speaker but with the volume high. Time for a little chat. The office walls on either side of the door they faced displayed Central America maps. I could view papers and a pen set and a cell phone on the desk. I dialed Pettis. The man behind him signaled with his pistol. Pettis tapped the speaker function and answered.

"Is this you, Tilly? Or Lee or whoever the hell you are?"

"It is. I'm downtown. There's been an incident. You may have heard."

"The incident is right here! This is life or death you son of a bitch. *My* life or death."

"Who's with you? The guy with a knife to your neck."

"It's a needle! *In* my neck!"

My question prompted the hitter to shift closer and whisper in Pettis's ear. The slim figure turned his head, full profile. Tig. The dread pirate Roberts from Abaco. His repositioning exposed Pettis's left shoulder and neck. A syringe protruded, plunged into the intersection of the two. A darkish liquid ready for injection. Pretty sure what it was. If Tig shot a quarter of the syringe into Pettis, instant death.

But this didn't jibe. Tig wasn't capable of operating a conspiracy on this scale. He wasn't the mastermind. Just another pawn, another killer hired by the head guy. And the head guy kept his layer of separation in play. Damn. But answers, less than full reveal, might be pulled.

"Don't worry about who's with me," Pettis continued, prompted by Tig. "Just get your ass here."

Tig knew my name. He'd been told. And likely informed about the bounty. So his job was simple enough. Get Case Lee to walk through the door. Shoot me. Inject Pettis. Collect a million bucks. Conspiracy covered, loose ends tied. Tig the dumbass hadn't figured out he also represented a loose end.

"Well, the deal is I'm not anxious about heading your way unless I know who I'm meeting." The rifle's sight steadied on Tig's head, finger light against the trigger.

Tig whispered into his victim's ear while the heavy pistol was lowered and rested on the desktop, still pointed toward the door.

"He's someone who will stop all this. Someone who will answer your questions." Tig whispered again. Pettis returned the slightest of nods. "And I'll pay you. A hundred grand to get here. A win-win situation."

Freakin' amateurs and idiots. But this vignette reeked of larger ties, deeper dark waters.

"Ask your friend who his boss is. Give me a name."

Tig gripped the syringe with his left hand and whispered. His face contorted, filled with vicious intent.

"This guy's the boss! Swear! Look, we can work a deal. Just *get* here."

I ran through angles, ploys—and wished like hell I had a better line of questions. Questions which would elicit an identifier, a clue. Didn't have it in me. Brief thoughts of Bo's condition pinged, as well as the senseless loss on a mass scale down the hill. Maybe I was mentally thrown after the last hour's trauma. Or maybe I sucked at Sherlock Holmes work.

But one item stood both discordant and clear. Pettis knew more than he'd shared with me at the hotel bar. He'd held back. And the odds of Tig revealing anything in the current situation were poor. It was time to end this segment of the hostage situation.

"Okay. Hang tight. On my way." I remained focused on Tig's head as my trigger finger applied pressure. "Just one thing, Pettis."

"What? What?"

"Don't move. No matter what happens, don't move."

A sharp rifle crack. Blood and brain matter hit the walls opposite the desk. A wide splatter mark surrounded the office door. More blood flew against the side of Pettis's head. Tig's body slid to the floor.

"Don't move Pettis!" He'd remained frozen, which wouldn't last long. "Do *not* touch the syringe. Wait sixty seconds for me. If you try and remove it you'll die. Wait for me. I'm a professional."

He did. Bought my BS lock, stock, and barrel. And it was quite the scene when I worked my way over to Pettis's place and entered the office. A mess. Blood and brains across the desktop and blown across Pettis. He sat sphynx-like, long slow blinks, mouth open.

I make a conscious effort not to be a jerk. But the last hour's events stripped away any semblance of social niceties. A short distance downhill showcased the mass deaths of innocents and life-long trauma for the survivors. And here I stood, fiddle-farting around with deals and big bucks. But the alarm bell continued ringing—and I would get answers.

"You don't look well, Jordan. Got a bug?"

No response, frozen, hands palm-down in blood and gore. I leaned the rifle against the desk and positioned behind him, the floor sticky with a sheen of Tig's blood. Speaking into his other ear, I placed a gentle hand on the syringe.

"Here's where an element of trust should enter our relationship. You agree?"

A whispered, "Yes." He wouldn't move much more than his lips.

"So you'll have to trust me when I say I'll push this syringe plunger if you upset me."

His shallow breaths increased frequency as panic ratcheted higher. A turn of events for Pettis both unexpected and most unwelcome.

"You'll be dead inside three seconds. This is the stuff that killed Bettencourt."

Silence, harsh breath.

"You don't want me upset, do you Jordan?"

"No. I swear."

"Good. Did you know this guy? I mean, you're wearing a great deal of his brain matter. You must have been close."

"No. Swear. Never seen him."

"What did he tell you about me?"

"Your name. Only your name. And that he wanted you here."

"So he could kill me?"

A no-win question, but Pettis could sweat a bit more. He remained silent.

"Guess you don't trust me, Jordan." I applied hand pressure to the syringe, pressing it deeper, while keeping my thumb off the plunger. I was surprised a small measure of poison hadn't already entered his body. Maybe it had.

"I do, I do." He hissed the answer. "Yes. So he could kill you."

"That wasn't very nice of him. Or you." I paused a few seconds and upped the ante. "But let's move on. Who instructed you to get me to St. Thomas? And get me here right now? In time for this slaughterhouse attack?"

He didn't hesitate. "A guy named Jones."

"I'm very interested in Mr. Jones."

"He contacted me. I swear."

"Do tell."

"Look. Look. He's CIA! I probably shouldn't even tell you that. But he showed me his ID. Swear."

Here we go. Spooks. Maybe.

"Did you take a close look at the ID?"

"It said CIA. In big letters."

"His name. Did you see a Jones anywhere? Don't lie."

The aroma of death filled our space. Tig's remains saturated the air. You never got used to it. Pettis's breath blew harsh.

"No. No, I didn't read the fine print. So what? He *knew* things."

"Did the body next to you mention Jones?"

"No. Why would he?"

Great question, you mullet. "Tell me exactly what Jones told you."

"He said he'd heard of me, and the Costa Rica deal. He's CIA!"

"Yeah. Got that part. What else?"

"It's why he contacted me. He'd heard about the deal. We met at a restaurant here in town. He said there were lots of big players interested in the deal."

"Okay." Jones would have played him like a drum during their discussion.

"Pull the damn syringe! We can talk then."

"Nope. What else did he say?" Mr. Jones of the CIA or Friar Tuck of Sherwood Forest—whoever the SOB was, he'd tried to kill me. Now, four times. Mr. Jones and I would meet. Not his choice. Mine.

"I told him my life was in danger. Investors were being killed. He was concerned! I mean really concerned for *me*."

I bet. "What else."

"He asked if I had protection. I told him the FBI wouldn't pay any attention. And I told him I'd hired you. Jack Tilley. To investigate."

"Did you tell him about Global Resolutions?"

"No. I swear. Come on. Pull the syringe. Please!"

"Soon, Jordan. Soon. Keep talking."

"That's it. I told him I'd hired you. And gave him your name. Which I guess isn't your name. But that's it!"

"And?"

"And he was concerned. I told you, he's CIA. He said he'd heard things. Things about my safety. And to get you here for protection ASAP."

"You didn't think it was weird?"

"Why? Why was it weird? C'mon, pull the syringe."

"So it didn't appear strange Mr. Jones would contact you?"

"Look. The FBI wouldn't listen. And your report hinted at trouble. Trouble in the Bahamas. And trouble on Long Island. So I knew you could handle yourself."

"Did you tell Jones about the report?"

"Only that you could handle yourself. I swear!"

"So he encouraged you to get me here. Right away."

"Yes. Yes. Protection. He was concerned about me. I swear. C'mon man. Pull the syringe. Please. I'm begging."

"You didn't find it weird some guy from the CIA shows up and wants to meet?"

"This is his area! He told me. The Caribbean and Central America."

How freakin' convenient. So a Mr. Jones ran this show. The Bahamas, Long Island, and now St. Thomas. Plus four operators who tracked us from the Clubhouse. But why? Why start whacking people over a business deal? But that wasn't the big question. How the hell did this play into the terrorist attack? Oh man. It stank to high heaven. The whole damn thing.

Now, what to do with this idiot. Simple enough—shut the lid, insert the fear of God, paint a nightmare picture. "There's another thing, Jordan. Another thing you'll have to trust me on."

"Anything. I swear."

"You've never heard of Case Lee."

"Fine, fine."

"And I was never here. You don't know who blew this guy's brains out."

"Got it. Pull the syringe. Please." Pettis didn't display acceptance at his situation, but rather resignation. He'd be his usual self in short order.

"You'll have to trust I'll be upset if you slip up and associate me in *any* way with *any* events."

"Got it. Got it."

"And know this, Jordan Pettis." I spoke close against his ear, voice ice-cold. "You've never met anyone like me. That's a fact. And if you ever reveal *anything* about me, I will find you. Anywhere on this planet. And I will blow *your* brains across the room."

Silence. A slight nod as reality settled. "Understood. Believe me, understood."

I slid the needle out.

He slumped, moaned, and asked a question. "Can I stand up?"

"Anything you want. I'm not here, remember?"

He stood, stepping away from the gore surrounding the desk. I jabbed the syringe into Tig's body, emptied the liquid, and broke off the needle. A smoke trail, added confusion for any investigations.

"Why'd you do that?"

"Do what, Jordan? I'm not here."

"Right. Right. Sorry."

I kept the syringe, tossed into thick landscape bushes down the road. Rifle retrieved and a final glance at the venture capitalist. No words. He turned his head, looked away. Pettis stared at Tig's condition again. Because I wasn't there.

Chapter 24

I headed downtown to lend a hand and seek Bo. Took it slow and tried piecing it together. Too many thoughts rattled around my head, horror-tinged and disconnected and awash with questions. This Jones guy Pettis mentioned held answers. Maybe. Connections, ties. Thin ties, opportunistic ties—I couldn't wrap my head around it. Not now.

It was still early evening. Unbelievable. So much had happened, so many major events. I returned to the area of town where I'd last seen Bo. The area was filled with islanders, tourists, police. And more than a handful of Delta operators. Each chipped in, lent a hand. The wounded were treated as best as possible, bleeding controlled, hands held and comforting words expressed. Then they were loaded on vehicles and sent toward the airport. US military planes were coming, physicians and nurses on board. Once loaded, lives would be stabilized until back in the States for full treatment.

Other incoming flights would pour in soon enough and deal with the aftermath. FBI, Homeland Security, political appointees. The media hauled it toward St. Thomas as well, sure as the sun would rise. And most Delta operators would take the last planes out, before daylight. They'd done their job and would fade back into the shadows.

"Next available vehicle, ma'am." It came from an operator near an older woman lying on the sidewalk. She had wads of bandages and restaurant linen napkins around her upper chest area, near the collarbone. The operator caught my eye. I nodded back. He moved on to help others. I took a knee near the senior citizen.

"What's your name?" I asked. She was in severe pain but not shock, and her face held a hard and determined set.

"Lois. Lois Dunham."

"Where you from, Lois?" I held her hand and kept an eye for an available vehicle. The blood had congealed around the shoulder wound, but she required medical help ASAP.

"Warren, Ohio. Near Youngstown."

Steel and manufacturing country. Tough folks, resilient.

"Well, Lois. I'm going to get you on the first vehicle available. Can I make a suggestion?"

"Sure. After I ask a question." She lifted her head off the sidewalk and locked eyes.

"Ask away."

"Can I have that pistol sticking out of your britches? I might run across one of those bastards between here and the airport."

Wrong, perhaps, to crack a smile given the environment of death and trauma and tears, but I couldn't help it. "I think you're covered pretty well on that front, Lois. And my suggestion is you stay awake during the trip. It helps. Helps you hang in there. I have a little experience with these matters."

"Oh, I'll be awake all right. They aren't blindsiding me again."

Two men approached—an islander and a tourist. "There's room in this vehicle. A quick airport trip and then the mainland."

They lifted Lois with gentle hands. She grunted once and squinched her face. Eased into the back seat of the sedan, she pointed toward my pistol and asked, "So, the answer's no?"

"You hang in there, Lois."

She lifted me, gave heart and a pinpoint of positive light. I wandered toward a bistro across the street where activity bustled. The wounded were carried on makeshift stretchers to pickups and placed on the truck beds. I stood aside until the entrance cleared and then stepped inside. A slaughterhouse. Bodies, blood, the stench of death. Bo worked among those saving lives, covered with blood. I blew a hard exhale and waited for a pause in his activities, washed with relief. He stood as I approached.

"Any of it yours?" I asked, pointing toward his blood-soaked clothing.

"It's all mine, my brother." Eyes radiated depthless sadness and pain. His body slumped, the universal weight of such horror across his shoulders. I didn't figure he was wounded—the "all mine" was a metaphysical reference.

"Was worried about you."

He looked about the immediate abattoir, back at me, and shrugged. "I worry about all of us."

"Yeah, I know."

He grabbed a cloth napkin from a stack on the small corner bartop. People bustled, volunteers worked, the wounded carried outside awaiting airport transfer. Bo wiped his hands, smearing fresh blood over dried. His shirt front stuck to his chest and belly, crimson. Red speckles crossed his face.

"Here, bud. Let me help." I grabbed a few cloth napkins, went behind the bar, and soaked them with water. The scene of Bo's back, drooped, helpless as the wounded and dead were lifted and moved from the small enclosure said it all.

I started with his face and asked him to remove the soaked shirt. He could go shirtless until we returned to the hotel. I wiped him down and cleaned him, ending with his hands. He stood still and offered no resistance.

"I take it things were pretty active in this area of town." I'd never seen him like this. Plenty of death and blood and gore connected our common past. But not with innocents. Tourists, locals. Folks on vacation and the folks who helped them enjoy their time. Our Delta days were spent stopping the bad guys before they could act. Before this could happen. And no slam on the operators who showed and stopped this group of killers. If they knew of Trinidadian opportunities to cut this off, they would have taken care of business. But this attack, after all the years since 9/11, held a pall of inevitability.

"Slowed. Everything slowed," he said and looked into my eyes for answers. I had nothing. "A slow-motion horror flick. It couldn't be real. I shot the bad guys while they shot civilians. It makes no sense." He gripped my hands. "And I worried about you. Thought I'd see you stretched on the street, cashed in."

"I went to the cruise ship. Bad news all around. Looks like right here."

Sad eyes blinked back. "I need some air."

I led us outside. All around, among the carnage, mercy and spirit and grace. Locals and tourists. Good and fine people consoled, triaged, helped as they could.

"Well, we've faced it before," I said, broaching one of the universal questions often mulled during active Delta Force days. Evil as a real and vile force among us. Without acceptance of such a possibility the actions of certain fellow travelers on this earth held no explanation.

"You ever read Hobbes?"

"No, Bo."

"The state of nature. Life. Nasty, brutish, and short."

"Okay."

"And this," he said and waved a hand toward the street scene. "Nothing but affirmation. Affirmation of death and chaos, a Hobbesian life unchained."

The breeze blew warm and we stood for several minutes, silent. Law enforcement from the mainland would pour in soon. Followed by the press. And we required placing ourselves on the low side of things. An army of badges held zero appeal.

"Let's hit the hotel," I said. "Clean up. We have to fade into the woodwork."

The scooter remained the only available transportation. We drove up the hill, retrieving our duffel bags from the hotel bar. Patrons and staff fell silent as two well-armed, blood-splattered men strolled in and retrieved the empty duffel bags. Center of attention was the last thing we needed.

I stood under a hot shower longer than necessary. Much longer. The "Whys?" and "Hows?" flooded as water cascaded down my face. Bo was the perfect sounding board, and I required expression and digestion of thoughts aplenty. We agreed to meet in the lobby and find another bar to have a drink. Our rifles remained in the rooms, although pistols were tucked in pants. A short walk together and we settled at another hotel's quiet bar.

"JJ?" he asked, a beer and Grey Goose ordered.

"She stayed with me. Joined the battle on the cruise ship."

"She okay?"

"Physically, yeah. A trooper. Swallowed fear and dived in, undaunted. Covered my back."

"Operators?"

"One. For the entire ship."

"I take it you shut things down."

"Not soon enough."

We sipped drinks and stared through the open window. Military transport—medical airlift—droned overhead, coming and going. Bo pulled his phone. "Sorry I missed your messages. Was walking through a surreal time and space."

"No worries."

"I messaged JJ from the hotel. She just messaged back. Wants me to call her."

He stared, waited for input. We held no option but to get off this island. Fade away. And sever communications with any and all badges. But she and Bo clicked, and I wouldn't toss roadblocks across their path. I returned a shrug, ambivalent. His choice.

They held a low, brief chat. Soft tones, affirming. He handed me the phone. "She wants to talk."

"A couple of Executive Assistant Directors are flying in," she said. "Way, way up the food chain."

"Okay." She'd regained a semblance of normalcy, her voice precise. But underneath, a sadness, a loss. One which would stick with her for the rest of her life. I knew. Boxed and tucked into a mental attic. But there. Always.

"We're holding an all-hands meeting at 5:00 am. A post-mortem. Is that an accurate descriptive or what?"

"Okay."

"And a game plan moving forward which will include handling the press. I'd like you there."

"Why?"

"I'm not real sure, Case. Insights, maybe. Thoughts. You were in the thick of it."

My initial reaction was no way, Jose. But answers—sought and missed and longed for—could be revealed during their meeting.

"Who's attending?"

"FBI, Homeland Security, CIA."

The last guest appearance sealed the deal. "Where?"

A large conference room at a beach-front hotel was reserved. Not a government building—the first place the press would head.

"All right," I said. "I'll meet you there. So how are you doing?"

"Walking around in a fog."

"Yeah. If it's any solace, it will clear. Eventually."

She signed off. We ordered another round, and I laid out the Pettis office vignette. Bo listened, nodded, and asked minimal questions during my soliloquy.

"It ties," he said after I'd finished. "A subset of a larger flow." He leaned my way for emphasis. "And this guy isn't afraid to drag a branch."

Cover his trail. No disagreement from me. This Jones character held informational pipelines that located the Clubhouse. And no doubt identified Case Lee due to a surreptitious photo taken on Abaco and fed upstream. Facial recognition software—with a top secret database for mining. Damn few players held those cards.

"Did JJ mention an a.m. meeting?" I asked.

"Yes, but no commitment from me."

"I'll go. Answers may lie there. Best if you don't attend. Too many opportunities for association."

"Sure. Fine." He sighed heavy. "We rubbed against the dark underbelly of the universe and it makes no sense. My failing, I suppose. A blind eye toward ugliness real and realized."

"I don't get it either, bud."

We sipped our drinks and paid the tab. On the walk back, I asked, "How does this affect you and JJ? A pretty strong vibe was working there before hell unleashed."

"We'll see. It casts her, and me, onto a different stage. I don't know how it mixes or resolves or if it should. But a deep spiritual component resides there. And trust. A tough commodity to find at the moment. I should drift those waters."

At the hotel, I called Pettis.

"Hello?"

Trepidation and uncertainty filled his voice. He knew it was me, the Omaha exchange still working.

"Picking you up at 4:30 a.m."

"What? Why?"

"A short visit. Don't upset me."

Chapter 25

Early morning. I took a taxi and parked outside Pettis's house. Stood on the front walk. The door slid open, he assessed my silhouette, and walked out. He kept silent until we reached the large hotel—site of the badges confab. He'd learned. I didn't exist.

We stood off the circular drop-off drive at the main entrance behind robust potted bougainvilleas trained up hotel columns. The air calm, insects called, and the first vehicles began arriving.

"Tell me if you see Jones. Don't screw this up."

No response. I glanced his way. An emphatic wide-eyed head nod returned.

One after the next, sedans and SUVs and taxis arrived and dropped passengers. Suits. FBI, Homeland Security. Grim no-nonsense the order of the day. JJ arrived with several others. Their IDs on lanyards reflected the hotel's overhead lights. No one glanced our way until a couple of remaining operators showed. They sussed our position, acknowledged my nod, saw no danger, and moved inside.

Another taxi pulled up, and a spook exited. Jeans, long sleeve button shirt, Ray-Bans folded and nestled in the shirt's neckline. Badge on lanyard. Still too much in the dark for decent viewing. As he strode toward the entrance, visibility increased. Flashback and a gut twist. The man was a spitting image of Tom Cruise.

"That's him. Jones," Pettis whispered.

"You sure?"

"Sure."

So a CIA spook ran the Costa Rica deal conspiracy and had Bettencourt and Whitmore killed. He'd violated the sanctity of the Clubhouse. Sent hitters after me and Bo. And intended to have Pettis whacked during the fourth attempt on me. The dude wanted the Costa Rica deal shut down, big time. Now to see what else he was involved in—before taking him out.

"Walk away. Stay in the shadows. Go home. And I require your jet later today."

"I'm leaving this island! What am I supposed to use?"

"Why are you making me upset, Jordan?"

"I even called the cops last night. There was no response. That body is *still* in my house. I'm not staying another night."

"Very upset."

His mouth opened then clapped shut. He slunk away, tripped on landscape plants, and looked back at me once, visibly upset. Schmuck.

I waited until the arrivals thinned. Over a hundred badges poured into the place, and I joined the tailing few. JJ met me at the door.

"Bo couldn't make it?"

"And good morning to you. Nope. He couldn't."

She hadn't slept. Dark circles under her eyes, fatigue and attempt at recovery on full display.

"Sit with me. They may ask me questions. I want you near me as back-up. Confirmation."

"Sorry, JJ. Not going to happen."

A quizzical expression, my answer unexpected. And unwelcome. "What?"

"I don't associate with badges. At least not the feds. No offense, but too many questions could bubble up. And obscurity is my middle name. I mean it."

"Then why did you come?" Hands on hips, one eyebrow raised. She was a stunner—given everything she'd been through the last twelve hours she would still turn the head of every guy in the house.

"Personal reasons. And let's leave it at that."

She remained frozen, wouldn't budge without my elaboration.

"We have a bond, you and I. Trial by fire. Right?" I asked.

Wheels turned as she mulled it over. "Yes. Fine."

"It's special, life-long, and I'm not blowing it by dwelling on the past. *My* past. So leave it, JJ. Just leave it."

Her body released, signaled resignation. "And you'll do fine in there," I continued. "If you are asked, I'm an unidentified Delta operator. Don't mention retired. A little loose with the facts, but not a lie. Okay?"

She glanced inside the room. A suit organized papers at the podium. Back to me. "Okay. Yes, okay."

"And you've never heard the name Case Lee. Or Bo Dickerson."

Her jaw clenched, lips tight. "All right." She'd stick to it. I trusted her.

We filed in. I worked my way to the massive coffee urn at a back table with an eye for Jones. One of the few operators remaining on the island joined me. We exchanged tight steeled smiles and nods of acknowledgement as coffee poured. No handshakes or bad-ass gestures or implied accolades. A job done, mission performed—sufficient in and of itself. Coffee in hand, I sat on the back row of folding chairs. The double doors were pulled shut and locked. The meeting started. A high-ranking FBI suit addressed us.

"First, a few knowns. Thirty-three terrorists. Dead. Three others wounded but alive. There may be others who haven't engaged. If they exist, we'll find them. Eighty seven locals and tourists. Dead. Another seventy two wounded. Evac to the mainland has been completed."

He paused, scanned the room, and continued. "ISIS. The Islamic State. We know this due to the remarkable work done by the head CIA Caribbean operative. I'll introduce him in a minute. You will all understand he will maintain the lowest of profiles, no names mentioned with the media. And he will be leaving in a few minutes."

The suit went on and explained the terrorists originated from Trinidad. A weird geographic and situational anomaly. Trinidad and Tobago had the highest recruitment rate for ISIS in the western hemisphere. He stated the "whys" and "hows" would be covered later. I flashed back to Tig and his Trinidadian accent.

The three surviving terrorists had talked, and the FBI pieced together the grand plan. Three dozen Trinidadian ISIS fighters planned on taking over St. Thomas. A US territory. Hold the locals and tourists hostage while they established an island caliphate. Insanity.

"While there is little to be considered good news, one fact, one acknowledgement, is clear. Case Officer Roger Stinnett of the CIA obtained intel, established a potential location and timeline, and positioned Special Forces accordingly. Without Case Officer Stinnett's efforts, the outcome would have been much worse. Worse by a factor of ten, at least. So let me take a moment and acknowledge the man."

Stinnett, a.k.a. Jones. He stood, his chair at the front row. Applause sincere and extended filled the room. A half-smile, nodded returns, a touch of humble just-doing-my-job. Several suits in the audience gave him a standing ovation. As he scanned the room and received continued applause, he slowed and checked the lone individual in the back not clapping. Not clapping and wearing a deadpan expression. It took a second or two given the incongruity of my attendance, but recognition came. I matched the photo he'd acquired.

I raised my paper coffee cup toward him. Hi, asshole. His smile disappeared, replaced with confusion and uncertainty. And something else. An all-too-brief glimpse of fear. I should have been dead, blown away by Tig, my body occupying the same room as a poisoned Pettis. His jaw clenched as reality was absorbed. That's right, you SOB. That's right Mr. Hero. Case freakin' Lee.

He recovered, pasted on a less sincere expression of accolades received, and sat back down. No one in the room noticed our three second eye-lock. Except for JJ. She turned in her seat two rows forward of me and raised one eyebrow. I kept the deadpan expression plastered. No visual clues. An important thing when intent involved someone's demise.

Crystalline clarity arrived, bright and sure. Stinnett was a rogue operative. Why and for who was still unanswered, but the moment's hero operated outside the realm of CIA case officer. He hired hitters. Ran an off-the-books conspiracy. And wanted me dead. Right back at you, bub.

Five minutes later, as the head suit spoke about the aftermath of the attack, their operational framework, and media management, Stinnett stood and performed a discrete exit through a service door at the front of the room. Along with two FBI agents. I rose and unlocked the main entrance double doors. Scooted toward the service area of the hotel. The main entrance door opened a second time as I checked for behind-the-scenes entrances and hallways.

JJ ran and caught up, on fire. "You want to tell me what is going on? Like right now?"

"Nope."

On the left, a hotel staff member exited a discrete door. I took it, a long hallway running parallel to our conference room. Pipes overhead, walls white, and the door at my back never had the opportunity to close. JJ on my tail.

"How about I arrest your butt so we can talk," she said to my fast-striding backside.

"Good luck with that."

At the far corner I paused and raised the pistol from my waistband a bit. Ensured it could be quick-drawn. I sensed her riled presence at my rear, inches away. "Aren't you going to be missed in the meeting?" I asked.

"I'm so low on the pecking order the short answer is no. What are you doing and why? And stop being an ass."

On the right, along another long hallway, metallic exit doors clanged. I headed toward the sound. Along with JJ. She positioned alongside me and addressed the side of my face. "Well?"

"The one big item, I'm learning, is full tilt at the moment."

"What one big item?"

I paused before exiting. Stinnett was still with the two FBI agents headed God-knows-where. I could have my own personal agent as well. Momentary cover. But I wanted him alone.

"Nothing is ever as it seems."

Shaking JJ and Stinnett's two FBI agents became paramount if the opportunity for direct action appeared. I'd have to lose her when the time came. Plus the gravity of confronting and perhaps killing a CIA operative was no small thing. Especially our hero, the man of the hour. Rock, hard place.

"You been taking lessons from Bo?" she asked.

"Funny. Walk with me, JJ." No other viable operational plan presented.

I threw the service exit open and stepped into the pre-dawn darkness. The town was quiet, still in shock. I sought sound and movement. Both came together. A sedan pulled away from the hotel and headed east. Too dark, until they passed under a streetlight. I could make out three passengers.

"You have a vehicle?" I asked. "If not, walk away because I'm going to steal one."

It may have been the trust, the bond, developed through combat. Or simple curiosity. It didn't matter. She dropped the badge protocols.

"I'm parked over there. Let's go."

We both dashed, she drove, and I asked her to find and follow the vehicle. She didn't hesitate. We hauled from the parking lot and took the same road. JJ goosed the accelerator until we gained on distant taillights. Taillights which now showed a right blinker and brake lights.

"What's there? Where they're turning?" She'd know. This was her turf.

"Yacht club."

Scenarios flashed, opportunities sought. Not a helluva lot I could do with three badges present. But I could eyeball the guy, assess, probe weaknesses. And maybe take action.

"You've met Stinnett?" I asked.

"He briefed me when he arrived here two days ago. About the possibility of an attack. I sent it up the chain, but was told to, in essence, chill. My bosses didn't bite."

She turned right. The sedan we tailed parked at the entrance to a substantial pier. A lone figure strode under the pier lights toward a line of tied-up yachts. Two figures stood alongside the vehicle.

"They're sure biting now."

"My hope is they don't shoot the messenger."

Our tires crackled over gravel. "Slow approach, JJ. No alarms."

"You want to provide a few details on what is going on?"

"Nope."

She pulled alongside the other vehicle, opened the door, and while standing raised the FBI badge up to the overhead dock lights. The two FBI agents removed their hands from inside dress jackets, prepared to draw and fire if necessary. I exited.

JJ didn't know them and introductions were made among the three. I raised a casual hand greeting and began to stride past them, onto the pier.

"Whoa," one barked. "No access for a few minutes, sir."

"Who's this guy?" the other asked JJ.

The first one positioned himself in my path, officious and unyielding. The FBI badge dangled on his chest and glistened with his movement. His stance proclaimed no trespass. Oh man. Three FBI agents, one rogue CIA operative, and one guy who wanted nothing to do with the FBI and everything to do with the spook of the hour. And now their question directed at JJ. A seminal moment.

"Tilly. Jack Tilly," JJ said. "A friend. Helped me last night."

Bless her. "And what's your business here, Mr. Tilly?" my blockade asked.

"Roger and I are old friends. Thought I'd say goodbye. Just a quick visit."

A flawed plan but it was all I had. Walk the pier while the three FBI agents stood around. Say goodbye to Stinnett. Maybe the sleeper hold again, held way too long. Then call down the pier from his yacht, ask for help. Ol' Roger has had a heart attack. But it would appear too weird, too suspect for the badges. Man, I needed a break, a bit of luck.

"Case Officer Stinnett was explicit with his request. No one allowed nearby. He's departing the island."

I bet. "Just a quick chat. Couple of minutes."

"Sorry, Mr. Tilly."

Son of a bitch. Dual diesel engines fired far along the pier, rumbled in idle, warming up. A vague figure appeared back on the pier, untying lines.

Frozen, with no viable options. Rock. Hard place, again. A plan formed. A poor plan, but something. A ray of hope. I could wait them out. Wait until Stinnett pulled away and the badges left. Steal a boat. Chase him down. Deal with him on the high seas.

A lighter flared as the badge near JJ lit a smoke. I focused on Stinnett's yacht. As it edged away from the pier I gained a decent visual of the profile. An ocean cruiser. Seventy footer. Two million bucks, easy. And I was more than pretty sure the CIA didn't pony up for it. And more than sure Stinnett's salary wouldn't cover the cost. A loaner or higher odds, a gift. A bribe, plain and simple. The FBI agents glanced toward the departing yacht. They must have figured it was funded from the CIA's black ops budget. Yeah, boys, the Company funds a litany of strange things. But a multi-million dollar yacht for a case officer's play toy wasn't one of them.

Stinnett didn't lollygag around making his exit. The diesel engines throttled up and their low rumble echoed across the water. I scanned other docked yachts. Nothing the size of Stinnett's, but potentially faster. If he didn't get too much of a lead. And if I absconded with one that held sufficient fuel.

JJ and the other badges chatted, my pier access now open. At one point, she caught my eye and mouthed the word, "Sorry." I appreciated it. But stealing a yacht in front of them wasn't an option. Among other things, this was US turf. They were badges. And would take the theft of a yacht seriously. And ask far too many questions regarding my relationship with Stinnett.

They talked among themselves for a full twenty minutes. Lots to talk about. Stinnett's running lights faded, as did my opportunity.

A run-down and worn-out former operator stood in the pre-dawn Caribbean dark, operationally frozen and frustrated, fists clenched. Run, you bastard. But CIA or not, I'd find you. And when I did, hiring someone else to do my dirty work wasn't on the menu.

Chapter 26

We sat in her vehicle after the other two badges left. Windows open, the fresh breeze lifted several fly-aways around JJ's face. A classic Caribbean dawn. Warm air movement created ripples across crystal-blue water. Boats bobbed at the pier or at anchor, palm trees swayed. A postcard idyllic scene. Less than twelve hours earlier, a massive terrorist attack. You wouldn't know it.

"What can you tell me about Stinnett?" I asked. Fatigue, a bone-tiredness, settled as a wet fishing net. A quiet moment and head-shake amazement at once again landing smack dab in the middle of these situations.

"I was going to ask the same thing," JJ said. She slumped, head back, eyes closed. "And you could view what I just did as lying to fellow agents."

"Not a lie. A bit of obfuscation. There's a difference. And thanks for the cover. Sincerely."

"I've got to get back," she said and straightened. She checked the rear view mirror and opened eyes wide, sussing the reflected tired factor on her appearance. "There's lots of work, lots of clean-up."

"Stinnett?"

"It's classified." A quick glance my way. Her eyes also displayed a touch of sadness and resignation.

"I know. And I lived in their world for years. All I'm looking for is background."

"Does this have anything to do with Pettis?" she asked.

I shifted the conversation, a benefit for us both. And I was worn out, aware how desultory my voice sounded. Concerned it came across as don't-give-a-damn. Not the case.

"The Trinidad thing. Highest recruitment rate of ISIS fighters. True?"

"Yes. We've known about it for a while. Now what does this have to do with Pettis?"

"Just tell me where he's based. Which Caribbean island?"

A quick answer, honest and blunt. "I don't know."

I stared out the window and considered the obstacles presented the last forty-five minutes. They *could* be construed as a lucky break. Hot emotions propelled unwise actions. You couldn't whack CIA agents without more than careful consideration. I knew. Spookville maintained a strange and violent protective bubble. Yeah, he might be dirty, a rogue, but he's our dirty rogue. We'll handle it. Stay away.

I'd tread with care. Work this out. And make sure US-based Feds never received a whiff of the whole mess. JJ's questions about Pettis cracked open too many doors. And pulled a new friend into uncomfortable decisions. Enough. I'd handle it.

"Let's head back, JJ."

She started the car, sat still, and turned the key back off. Something else weighed. She shifted toward me and asked the next question.

"So what's the deal with Bo?"

A legitimate question on many levels. And not surprising. They clicked, and she sought inside intel. I'd shoot honest as possible, within bounds.

"My blood brother and closest friend."

"I mean, what's his background?"

"He can tell you that. We go back a long way."

"Look. This is a little weird, I know. The timing and all, given what's happened around us. But I'm asking about his relationship background. Is he married? Girlfriend?"

"No and no. But he's special, JJ. And I don't mean the cosmic worldview stuff. Although that's part and parcel and real enough." I mulled over a descriptive of my best friend. "Bo is an old soul. There's wisdom buried there, and insights. And love."

Two vehicles cruised along the road outside the yacht club. Charlotte Amalie stirred. A semblance of normalcy cast hope after last night's events.

"I guess what I'm asking about is stability. Or maybe his ability to commit. He has this vagabond thing going." She shook her head, shot me a quick smile, and started the car. "And I sound like a high-schooler. Never mind."

We drove a sedate twenty miles an hour toward my hotel. I stuck a hand out the window and surfed with the pressing air. Perhaps it was fatigue or obligation or heartfelt concern, but a pull to provide insight drew my response.

"Bo is on a bit of a quest right now. He always searches, but right now, in this time and place, he seeks something. Maybe the stability you asked about. Maybe a new path." I laid my head back. "A lousy answer, I know. But it's about the best I can do right now."

She nodded and chewed her lower lip. A tough business, describing Bo. And tough doing so without violating his privacy, his personal thoughts shared. We pulled up to the hotel, and I cracked the door.

"Thanks for the ride. And I think it's great you have an interest in Bo. Pretty sure it's reciprocated." We shared tired stares. "Acceptance. I guess if there's any one thing about Bo, call it acceptance. He's the real deal, with no artifice. And I love him for it."

Smiles, sincere and heartfelt, were cast both directions. I waved goodbye.

The hotel's small café stood open and coffee called. Coffee and cogitation. Clandestine operations loomed. Well, I had an insider for that world. And this required thought, planning. Take out a CIA operative. One who'd prevented a terrorist assault from a ten times worse outcome. Who'd helped eliminate a large collection of ISIS fighters. Stone-cold killers. So I gave him his due. Well done.

But also a CIA operative who'd taken payment for commercial services from an unknown source. And who'd continue his attempts at murdering me. A blatant assault, as I'd prepared to perform at the pier an hour earlier, wouldn't do. Welcome to my personal high-wire act.

I texted Jules and requested a meetup, late afternoon. I had no other choice. Well, there *were* two other choices, neither of which fell heavy on the take action table. One option—activate an unofficial pipeline to the head of the CIA's clandestine operations. With no guarantee of action, much less results. A tug of obligation and respect kept this option present, possible.

The second option was a non-starter. Walk away. Hope for the best. Pretend Stinnett wouldn't try whacking me again. Fat chance.

Five minutes later Bo arrived and sat across the table. His eyes reflected a disconcerting flatness. I reviewed the morning activities. Stinnett the hero and Stinnett the yacht captain. Bo's body slumped, both forearms on the table as he spun a salt shaker.

"My strategic whiteboard isn't wiped clean at the moment, my brother," he said. "So let's start with the mundane. What's a vessel like that cost?"

"Couple of million. At least."

"So he's dirty. If the Company gets wind of it, they'll handle the situation."

The unofficial pipeline option. "Maybe, maybe not."

"She'll listen to you," he said, rearranging the salt and pepper shakers.

"Yeah, but the trust factor—both ways—stands on shaky ground."

Bo knew Marilyn Townsend. The secret head of the CIA's clandestine operations. All my Delta brothers knew her. She was a high-ranked clandestine operative during our Delta days. We'd worked with her—hammer for her pointed-out nails—and recognized her type of person, her character. The perfect spy master. Cold, ruthless, mission-focused to the point of disturbing. And I'd met with her recently. We'd held a terse discussion about a little matter of her playing me like a New Guinea drum.

"I take it you're not considering a quick skedaddle out of the picture, either," Bo said.

"Nope. This guy will keep coming after me. The people who provided his multi-million dollar toy will make that abundantly clear. And my gut says he knows about the bounty. Used it as leverage."

"Seems like half the spooks we run into know about the bounty."

"Yeah. The ever-present migraine. But that's not the current focus."

"Jules mentioned the Chinese. You see their hand in all this?" Bo asked.

"No. They wouldn't touch anything related to ISIS. Stinnett works for another commercial entity."

The waiter brought more coffee. And a carafe of hot water along with a wide selection of tea bags. While Bo perused the selection, he asked, "Honey? And if so, may I ask what kind?"

It threw the islander waiter, who shrugged at the question with a smile. Who knows and it'll be okay and it's just tea, mon. A smile delivered toward us, sincere, twelve hours after wide-spread horror visited his island. Life would go on. Man, I loved the Caribbean.

While Bo engaged the waiter, I called Pettis. "Need a plane ride. One hour. To Norfolk, Virginia. Any questions?"

"None." He hung up.

Bo raised an eyebrow at the Norfolk destination. "The Clubhouse?"

"The best starting point I can think of."

"Fair enough. But consider this, Mr. Bond. Once she starts the wheels turning they won't stop."

"Yeah. I know."

"Before you light her fuse, consider the other options."

"It's a self-serving fuse, Bo. I admit it. Direct action. Because it's my ass on the line."

A sad smile and deep sigh. "So let me toss something new in the mix. First, you know I'd bleed out for you," he said.

"Yeah. And likewise. Nothing new there."

"What's new is my path. It isn't toward Norfolk."

"I know. Wasn't planning on you joining."

He dipped his tea bag and added honey. "But joining or not I have to reiterate the big thing."

"Jules has the market on those."

"No she doesn't. The real big thing is my expectation of you. Because you're hard-headed, my Georgia peach."

"Okay."

"And wherever your new path leads, you'll try and fly solo."

"Didn't in New Guinea."

"Because of the odds. This is different. One guy. Somewhere on the great blue sea."

"Okay."

"So in lieu of flogging you like a rented mule over your Lone Ranger tendencies, I'll tack on a personal request. A personal expectation."

"You're pretty feisty for this early in the a.m. And for someone wading through an existential crisis."

"A simple request. So it fits in your mental wheelhouse," he said with a half-decent smile. "Take me. When clarity washes the mission clean, call me. I'll answer."

"You always do."

"But only if you communicate."

"Then watch for those cosmic messages you're so fond of."

He ignored my comment, and his face acquired a look each of my Delta brothers recognized. Bo, our spearhead. First in. Willing, able, fearless. It was fine and good to see. Fire, life, readiness. A slice of personal comeback as we addressed familiar turf.

"Call me. I mean it." Delivered with the utmost sincerity and more than a little attitude.

A two-way unblinking stare.

"We'll see."

A genuine smile and light chuckle. "Do I have to kick your butt before breakfast?" he asked.

"Speaking of which, let's order something. Then I'm outta here. I take it you're staying put?"

He sat back, gave his teacup a slow spin, and stared at the tabletop. "I don't have an option. Something happened here. It was the correct path arriving here. But something broke."

"Broke?"

"The question is whether it requires repair or discarding. A decision somewhere between monumental and trite. I'm wrestling with that."

"What about JJ?" I asked. I'd reveal our earlier conversation.

"Part of the larger swirl. With, perhaps, a perception issue."

"Okay."

"This formerly magnificent creature before you might be perceived by others as defective. On what scale and to what depth is an unknown. Which brings us to the mysterious case of JJ."

"Of all the gin joints, in all the towns, in all the world."

"That's love lost, Clouseau. We're talking love found. Or love passed. Ships in the night."

"She's interested in you. Told me."

"Interest as in the albino monkey at the zoo or as Bo Dickerson, suave man of mystique?"

"She asked about your relationships. I lied. Neglected to reveal the lost years when you traveled with the circus. And their troop of gypsy acrobats."

"Better that than the reality."

"Speaking of which, our reality stands on thin ice, my brother. She's a badge. A Federal badge."

"Only forward. My path ahead. The one behind will reveal no trail. You have my word, goober."

"Thanks. And I want you happy. If she's part of the happy meal, good on you. Hundred percent behind it."

"The question is whether the universe is behind it. Time. Time and acceptance and healing will tell the tale."

"And love. Whatever happens, Bo, you've always got that. Coming from multiple sources."

He glanced around the room and stretched his neck. I could discern a vertebrae pop. We held a dead-serious eye-lock.

"That's my keystone, brother. Without that, the arch tumbles."

The airport taxi drive brought an expected response. The Clubhouse was open for business early, the message from Jules anticipatory.

Expecting you.

I bet. The terrorist attack was public and her network would now hum like overhead power lines. She would already have established ties, connections. And plotted revenge. Because Stinnett hadn't just gone after me. He'd violated Clubhouse sanctity. And that wouldn't do at all.

Chapter 27

The stairs squeaked at every step. I'd laid my rucksack and duffel filled with special tools on the dry cleaner counter. Both disappeared, the Filipino behind the counter expressionless. Two knocks, the metallic clank, and dual shotgun barrels greeted me. I performed the empty pockets 360 display and shut the door.

"You sojourn alone. We shall arrive at your compatriot's whereabouts shortly. But first, how is he?" She used the weapon as a pointer and indicated a chair.

"Mulling life. Rudder repair."

"A man of resiliency, no doubt. Our little tête-à-tête was most enjoyable."

A quick pass through other Clubhouse business. Recruitment endeavors.

"Now," she continued. "Brass tacks. We have serious business to attend, Mr. Lee. With little room for the usual pleasantries."

She enhanced her statement with an uncomfortable display. The shotgun clattered on the desktop, an emphatic gesture. And one with both the loaded weapon's barrels still pointed my way. A drawer opened, cigar produced, the upright KA-BAR knife utilized. A lit kitchen match and smoke blown toward the ceiling completed the ritual. I waited.

"As you know, this poor wretch before you has been violated." She referenced the hitters who picked up our trail after leaving her establishment. Jules puffed the cigar. Her squinted eye glistened, face resolute, and she spoke with granite surety. "It will not stand."

For the umpteenth time I jotted a mental note—stay on Jules's good side.

"Yeah, well, there's also the little matter of the same guy's attempts at killing me. Four times."

"Hence the importance of our alliance."

She'd never used the term before. Alliance. A good thing in the short term. Over the long run, another question altogether. But the conversational tenor indicated one fact bright and clear. This wasn't a transactional discussion. The gravity of the situation and subsequent plans were far beyond money. The abacus would remain still.

"Describe recent events for me," she continued. "Begin, with great detail, your last exit from the Clubhouse. Leave nothing out."

I opened the kimono wide. Included details of the four hitters Bo and I battled after leaving her place. The St. Thomas meeting with JJ and Pettis. The discovery of Delta operators. The terrorist attack, although I brushed over gory details and individual actions. The Tig and Pettis scene. The FBI and Homeland Security morning meeting at the hotel conference room. And Roger Stinnett, including his watery escape. The Bo and JJ relationship remained unspoken. Not Clubhouse business.

"No indication of nationality regarding the four assassins?"

"None. No ID, standard special ops weaponry. No hue or cry that would indicate their language."

"Pity."

"I suspect the bounty played a role."

"No doubt. An added facet. But a mere sweetener," she said and puffed the cigar.

"That yacht is a hell of a sweetener."

An attempt at moving the conversation toward the end game—Stinnett. But the yacht reference presented a potential prickly patch. For all I knew, Jules fostered several happy campers around the world with boats or vacation cabins or mortgage-free houses. Campers under the employment of the CIA, MI6, Russian SVR, or name your own acronym. But Jules exhibited no reaction and stuck to the current mission.

"It would appear our subject du jour has fled the field of battle," she said.

"Well, in retrospect it was a good thing the FBI stopped me at the pier. Handling Stinnett at that time would have put my butt in a sling."

"An opportunity lost, nonetheless."

"Sling. My butt."

A soft cackle returned.

"So paint with numbers, Jules. I'd appreciate a little clarity so we can move forward."

"Multiple birds, one stone."

"Okay."

"You, dear boy, proved a difficult removal. A remarkable trait, often exhibited and always admired."

"A trait I'd like to foster."

"You and Mr. Pettis represented final obstacles. Obstacles on a full stop of the overland route through Costa Rica."

"Yeah, got that."

"So, under the cover of an unrelated terrorist attack, actions were taken."

"Unrelated?"

"There is an intersection of motivations, admittedly. Which is different than related."

"If you say so."

"I do. With the operational cover of extreme bloodshed, both you and our venture capitalist could be removed."

"Killed."

She wafted a hand at the more blunt assessment. "And, I should add, the young Trinidadian who attempted a medical procedure on Mr. Pettis would have met the same fate. In short order."

"Fair enough. Loose ends tied, the Costa Rica deal shut down."

"Indeed. Mr. Stinnett's sponsor satisfied. But there are other considerations." She leaned back, smiled, and puffed the cigar—added theatrics for a Clubhouse presentation. "Are you familiar with the region's geography, Marco Polo?" she asked.

"Yeah. I'm not an idiot, Jules."

A faux-shocked expression. "Nor would I ever deign to imply such. But consider. The Caribbean Sea. Bound on the east with a string of islands. Including Trinidad at the southern point."

"Okay."

"And bound on the west by Central America. Which includes Panama. Now, let us consider likely targets for a large band of island-based jihadists within the context of a larger picture."

"St. Thomas, for one."

"Yes. A political statement against a US territory from delusional zealots."

"Those slaughtered locals and tourists were sure more than a political statement. Blood flowed in the streets."

"I'm sure it did. Terrible, to be sure." She presented an empathetic expression, practiced perhaps, and continued. "But for our purposes, let us back away from experiential carnage. And adopt the perspective of threat assessment."

I stared back, unblinking. "Do these weeds we're heading into hide Stinnett? Because that's the lone threat on my dance card."

"If only it were so, dear. Although I do admire, as always, your focus on the immediate."

Head claxons rang. She intimated other and perhaps larger threats lurked on the horizon. Not what I wanted to hear.

"So what am I missing?"

"Amalgams, perhaps. And we shall return to my earlier assertion. One posited during Mr. Dickerson's visit."

"Okay."

"You have focused, rightly so, on Mr. Stinnett. And to a degree, his sponsor."

"Another commercial interest. Hell, for all I know, one of Pettis's competitors on Sand Hill Road. A competitor who found a CIA operative willing to moonlight."

"Indeed. Now as to both amalgams and threat assessments."

I sighed. "Is there a CliffsNotes version of this you might want to share?"

She raised a single eyebrow. The one under the eyepatch. It presented a disconcerting affect, planned and practiced. She laid the cigar at the desk's edge, placed both elbows on the well-worn surface, and scooted forward in her chair. Somewhere, an AC vent hummed.

"This is beyond serious, Mr. Lee. For our actions will engage multiple players. Large and dangerous players. Starting with the Chinese."

Oh man. I'd fought it. Refused consideration. The Chinese. But this was Jules. She knew. She always knew. Acceptance washed, depression settled. I sighed, loudly. Oh man and oh well. Time to rip the bandage off with a single pull.

"Tell me."

"First, amalgams. Do you not understand how our large Asian friend conducts business?"

"Yeah. Yeah I do."

They took the long view. Their government's goals were their commercial companies' goals. A government and commercial amalgam. I was a moron. Shunted the obvious aside, convinced a commercial entity drove the Costa Rica conspiracy. Well, a commercial entity did drive. The Chinese government. And the MSS—the Chinese clandestine services—were an extension of state commercial interests. And the bridge to Stinnett.

"Stinnett works for the Chinese," I said. Plopped on the table, waiting for disagreement. None came.

"You and I must walk a fine line, lad."

Point taken. The MSS, similar to Russia's SVR, were ruthless. If they got wind of the Clubhouse's hand in Stinnett's demise, Jules would deal with much more than a sanctuary violated. And the last thing I wanted was the MSS aware and in pursuit of Case Lee, Esq. The Russians already held that position, and I much preferred the field winnowed rather than added to.

"All right. Give me the threat assessment perspective, Jules. While I endeavor maintaining this façade of calm."

She relit her cigar, the kitchen match emitting sulfurous fumes, and sat back. The situational elephant recognized and accepted, she held free reign for painting a bigger picture.

"Threats toward cash flow. Trillions of dollars' worth of cash flow," she said.

"The Panama Canal. Operated by the Chinese."

"Yes. The perfect objective for terrorism if commercial disruption were the goal. Much to the relief of our Asian friend, the merry band of now-deceased jihadists chose a soft target for their endeavors. A tourist island."

"Glad they're relieved."

"Think as they would, dear. Set personal emotions aside."

That wasn't going to happen. "So the Chinese sent their well-rewarded proxy to shut down the Costa Rica project."

"Yes."

"And encouraged him to eliminate a future terrorist threat to the Canal," I said.

"No."

"No?"

"I doubt very much if Mr. Stinnett informed his sponsor of the impending attack. Let us not forget who signs his actual paycheck. He performed his day job, as it were. Corralled intelligence and arranged for your brethren's placement to thwart the attack. Then leveraged the unfortunate event and constructed deep cover action regarding Pettis. And you. An admirable play."

"Yeah. Admirable."

"From a professional perspective." A brief appreciative smile. "And taking credit places him in greater stead with both his employer and sponsor. It solidifies his position. All that said, it does *not* alter the fact he violated my sanctity."

Stinnett as the layer of separation between the Chinese and stopping the Costa Rica project. Hired hitters as a layer of separation between Stinnett and multiple killings. Lots of clean hands. So what drove the guy? Beyond money? This was treason. Another reason to whack him.

"So he was bought. Money. Is it that simple? We're talking treason, Jules. A death sentence."

She stared at the Cirque du Soleil poster and ruminated. "A world of possibilities lay there. Money, sex, power. Perhaps there were past indiscretions used against him. Or perceived slights and bitterness toward his home country."

She shook her head and sighed, silent for the moment. The single overhead light bulb's pull chain performed a slow dance with the AC currents. I waited. She continued. "To claim I have seen it all is perhaps too broad a brushstroke. The rationale behind such actions often lay beyond normal thought processes. But our Mr. Stinnett has greater problems now."

"Well, yeah. Me."

"A formidable challenge for him, no doubt. A challenge made clear with the knowledge you remain alive. In the future, dear, please consider keeping such awareness away from the quarry. It does tend to make things easier."

Point taken. There was little reason for exposing myself at the FBI's morning meeting. The lift of a coffee cup as Stinnett recognized my face. On the other hand, I wanted the son of a bitch to see who was coming after him. A personal motive. Which didn't lessen the truth of Jules's statement.

"As for his greater problems," Jules continued. "If our Asian friends receive wind of your continued existence, they may decide to take action."

"The MSS after my ass. Just freakin' great."

"And after the posterior of Mr. Stinnett as well. Even given his other successes, he failed to eliminate you. And Mr. Pettis. They do not look kindly upon such things."

"So all the more reason for handling Stinnett now. Before he comes after me again. And before news I still walk among us breaks."

"Indeed. A sense of urgency." She cocked her head and puffed the cigar. "Let us shift the conversation toward next steps."

"Okay."

"We shall discuss retribution. An apt noun. For both of us."

The heart of the matter. Retribution. Fine, we'd discuss it as planned. With acute awareness I represented a degree of separation for her and the Clubhouse. Important for Jules because the CIA was a valued client. They purchased Clubhouse information and paid good money. She stood in fine stead with the Company. So Clubhouse retribution required a hands-off buffer. Me.

It was dangerous turf, and Jules would remain clean. But her position wasn't without risk. If word leaked she aided and abetted the removal of a Company operative the consequences were severe. Hence the alliance comment. Partners. Sink or swim together.

But Stinnett's removal was her goal, and no doubt about it. The rogue agent broke Clubhouse rules. Neutral turf, and neutrality violated. The punishment absolute.

"First, a location. I shall assume this responsibility," she said, her tone cold and final. "Our clandestine culprit has a home base."

The statement implied I would handle the rest.

"Okay."

"It may take a few days. May I assume you will initiate action once a location is ascertained?"

"You know, there's an alternative."

I wasn't backing off the desire to act as cleaner. But a personal trigger pull wasn't the sole option. The best option, perhaps, but the Norfolk flight afforded me more consideration of an alternative Bo and I discussed.

"She is not of our tribe, dear," Jules said, with full understanding of the alternative. The Marilyn Townsend option. As always, she was a step or three ahead.

"A turncoat in their midst," I said. "They might hand it over to their wet work group."

Wet work. Assassins. Killers.

Jules shook her head and adopted a school teacher attitude. "As a last resort, perhaps. But it would not constitute their initial play."

"How so?"

"Because, dear boy, our Mr. Stinnett has an informational pipe into China's clandestine world. The MSS. He feeds them."

"So?"

"So their first move will be turning him. A double agent. Acknowledge his behavior, confront him, and offer an alternative to instant termination."

"For him to feed MSS misinformation?"

"Of course. A tactic stretching back a thousand years. And still around, I should add, because of its efficacy. With the added bonus he might extract valued information from them."

She smiled, puffed the cigar, and added, "Unless the Chinese learn of his new role. In which case they may feed the Company false information as well. Think of the intrigue!" She cackled longer than necessary.

Yeah, funny. Although her picture of constant permutations and shifting sands buttressed the argument for a short and final solution.

Jules returned to tribal chieftain mode. "And consider this. She is not inhuman. While you two may have a working relationship, she will resent the bearer of bad news."

Marilyn Townsend. Director of the CIA's operational clandestine services. Someone known to a small handful of people on this earth. The world's head spook. And, yeah, she might resent my message. I respected her, but our relationship—since the New Guinea job—bordered on adversarial. At least from my perspective. Townsend lived so encased, so mission-focused, she likely considered me a tool. One used when opportunity presented. As for her personal feelings toward me, I'd never know.

I sighed. "You may be right."

"I am right, dear." Convinced she'd buried any alternatives to personal retribution and the mission forward established, Jules fired up the informational plucking machine. This was, after all, the Clubhouse. "Now, tell me of this FBI agent on St. Thomas. The committed Julie Johnson."

I added little to my earlier descriptive. And reflected I may have already said too much.

"And back to your compatriot. The delightful Mr. Dickerson. Where might he be at the moment?"

"Still on St. Thomas."

"I see."

I couldn't contain a grin. "You are a true and genuine piece of work, Jules."

"I am a simple and honest broker of information. A mere speck among games writ large. And you, Don Quixote, must avoid jousting with windmills. Focus. The time is at hand. I shall provide you a location anon."

The mechanical clack as the door unlocked signaled the meeting over. I would wait for her spider web's tingle. A location for Roger Stinnett. Then I would kill him. Before exiting I turned and sought something. Solace, perhaps.

"It started as a simple job. Low key."

"I know." She adopted the tone and appearance of true empathy. A connection. Real or not, I appreciated it. "As is so often the case among our tribe. Chin up. You rank as among the most solid of characters, Case Lee. Hold the course. And take succor knowing there is no alternative."

Chapter 28

A mile from the Clubhouse, a quiet coffee house. I gathered thoughts and considered next moves. Fought a hollowness, a general attitudinal malaise. I didn't appreciate the emotional state one little bit. Could have prompted myself to man up. Life could be a lot worse. But I couldn't shake the weighted role of Case Lee, hitter.

Revenge made for a lousy motivator. Yeah, the guy tried killing me. Multiple times. Which placed him among a crowded field. Would he continue the endeavor? The sixty-four-dollar question. If so, then strike first. But his continued pursuit wasn't a given. Unless the idiot Pettis resurrected the Costa Rica deal. Which he might. An ugly thought came, passed—I could have manipulated the Pettis and Tig vignette, the poison injected before I squeezed the trigger. Prompted with the right words during the cell phone conversation as Tig listened.

And Stinnett belonged to the Company. Talk about a can of worms opened wide. Alerting Marilyn Townsend of a traitor in her midst would initiate a laser-focus on both Stinnett and yours truly. Thoughts of the Company trailing me with unknown intent sat heavy. Oh man.

We all require sounding boards, I supposed. I was blessed with several. Mom remained a prime candidate for personal issues. But this fell far outside her realm. Which left Bo, Catch, and Marcus. Bo would ruminate and offer off-trail possibilities. This situation wouldn't accept metaphysical considerations. Catch would deliver his usual succinct statement. Give me the guy's location, what he looks like, and go sit on the *Ace of Spades*. Problem solved. But this was my business, not his.

Which left Marcus Johnson, former Delta Force team lead. Always rational, sound, and sage. A wise man. I accepted a coffee refill and ensured the quiet corner I occupied remained so. Then placed a call to the rancher near Fishtail, Montana. It was summertime, and he'd be in full cowboy and cattle mode.

"To set the stage," he started. "I'm working on the tractor. The Beartooths and Absarokas stand clear and cathedral-like in the distance. And it's warm. Warm enough for your Pollyanna can't-stand-the-cold self. So when are you arriving?"

Man it felt good hearing his voice. And an easy image for the mind's eye. Tall, lanky, shades of gray showing under the worn Stetson. Working on ranch equipment, hay season in full swing. The Beartooth and Absaroka mountain ranges were far distant. Glorious peaks well above tree line. And miles and miles of nobody.

"Soon. But this is a consultative call."

I'd visit him three or four times a year. But not during winter. Hence the Pollyanna statement.

"I'm pricey. And this tractor needs new parts. So the wailing couch awaits."

"And I'd take it, except you'd prop those snowshoe-sized feet near my head. Liable to pass out from the smell."

"The aroma of hard work. Something you *would* crinkle your nose at."

We both laughed. The sound of a wrench dropped into a tool bucket said I had his full attention. I told the tale. Alone in the isolated corner of a coffee house and using a 256 bit encryption phone, I still couched the affair with the ugly burrs ground off.

"Is this a poor time for the talk?" he asked after absorbing my activities.

The talk consisted of me settling down in Montana and starting a new, sedate life. I'd pointed out, more than a few times, the bounty on our heads held little truck with geography. Marcus waved away any such considerations. Bounty hunters could come. His wide-open space offered a degree of warning. At which point he'd handle business. I wasn't as sanguine about remoteness as a warning system.

"Is it ever a good time?"

"Right about now would seem appropriate."

"Later, Yoda. Bigger fish to fry at the moment."

"Then let's drill to the basics. The treasonous aspect is sufficient for a bullet to the head."

"A fine motivator, granted. Plus the attempts on me."

"Nothing new there," he said.

"A comment used much too often. And high odds he knows of the bounty."

"An unknown. Let's keep the bounty out of the immediate picture." His Zippo lighter clacked open as he lit a cigar.

"Two big sticking points," I said. "He's CIA. And as of the last twenty-four hours, a hero inside the Company."

"And the other issue?"

"Feels like a hit job. Reeks of wet work."

"Well," he said with a fresh-cigar-in-mouth inflection. "If it gnaws at you that leaves one choice."

"Maybe."

"Son, you don't even know where this guy lives. You said he was over Caribbean operations. Lots of islands, lots of blue water."

"I'll know soon enough," I said, aware where the statement would lead.

"The witch?"

"Her name is Jules, and she's provided ample help in the past. As you well know."

"She's a damn witch who drags you through illegal and prickly turf. And you wonder why you don't find less dangerous work? What the hell do you think she deals in? Popcorn sales?"

Marcus held grudging respect for the CIA, and a great respect toward Marilyn Townsend. He long ago internalized the need for the Company, and for a strong leader among them. The Clubhouse failed any and all such benchmarks in his book. The Clubhouse was a commercial endeavor which played games and moved chess pieces without the hint of a nobler perspective. I skirted his commentary.

"So I'll have a location. Then what? *That's* what we're discussing."

"Still just one option. You owe her the information. Her shop. And she'll clean it."

He was right. As always. Jules wooed me with tribal affiliations and potential downsides. But Marcus nailed the heart of the matter—it was the right thing to do. A sip of coffee delayed the admission. "Yeah. She'd handle it. But she might try and turn him. Insight as per Jules."

A light poke, and I waited for the sigh, the pause. It arrived, along with a hack and spit.

"Even if she did flip him, part of their new and improved treasonous relationship could involve hands-off regarding you," he said.

"So I should ask for that? Oh and Marilyn, please ask the guy not to hurt me. Is this what happens when retired Delta operators reach a certain age? They begin swallowing wussification pills by the handful?"

"Stop being your usual idiot self. Tell her what you know and tell her your concerns. Then back on your decrepit old tub and hit the Ditch. Or better yet, come to Montana. Where I will personally demonstrate my state of wussification."

"Not enough Epsom salts in Billings to facilitate your recuperation. And if I contact her and spill the beans, there's still no guarantee the situation stands resolved."

"Since when has life tossed guarantees your way? Or mine? But bottom line, you know it's the right move."

A slurp of coffee, a sigh. "Yeah. You're right. I could say you're always right, but it would detract from the reality of blind pig, acorn."

"Shut up, do it, and get your sorry ass to God's country. I could use help with the hay."

We signed off, and I swirled coffee dregs. Unlike Jules, Marcus held no ulterior motives. So I dialed Townsend while my former team lead's impetus still held its effect. We'd exchanged numbers in the recent past so she knew who called, but as always waited for me to speak first.

"Director."

"Mr. Lee."

"You've got a rogue."

A long silence. She would consider continuation of the current conversation or if this required a face-to-face. She chose the latter.

"Are you available?" Translation—was I near D.C.? Or more accurate, Langley. A four hour drive.

"Yes."

"A restaurant?"

"Nope." A crowded venue made great cover, granted. It also allowed her people close proximity. Too close.

Silence. A long one.

"Ah, yes. I'd forgotten your predilection toward the outdoors."

"There's a reason for that."

"Which we shall not waste time discussing. Clemyjontri Park. Tonight. Eight."

She ended the call without waiting for a response. I pulled the laptop and found the park. A mile from the CIA's Langley headquarters. Great. Just freakin' great. She'd have an army of spook underlings behind every rock and tree on the place. So be it.

I maintained multiple Uber apps—each with a different identity and credit card. A rental car wouldn't do, even using a false identity. Too many cameras, too much gathered information. A young man driving a late model Chevy leapt at the opportunity for a four hour paid trip. I gave a false D.C. destination and would have him drop me off a half-mile from the meeting spot. In a few hours, sunset. It marked twenty four hours since the Charlotte Amalie slaughter started.

"Instead of dead-heading it back home, I could use a return ride," I said from the front passenger seat. The rucksack occupied the back seat, duffel with the HK between my legs, the pistol in my waistband.

"You bet. How long is the wait time?"

"Not long. An hour."

"Happy to. Do you have some kind of business in the D.C. area?"

"Yeah. Some kind of business."

"At night?"

"The world doesn't sleep."

"It must be interesting work."

"Yeah. Interesting. Keeps me on my toes."

I napped as we headed north, toward the belly of the beast.

Chapter 29

The park covered two acres, a kids' elaborate playground the centerpiece. No civilians, but sufficient moonlight highlighted a dozen dark, solid figures around the slides and playhouses and jungle gyms. Each would have full automatic sub-machine guns hidden under their jackets. And each wired with an earpiece and microphone. My arrival across a groomed grass acre would be noticed. Big time. A good thing, as surprises were off the menu when it came to protecting the world's head spook.

She occupied a parents' bench near the playground equipment. An upright figure, still, except for the occasional hand raise with a cup of hot liquid. The steam showed in the night. Two suits approached me at fifty yards. It was two minutes after eight.

"Lee?"

"Yes."

"I hear you don't go for pat-downs."

"You heard right." The Glock remained in my waistband.

"I don't like that."

"Should I play the world's smallest violin?"

He glanced at his partner, and back to me.

"You're a funny guy."

"You're in my way."

Another glance toward his partner, then two side-steps back.

"Still in my way." I wouldn't tolerate any physical attempts at corralling me. I could take them both, no worries, but it would set poor stage dressing for this little play.

They each took another two steps back. As I moved forward the quiet one said, "Asshole," just loud enough to hear. I tossed an extended middle finger over my shoulder and entered Spookville's inner sanctum.

"Mr. Lee. You will pardon me if I don't rise."

Marilyn Townsend took a bullet to the hip during a field ops, years ago. That, and the rumor she was a stone-cold cribbage player, the sum total of my insider knowledge about her. Which was more than members of congress or anyone in the media. They didn't even know her name.

"Not a problem. Good to see you, Director."

"And you. Sit. Would you like coffee? It's pre-sweetened and with a dollop of fresh cream."

Her cane rested within reach a bit farther along the bench. High odds it was weaponized with either a blade or a firing capability.

"No thanks." Rule one through nine. Never eat or drink around high ranking spooks. Too much opportunity for a dark cellar wake-up call.

"Pity." She sipped and waited, eyes hooded and head cocked. I sat five feet away.

"Roger Stinnett has gone rogue. The Chinese."

Traffic a quarter mile away failed to overcome the summer insect symphony. The night air draped sticky, filled with the aroma of fresh-cut grass. Townsend sat still as if she hadn't heard me. I waited.

"A more serious allegation could not be levied," she said, and fell silent again.

Head games. She'd attempt positioning me as an unsure neophyte, filled with hunches and innuendo. Someone who jabbered and justified their allegation. I leaned back against the park bench, legs outstretched and crossed. Head back, staring at intermittent stars as summer night clouds passed. She took another sip of coffee.

"Word has it from your active duty brethren you were engaged on St. Thomas. Along with our mutual friend, Mr. Dickerson."

A course change. Proof of the Company's all-seeing eye. An intimidation tactic. She sipped again and set her paper cup on the bench.

"You sure make friends easy, Director. But he's out of bounds. This is you and me."

"I fail to understand your attitude, Mr. Lee. It borders on the adversarial and is most unwarranted."

"Not adversarial. Arm's length. New Guinea remains fresh on my mind. And body."

"Understood." A framework established, no great animus, full professional. She continued. "Now, shall we begin with the facts as you perceive them?"

I delivered short declarative sentences. Emphasized what I knew and what I didn't. Included and acknowledged gray area perceptions. No nuance, no subtleties. Just the facts, ma'am. Although I painted the outcomes of the attempts on my life in dark smoke. Didn't need her digging up those graves.

She sat stone still, absorbing. The statements and questions came after I'd laid it out.

"Case Officer Stinnett prevented a much greater tragedy. Solid clandestine work, the results of which are most evident."

"No argument here. He averted an even greater slaughter. Eliminated multiple jihadi terrorists in this part of the world. Which benefited us all. Including the Chinese and their canal. And, provided great cover if you can pull it off."

"It is hardly their canal."

"You and I both know they run the show. And have invested billions, to make trillions. And the Panama Canal remains a prime terrorist target. Stinnett has made the MSS very happy."

"How kind of you to lecture me on geopolitical happenings."

"It lines up, Director."

"You also base a portion of your assertion on a young foreign prostitute's cinema descriptive."

"Your boy *is* a dead ringer for Mr. Cruise."

"And a common thread among several attempts on your life, and that of Mr. Pettis, is your Trinidadian. A Mr. Tig Roberts."

The skepticism was expected and warranted. I'd made the gravest accusation in the clandestine world.

"Forget threads. Think land mass. Costa Rica."

"And how did you conclude the sponsor issue? China's MSS?"

Well, Marilyn, it was Jules. You know. Jules of the Clubhouse.

"I connected dots. You don't find it curious Stinnett pushed Pettis to have me in St. Thomas?"

"You explained a Mr. Jones, identity unknown, encouraged Mr. Pettis. Subsequent identification was obtained while hidden among the landscape in the pre-dawn darkness. With a very frightened Jordan Pettis."

"Stinnett freaked in the conference room. Ran like a rabbit."

"Your countenance, Mr. Lee. The lone individual not applauding. The operator look. An anomaly among that crowd and danger for any low-profile case agent."

"My look?"

"I know it well. You do remember we crossed paths multiple times back in the day?"

"And that's the *only* reason I'm here."

My statement settled for a while. And then Marilyn Townsend offered a gesture I'd never forget. She raised her coffee as a salute, and nodded. It was sincere, the real deal.

"I do not doubt your sincerity," she said. "Yet those dots you referred to have tenuous connection."

"And the yacht? A line item on your black budget?"

"Borrowed, leased, or confiscated during an operation."

"The pieces fit, Director."

Ten seconds, locked eyes, shared unblinking stares.

"I will not discount your assertion, Mr. Lee. Not in the slightest, due to the gravity of the claim. Activities will be initiated tonight."

"You'll find I'm right. The question is, what action will you take?"

"Hardly your concern."

"Very much my concern. He will continue the attempts on my life. His other boss wants the loose ends tied. Pettis. Me. I have a lot more concern about the latter."

"Understood." She drained her cup, placed it inside my unused one, and ensured the thermos top was screwed tight. When she reached for her cane, instant movement from nearby suits. They approached, I stood.

"May I assume all communication regarding this ends here? Tonight?" she asked, rising. The cane tapped the concrete walkway twice. A signal or affectation or engagement of the weapon system—I'd never know.

"You may. It's Company business. Under the assumption you'll handle it appropriately."

An agent scooped up the thermos and cups. Another extended a hand to assist her. She waved it off.

"Know this, Mr. Lee. If facts present themselves as supportive of your claim, the situation will be handled." We locked eyes a final time. "Handled most appropriately."

She turned and worked her way toward a nearby parked fleet of large black SUVs. I remained, and walked among the playground equipment. Hoped no Company wet workers lurked. I carried the uncomfortable awareness a long-range night scope could have me in its crosshairs the entire time. Fifteen minutes later I retraced my steps across the park's cut grass. Helluva way to live.

Chapter 30

After the Townsend meeting, I spent the night in Chesapeake then caught a different Uber using a different account the next morning. Three hours to New Bern and the *Ace of Spades*. I couldn't quell the Jules assertion that Townsend would flip Stinnett. Use him as a tool against China's MSS. Which left me exposed. And aware Townsend would never communicate on the subject. Ever.

It was three days travel toward Charleston, and I took my time. There was no word from Jules regarding Stinnett's location. Expected. It required a deep, deep dive on her network.

Salt marshes, rivers, hemmed-in canals—components of the Ditch. The days were warm and fine, the nights pleasant. At a small North Carolina Ditch town I tied the *Ace* at dusk and dipped into the lone establishment's offerings. Ordered a burger and fries while I nursed a cold beer. Contacted Bo, curious and with mild worry.

"How's island life?" I asked.

"A toehold. Solid so far."

"And JJ?"

"A major contributor of the solid aspect. Where be ye?"

"A recuperative spa on the banks of the Ditch."

"A reasoned choice. So tell me a tale, goober."

"Not much to tell. The *Ace of Spades* lifestyle, headed south."

A fair statement. The *Ace*. Lazy days, quiet nights. Home.

"A fine path. And any hints on future directions?"

He enquired about Stinnett and actions, if any, I planned to take. Good question. The Caribbean job lacked finality. A muddied end, nothing definitive. The lack of closure gnawed.

"None. I'm letting the dust settle."

"Due to torn sentiments?"

"In a way. I'm letting the universe drive."

We both laughed. "My Georgia peach learns. It has been years in the making, but solid improvement. I'm proud of you, laddie."

He sounded so much better. Back on his feet. Laughter rose from across the small barroom as old friends enjoyed a tale. The barkeep wandered over

187

and lifted a chin, questioning whether another beer was in order. I nodded an affirmative.

"Tell me a little about your path. You hanging in St. Thomas?"

"I'm not allowed to flee. There's an FBI agent demanding answers."

JJ's voice, the words indiscernible, sounded across the line. As did the soft laughter of two brand new lovers. The sound tugged at old memories.

"Well, tell her hi for me."

"You tell her. It's inexplicable, but she wishes direct communication with your plodding self."

JJ came on the line. "Case? Tell me how you're doing."

"All good. At a spa."

"And I'm brushing up for my quantum physics dissertation." We both laughed. "Bo told me about your long wet stretch of home."

A slight alarm rang. I wasn't fond of anyone outside my family and blood brothers aware of my living location—albeit one several hundred miles long. But if Bo shared this facet, what else was revealed?

"Did Bo also mention it's not something I want spread around?"

She paused. I'd intended keeping my voice light, conversational. Her pause indicated my tenor contained a bite.

"I understand. If it helps, this redhead ragamuffin is plenty reticent regarding you. Or regarding himself for that matter."

"Men of mystery, JJ." An attempt at levity to bring the conversation back toward an even keel. "We don't reveal our secrets."

"And you're both doing an excellent job at it. Secrets aside, there is one thing I neglected telling you."

Again, whiffs of alarms. I was speaking with an FBI agent. The Company and its elements were one thing. Foreign affairs. But the feds impacted home turf. Turf holding more than a few past items that didn't belong exposed.

"Okay."

She hesitated again, perhaps perceiving my shields raised.

"It's not a big deal. Well, it *is* a big deal but not something to get your hackles up about."

"Okay."

"I never said thank you. And I should have. Multiple times. I don't have any excuses for it, but maybe you'll cut me a little slack. I was overwhelmed."

"An overwhelming experience, for sure."

"Amen to that. But thank you, Case. You're a special breed. I suppose all your type are. Including this peculiar man alongside me."

"Peculiar may not be the most apt description," I said. A conversational avenue led away from me, and I took it. "Unique, maybe. Different, for sure. And I should have left you the Bo-speak translation guide. You'll need it."

We both laughed, a fine and good sound, relieving.

"Send me a copy when you get a chance. It will cut down on the eye-rolling."

Delivered with a chuckle. And a muffled Bo response which prompted more laughter from their end. It resurrected more painful memories of my wife, Rae. Gotta learn to get over it, Case.

"I'll send it your way via sea cargo. It's a massive book, unabridged."

"I believe you. And speaking of Mr. Cosmic Thoughts, he wants a final word. You take care, Case. I mean it."

"You too, JJ."

"A reminder," Bo said. "One both short and sweet. If the path leads offshore, you will not fly solo. Thought I'd reiterate a given, mon capitaine."

"Thanks." I meant it, but this short stretch of conversation required a nail-down. "And this remains between you and me. Locked down tight."

If Bo and JJ remained together, her vocation constituted a relational element I'd have to get over. But in the meantime, concerns remained.

"As tight as blood, my brother. Kiss your mom and CC for me."

We signed off. The jukebox sang of Tennessee whiskey, a couple danced in a corner, and I felt a lot older than my years. It wasn't an altogether bad feeling. Perhaps poignancy-driven, introduced through Bo's words. A yearning, undefined. But the moment, this place and time, rounded the track at a good pace, and I held no major complaints. Life was good, and the nagging pulls of incompletion and loss faded with each beer.

Underway the next day on the Santee River, I skirted Bulls Bay and closed on Charleston. A thunder-buster blew in from the Atlantic and passed over Dewees Island and the *Ace*. Bursts of wind, thunderclaps, a deluge of pounding rain. The foredeck tarp snapped up and down, spilling rainwater. The La-Z-Boy throne received gusts of wet wind. The tomato plants leaned, recovered, leaned. The wheelhouse offered protection until I nudged against a marsh bank and killed the engine. Stripped of clothing, I stood at the back deck and received the full brunt of the storm. It was glorious. Rolling booms overhead, lightening cracked, gale force winds whipped rain. It did a person good standing naked among nature's violent elements. A strange emotional mixture—fear, awe, joy. And it helped place my world in context.

Twenty minutes later it passed. Moved on. I drip-dried, face lifted, a smile of gratitude. Life rolled on and it was best to accept the road contained bumps and potholes. So be it. I'd deal with it.

A couple of hours from Charleston the sun broke through and a cheese, onion, and tomato sandwich waited. With the sun, the steam bath started, and Marcus called.

"What's the status?"

It was hard changing old habits. Our former team leader demanded an update. I'd called him with an issue, a recommended course of action delivered, and now a follow-up. I couldn't keep a large smile away.

"What happened to deep concerns over my wellness?" I asked.

"My apologies. How are you? Caught any new skin fungus from your rotting tub?"

"That's much better. I'm fine, thank you. And you?"

"Waiting for a moron to give me answers. Thanks for asking."

"Will you remember them when I do? What with your encroaching decrepit state."

"You make me want to crawl through this phone."

"Have at it, Obi Won."

"Shut up and tell me."

I did. Marilyn Townsend's name wasn't mentioned, but the pronoun "she" sufficed. I also added her commitment for action.

"Good. Good," he said. "Now the big question. Are you going to let her handle it?"

"I'm vacillating."

"Understood. And I get it. Which leaves two options."

Here came the Marcus Johnson declarative express. Man I missed the guy, and the plastered smile remained.

"Do tell."

"Don't be a smartass. Option one. Wait it out. Action on their part will take time."

"Okay."

"And stop with the okays. It irritates the fire out of me."

"Okay."

"Were you this big of an ass pain in Delta? I don't recall it."

"Old age, memory loss, the list grows."

He ignored my comment and plowed ahead. "Two. If you decide to take action, I'm coming."

"I appreciate it, Marcus. Sincerely. But Bo has already insisted the same thing. So you'd have to work with him again."

"A challenge, no doubt. But not insurmountable. How is our space cadet?"

"He remained on St. Thomas. With a new girlfriend."

"Nothing new there."

"Oh, you'd be surprised. There's plenty new there."

"Like what?"

"Like she's an FBI agent."

A short silence before he replied. "Great. Now we have to dodge flying pigs."

"They seem to click."

"I can't even wrap my head around it. So back to item number two. Call me and I'll head your way within hours. With or without our cosmic cowboy engaged."

"I appreciate it."

"Don't appreciate it. Do it."

Rare was the day when I didn't contemplate how blessed I was with friends like this. Prepared to enter the gnarliest of situations—situations of my creation—and cover my back. I didn't deserve such brothers.

"Will do. Has it stopped snowing there yet?"

"It's summer. Are you on drugs?"

"A Montana summer doesn't preclude snow. Remember the pack trip into the Absarokas? Fourth of July? I'm pretty sure the white stuff we woke to was snow."

"The ranch isn't at ten thousand feet."

"Sometime next month. Promise."

"I'll hold you to it."

We signed off. The *Ace* chugged past Fort Sumter and entered the Ashley River which ran alongside the Charleston peninsula. I would let Mom know my ETA, and insisted on taking her, CC, and her beau, Peter Brooks, out for supper. She would have none of it. We'd eat at home—restaurant fare lacked the appropriate recuperative powers. She revealed the menu and solidified her unyielding position.

Crab cakes from fresh-caught blue crabs. Collards cooked with fatback, the translucent shimmer of the pot liquor perfect for dipped cornbread. And red velvet cake. Just because. Whatever might ail her only son—wanderlust or internal turmoil or relationship challenges—a home-cooked meal set a firm foundation for repair. Fine by me.

I tied the *Ace* at one of three facilities I rotated through at random for each visit, avoiding patterns. The reunion was joyous as always. Mom hugged and kissed me, mussed my hair, shed a tear. Peter shook hands, his left draped over the handshake. CC, my mentally challenged younger sister, latched onto me, arm wrapped tight around my midsection. About as fine a feeling as you could want. Her dog, Tinker Juarez—a mutt of indeterminate lineage and CC's constant companion—jumped, barked, and rubbed against my legs.

Sanctuary. Beyond a concept and brought to full fruition in an old Charleston neighborhood. Where woes and troubles were sloughed off and love blanketed. A moment of respite, acknowledged and appreciated. An all-too-brief slice of time where the simple act of being held golden and joyous. A small slice of heaven.

Chapter 31

"Let me help."

We stood in the kitchen, the aromas rich, as Mom held court. Tinker Juarez parked at the sill of the room, entrance forbidden except for a pass-through to exit the back door. We'd eat on the screened-in back porch as an overhead fan moved humid air.

"You can help by going out back with CC. And take Tinker," she said. "He eyeballs me with too much intent when I cook."

"I'm happy to lend a hand cooking."

"Go."

"Peter's helping."

Peter smiled and stood sentinel, prepared to perform whatever small task Mom asked.

"He has a pass. Because he understands his role in this kitchen. You don't."

"I'll behave."

"No, you won't. You'll do what I ask for a short while then give me palpitations fishing through my spice racks and asking questions. Speaking of which, tell me about Bo and this young lady. And why in the world are they on some foreign island?"

I hadn't mentioned St. Thomas as their location. The terrorist attack remained fresh in the world news cycle. A generic designation—a Caribbean island—was used instead. Even so, Peter caught my eye and raised his eyebrows. I returned a deadpan expression.

"It's a civilized island," I said.

"Barely at best, I'm sure. Is she as far out in the pasture as he is?"

"She has a government job." JJ's vocation would get probed at some point so I cast a benign cover early.

"I didn't ask about her job."

"At first I thought they were an opposites attract thing. But there appears to be a side of her that leans toward an expansive worldview."

"You mean weird."

"I mean in sync with Bo."

"Exactly. But I've included him in my prayers, and if the good Lord sees fit to move their relationship forward, I'm for it. I do love that strange man, as trying as he might be. Now get. Take the dog."

I grabbed a beer from the fridge and settled with CC and Tinker on the far side of the back porch where a large cushioned porch swing hung. CC and I added a slow pendulum movement to the swing while Tinker lay nearby, head toward the kitchen, nose working.

"Maybe tonight," CC said. "Maybe we'll see."

"See what?"

Her hand hold tightened and eyes widened. Her voice lowered, laced with awe. "Lightning bugs."

"Have you seen any?"

"Soft, Case. If we say it too loud they may hide."

I adopted a whisper. "I understand. So did you see any?"

"Sometimes. Not every night."

"Maybe tonight?"

"Maybe tonight." The lightning bug discussion over, her voice rose to a conversational level. "Tinker Juarez is mad."

"Why?"

"I don't know. He's mad at another dog."

"Which dog."

"Mrs. Ellensworth. Her dog. Abe."

"Do Tinker and Abe fight?"

"They do through the fence. When Tinker Juarez and I walk past."

"Maybe Tinker is protecting you."

"I don't know. But they fight." She lowered her voice again. "I hope they come."

I squeezed her hand. "Me too, my love."

Mom and Peter set plates, CC and I were instructed to sit at the table, and the four of us held hands while Mom delivered a prayer. Then I commenced overeating. The sun lowered, shadows lengthened. A breath of ocean breeze worked through the neighborhood and pushed a bit of the sticky air aside. The hanging moss along the limbs of the backyard's old oak shifted with the air movement—nature's wind vane.

"Tell us about your latest adventure, Case," Peter said as he served cornbread slices from an iron skillet to passed plates.

"Kind of boring. Investigated a proposed business deal. But I did travel to Long Island."

Safe ground and an attempt at steering geography away from the Caribbean. The earlier brush with Bo's current location threw sufficient warning spikes. Mom stopped eating and smiled my direction.

"Now, that sounds nice. A civilized part of the world. US soil. Can you get more such contracts?"

"Hope to," I lied. The joined slow death drive through tourist hot spots of vacationing people flashed, and left.

Peter, a history buff, regaled us with a few tales of Long Island's importance during the revolutionary war. Mom insisted I both eat more and save room for dessert. CC and I played a winking game where she giggled at my exaggerated faces. Tinker Juarez hung at the perimeter, alert for any food mishaps.

"Why don't you and Peter take a vacation?" I asked as we settled back, beyond sated. I considered letting a notch out of my belt. "I'll take CC for a boat trip."

"I think that's a great idea," Peter said.

"A boat trip!" CC added and tossed in a small seat bounce for emphasis.

"Give it a couple of weeks to plan and let me know the timeline," I said.

Mom glanced through the screen and considered. "Maybe. Maybe someplace cool would be nice."

"The Italian Alps," I said and kept the ball rolling. Mom wasn't hurting for money. I made sure of that.

"Not with all the terrorism going on," she said. A bit of a blanket excuse—Mom wasn't fond of places outside US borders.

"How about the great wild west?" Peter asked. "We could get up in the mountains. Idaho, Wyoming, Montana."

"They have grizzly bears," Mom said.

"Lions and tigers and bears, oh my." CC giggled at my statement.

"Hush, son of mine."

"Long odds of a bear attack, Mary Lola. You're digging for excuses," I said.

"I'll think about it."

And she would. Such weighty decisions required thought and planning. CC and I cleared the table and cleaned dishes while Mom and Peter relaxed. The classic Carolina pause for a semblance of digestion to take place before dessert arrived. The neighborhood sat still, quiet. Another dog barked a long block away. Darkness fell.

Mom brewed decaf coffee, large slices of cake were delivered, and we ate from old fine china while spread across the porch. Soft and muted conversation, allowing ample room for nighttime peace to settle. Tinker conducted a good scratch. Peter told a funny story from the insurance business, his voice adopting the languid rhythm of a southern gent. The cake, better than fine. The company, priceless.

Thoughts of Stinnett and Marilyn Townsend crept into my sanctuary. Corrupting thoughts of abrogated responsibility toward dealing with my situation, my unfinished business. Business I'd delivered, handed off, to a third party. Marilyn Townsend and the Company. With no assurances, none.

CC saw the first one. A full second of tiny bright fluorescent light. It blinked off then on again a few feet away as the slow flying insect moved through the night air. It brought an enthralled hush across the porch. Another lightning bug blinked and another. CC sat tall, mouth open with wonderment.

"It's magic," CC whispered. She placed her plate on a side table, extended a hand, and kept eyes glued toward the dark backyard.

I took her hand and pulled her closer across the porch swing, wrapping my arms around her midsection as she leaned back against me.

"It's a gift, my love."

She nodded and spoke awed soft tones to the larger world. "It *is* a gift."

A wave, huge and monstrous and unforgiving lifted and crashed against the moment. The tumultuous wave called, bellowed—you walked away, Lee. Walked away and endangered sanctuary, endangered your family. I had left deadly actions and consequences in the hands of others.

Stinnett knew of the Clubhouse, and sent operators. Killers. He may have known of the bounty. I gave it higher odds than Bo or Marcus. And with sufficient effort, focused effort, he might discover the whereabouts of Mom and CC. My family. Sanctuary violated.

"And I have a promise to make," I whispered into CC's ear. She turned her head the slightest, one ear toward my lips, and kept her eyes on the insect light show. "I promise many more gifts in the future."

CC leaned her head back and rested on my chest. One path lay ahead. The gravity of removing a CIA operative faded as commitment solidified.

There would be no Bo, no Marcus. I was going in. Protect the family. Tie my own loose ends. Sanctuary would not be violated. First, find the bastard.

I kissed Mom and CC goodbye and turned down a ride from Peter. Explained I'd rather walk and work off the red velvet cake and reminded Mom tomorrow's evening meal was without argument on me at a nice restaurant. And she owed me her travel plans.

"I understand Tibet is nice this time of year," I said, teasing.

"Hush. I'm not going anyplace where the men wear pajamas all day. I told you I'd think about it."

Peter followed me through the front door and kept pace for half a block. The offshore breeze increased and brought cool salty relief. Charleston threw bright light, but stars were still visible overhead.

"It's not my business," Peter said. "But I'll have my say."

I slowed, stopped, and shared a companion's look of concern.

"I'm not implying you were involved with the horrible events in the Caribbean the other day," he continued. "But you were pretty doggone good at bypassing the subject tonight."

He'd put two and two together. Knew about my background from Mom and made an assumption as to Bo's whereabouts. And mine. "That's a young man's game, Case. You might consider turning the dial down a bit at this point in your life."

I squeezed his arm and delivered a wry smile. "Great minds think alike. A major item on my priority list."

He returned a smile, turned, and patted my back as he walked away. I'd liked the guy from the get-go. He treated Mom with respect and love—and exhibited the same toward CC. A good and fine man. And there was no lie, no obfuscation regarding turning down the dial. But in the immediate future, crank it up, buckle up, and handle the situation.

I sat on the patched throne and nursed a Grey Goose. The *Ace* bobbed in her slip, the chop from Charleston Bay extending into the dock area. Thoughts of operational plans, a loose end snipped. And to hell with the consequences. My family, exposed. The river crossed, the decision final. A light groan as I eased from the throne for another vodka before bed. My phone buzzed an inbound message. Jules.

Jules had released the dogs, committed to her part of the deal. And she delivered. The entirety of the message presented with classic Clubhouse style.

Providencia.

Stinnett's location. Providencia. Wherever that was. It didn't matter. Sorry, Marilyn Townsend. Can't leave this in others' hands. Sorry, Bo and Marcus. My mess, and I'd clean it up. And you should have known, Roger Stinnett. After the first attempts at killing me, you should have known I was one of a handful of people on this good earth you didn't mess with. And now it was my turn, you SOB.

Chapter 32

Dark ops, dark attitude. Movement and action under the radar, dark to family and friends. Dark ops in the literal sense as well. Hunker down during daylight hours, movement at night. Which made for tight timelines and added risk. Stinnett could change locations at any time. His warning radar was set high after recognizing me. And he hadn't heard from Tig, a silence driving valid conclusions. He'd be skittish.

I considered my quarry. We'd met before. The high seas when I exited Nassau. The trailing vessel, ghosting my speed and course. He'd contemplated action against me as we played the Caribbean version of cat-and-mouse. But he chose to exit the arena. A cautious man, unsure of striking unless the odds were stacked high in his favor. His preferred method—hire proxies, hitters. Or given his spook tendencies, hire an underground entity who would in turn hire the hitter. More layers of separation. The same pattern of off-loaded wet work would apply at his home turf. He'd have guards. Armed guards prepared to kill. A given.

Providencia and San Andres. Sister islands, and as obscure as you'd find. The two islands were situated 150 miles east of Nicaragua, 450 miles north of Colombia. Tucked in the western part of the Caribbean. Both the property of Colombia. Go figure. San Andres was much the larger, in size and population. An eight by two mile remote destination for Colombian honeymooners and casual tourists. Access via one flight a day from Bogota, Cartagena, and Panama City. Spanish the predominant language, and its geographic isolation created a unique island culture.

Providencia was another matter. Fifty miles north of San Andres, it defined isolated. A former home base for the infamous pirate Captain Morgan, it was two miles long and wide. But unlike flat San Andres, Providencia held substantial steep hills. Its small population spoke English and a Caribbean creole, with Spanish a third choice. Intrepid tourists did visit Providencia, although the numbers were few. An idyllic place, with warm gorgeous waters and undisturbed laid-back surroundings. Two choices for getting there: an irregular prop plane flight from San Andres which made harrowing landings on a tiny airstrip, or a semi-daily ferry service across fifty open miles of sea. I'd rely on rubbing elbows with nefarious characters and take a third option.

My logistics were set—nighttime travel, payments off the grid. I chartered a small jet on my dime under an assumed name. Paid from a Caymans bank account tied to a corporation that didn't exist except on paper. My destination—Cartagena, Colombia. I'd walked those streets before, both as a member of Delta and a private contractor. The pilot would refuel in Cartagena and wait a few hours while I managed a transaction. Then carry me for a second leg. Destination, San Andres. Arrival, midnight.

Then travel to Providencia under the cover of darkness the following evening, via boat. I held no contacts for this final leg, but San Andres and Providencia operated a solid drug trade network, and a fast boat wouldn't be an issue. I ran in those circles when needed, both as Delta and now. A night trip was the key—arrival on a tiny island such as Providencia under bright sunlight wouldn't do. Without doubt, Stinnett received alerts of any new visitors, including tourists. And I sure didn't fit the tourist profile.

Cartagena would supply needed firepower. I considered packing my own. Rely on a thick stack of Benjamins to deal with Colombian customs and immigration. Often used, it still left a chance of major issues cropping up. The catch tended to lie with the distribution of the bribe among the immediate authorities. One argument over the split and I owned a major issue. So a fake passport and broad smile, arriving unarmed. But once there, I knew a guy.

I called Mom and let her know a business item blindsided me. I would return a couple of days later. She understood with minimal questions. Greatest mom in the world. Caught an Uber to Savannah—my charter jet pick-up point. I'd packed light and wore field boots, jeans. My rucksack held the essentials—a change of clothes, toiletries, and laptop. And a bundle of hundred dollar bills large enough to choke a mule. I tossed in my medical kit, a lightweight hammock, a handful of energy bars, and small bottle of water purification tablets. Good to go. After my transactional visit among the back alleys of Cartagena, I'd be better than good to go.

I left Savannah late afternoon, flight time three and a half hours. Landed in Cartagena at dark and breezed through customs. My fake passport matched the Cayman Islands credit card I carried. Told the pilot I'd return a couple of hours later for the two hour San Andres flight. Left the rucksack on board and carried two pockets filled with Benjamins. I was unarmed, vulnerable, and on edge. A taxi delivered me to the old walled city within Cartagena. Game on.

Situated on Colombia's Caribbean coast, the walled city was built in the 1500s. Spain ruled the roost at the time and the high walls—rounding the old central town for two and a half miles—enclosed narrow cobblestone streets, small plazas, churches, and old colonial houses. A shadowed hemmed-in area, much of it bustling with tourist shops. Plus a small section of tight streets and dark alleys best avoided. My destination.

The bright lights of tourist bistros and restaurants faded, as did the crowds. A stretch of seedy commercial establishments appeared. It held the grim look and feel of a Hollywood set. A tight area which would trigger the casual tourist to make a dead stop, perform a quick assessment, then turn on their heel and head back. I entered my personal shopping district.

Everything stone—the streets, raised sidewalks, facades of the tight-packed colonial houses. Light cast from the open doors of bars and small bodegas provided the sole illumination. It reeked of ancient filth, urine, despair, and death. I strode the middle of the cobblestones, footfalls muted, and headed toward a specific destination. A corner intersection, squeezed with irregular angles, offered more light than the narrow streets I'd passed through. A run-down bar occupied the intersection's prime real estate. Outside its entrance, two men leaned against a corner wall, a third faced them. They spoke with hushed tones as I approached, the lone pedestrian within this tight-hemmed area. A prostitute farther along smoked a cigarette. She stood straight and adjusted her bust line as I approached. Muffled chatter and champeta music flowed from the small barroom.

The man not leaning against the wall side-stepped into my path and spoke with broken English. He'd spotted a gringo, a North American foreigner, and hence an easy mark.

"Got a light?" he asked in broken English.

His two partners left their positions and eased behind me.

"Don't smoke," I replied in Spanish and endeavored stepping around his blockage.

He shot out a hand and attempted grabbing my arm. I didn't have time for this crap. I blocked his hand grab, took a quick leap-step toward him, and delivered a throat shot. Hand open and flat, the web between thumb and forefinger drove into his trachea. The will to fight leaves a man quick when he can't breathe.

I turned as he staggered backward and performed a quick shift toward one of the two behind me. They both displayed lock-blade knives. The one I moved against left his crouch, surprised at his partner's distress and my movement toward him. He straightened, locked his legs. Big mistake. People expected kicks toward their groin or solar plexus or head. You could find gold much lower. Another rapid side-step his direction and I slid onto the hard cobblestone street, delivering a boot heel to the side of his locked knee. Cartilage ripped, ligaments popped. He screamed and dropped as I popped upright and locked eyes with the third man.

"Are you really that stupid?" I asked in Spanish.

He eyeballed his two partners in crime, shrugged, and with great calm folded his knife and slid it back into his pocket.

"No. No I am not."

He left the other two and strolled into the bar without a backward glance. I moved on. The prostitute smiled and began an approach as I passed. The violence displayed before her failed affecting her focus on business. Lack of eye contact and my index finger side-to-side wag—the universal "not only no thanks, but leave me the hell alone"—stopped her forward movement. Old town's deep shadows covered my exit, the destination a few blocks away.

I took a cut-through alley to an obscure walled street. A single light shone from a small window behind a wrought iron grill. The door was of heavy oak and reinforced with more wrought iron. There were no signs, no indicators of a business establishment. The heavy latch lifted and hinges protested as they opened.

A bookstore. Antique books, scattered across rudimentary shelves and stacked atop heavy tables. The smell was musty, with a hint of decay. The proprietor, an old man, reclined in his chair, one leg perched on a desk. Pencil-thin, white hair brushed straight back, and lined leathered skin. His eyes, though, were bright and eagle-like as they captured my every move above reading glasses perched at the tip of his nose. A large and ancient bound volume lay open across his lap. We'd met before.

Chapter 33

"You appear well," he said. "Older and with lines of experience, but well."

"And you, Don Costa, appear well. Perhaps wiser, although I am a poor judge of such things."

I'd never know if Costa was his actual name, but the "Don" designation—an appellation of respect—fit the man. A learned gentleman who sold antique books. And world-class weaponry.

"Please do look around. And take your time. Such decisions require consideration."

Part of the routine. Peruse his books, pay well over market value for one, and then shop for firearms. It worked, and I didn't mind. Many of the stacked books were bound journals of Spanish explorers and Jesuit priests from the 1500s. Cool stuff.

I took as much time as the evening's schedule afforded. A decent interval expected and delivered. To hurry displayed disrespect for both Don Costa and the bound volumes before me. After fifteen minutes I selected a hand-written account of a 1544 Cartagena battle between the incumbent Spaniards and the French pirate Jean-Francois Roberval. Of particular interest were the hand sketches of sea and land battle movements.

"You have chosen well, my friend," Don Costa said. He turned the volume over in his hands as he rubbed the front and back leather cover. Having adjusted his position as I approached with the book, he now sat straight and formal. An appropriate posture for serious business.

"Peruvian silver, collected from the interior and brought to Cartagena," he continued. "It also brought the French, English, and Dutch. You will find this battle of particular interest."

"Interesting times."

"All times are interesting. Each passing slice of history is spiced with battles and men of valor. Steel on steel, my friend."

An opening conversational gambit, intentional. His Spanish carried a hint of Castilian lisp. I delivered a slow head shake and a sigh of despair.

"I regret the onset of another battle. It is most unfortunate. Yet it is my time to draw my own cold steel."

He removed his reading glasses and placed them on his open manuscript. "Is the cause noble?"

"I am protecting my castle, filled with personal Peruvian silver. My family."

"Ah. A righteous battle. I would hope your opponent holds close an element of virtue as well."

"None."

He stood. "Then swift, sure, and final the appropriate manner. Perhaps I can help."

"It would be most appreciated, Don Costa."

He first locked the front door of his shop. Then produced a key ring and eased past stacks and shelves full of books. Another thick oak door, narrow, tucked in a far corner of the small room. The centers of the stone steps leading down showed concave under the cellar stairway's naked lightbulb. Worn down through hundreds of years of foot traffic.

There was nothing haphazard about the display of firearms. A vast array of weapons from manufacturers across the globe—each hung from wall-mounted brackets. Rifles, pistols, and shotguns. Originating from the US, UK, Czech Republic. And Austria, Italy, Israel, Germany—the list long and expected.

I'd first visited here years ago with Marcus. Delta was assigned a dicey mission on the Colombia-Venezuela border. Elements of the preparation were spelled out for us—outfit our team with weapons untraceable back to a US operation. Not so much for having one of us killed or captured along with our firearms. But rather ensuring the small piles of spent cartridges we left behind could not be traced to Delta. For my current mission, this bit of cover also didn't hurt. What with whacking a CIA operative and all.

"May I enquire if you had anything special in mind?" Don Costa asked.

"As my opponent is without honor, engagement at a distance is a possibility."

"Of course."

"And this shall take place at night."

Don Costa crossed his arms, a forefinger to chin, and considered the requirements.

"Yes, yes," he said. "It is most fortunate I have the exact weapon. Of Hebrew manufacture."

He shifted position within the confined cellar and pointed toward an Israeli Tavor assault rifle with a night vision scope.

"And be most assured my friend," he continued. "It is both well suited and well prepared."

He meant sighted in, accurate. I removed it from the wall, inspected the mechanisms, and threw it to my shoulder. A fine weapon. I selected four extra magazines, loaded, and placed my choice on a small central table.

"Yet a possibility exists," I said. "A possibility I may face my opponent in a more honorable manner."

Up close and personal.

"Ah. Perhaps we should consider a weapon for such an event."

He led me toward a wall full of pistols. I chose a Taurus 9mm semi-automatic from Brazil. Along with an extra loaded magazine. I declined the offer of a suppressor. Big bang on this mission might hold advantages. Stinnett's armed guards might duck and run.

"A thought," Don Costa said. "A passing thought, and perhaps one not worth mentioning."

"I stand in your debt for the wisdom you have shown in the past."

A slight bow of his gray-haired head as response. "Perhaps a weapon or two with—how shall I say this—less finesse."

Explosive weapons. Fine and dandy. A waist-level drawer slid open and exposed a selection of hand grenades. I chose four Ruag fragmentation grenades, Swiss-made. I appreciated the concept of people who made fine watches were less likely to manufacture a grenade that blew up in your hand.

"And a final thought," he said. "As you may face this man at a distance, a man with no honor, the possibility exists he will hide. Hide as a coward and refuse facing you."

"The possibility does exist."

A corner hutch was opened and displayed a small selection of grenade launchers. I glommed onto an old M79. Why not? A Vietnam-era single-shot, shoulder-fired, break-action weapon. It launched a 40mm soda can-sized explosive charge 350 yards. Old school. I added it to the cellar's tabletop collection along with four high explosive rounds.

It was appropriate to stand with Don Costa and consider the selection. A perusal, an assessment—serious business. A full minute passed in silence. At last we exchanged grave expressions followed with eyes-closed tight nods.

"A fine selection," Don Costa said. "Sadly, an expensive one as well. And I hesitate mentioning the price of the extraordinary manuscript you have selected upstairs."

"It is painful but necessary to ask such a question, Don Costa, but what might be the sum total?"

He provided the amount and laid hands, palms down, on the table. He gave a slow shake of his head while staring at the weapons. An exhibit, expected, of how it distressed him so, asking such an exorbitant price.

Lips pursed, I hefted the Thumper and a Swiss grenade, followed with a heavy sigh.

"Perhaps it is best if I left without these inelegant choices."

Still focused on the tabletop, he too sighed. "I cannot allow a friend to march afield on such a noble mission as yours without adequate protection. No." He slapped his hands on the tabletop, raised his head, and we shared stares, unblinking. "I cannot and will not."

He lowered the price twenty five percent. Hands were extended across the small table loaded with lethal merchandise. We shook. Done deal and good to go. He tossed in a large bag of fine Colombian leather which held my purchases with room to spare.

Cash was transacted, and I slid the pistol into a front pocket, slung the bag over a shoulder, and followed him up the stone steps where he added the manuscript to my collection. At the front door, he turned and addressed me.

"May you vanquish your foe and protect your silver. If you fail, my friend, fail as a warrior of olden times. Valiant to your last breath."

I wished him well, hustled back toward the tourist section of the old town, and caught a cab for the airport. My pilot stood outside the small jet. As I boarded he said nothing about the large and loaded leather bag I'd acquired in the old walled city of Cartagena.

Chapter 34

The Caribbean Sea shimmered black and unknown through the jet's window. This small part of it represented enemy turf. While Providencia held Fortress Stinnett, the approaching island of San Andres might contain emissaries, early warning players. Arrival under darkness and obscure movement mitigated this advantage.

The airport sat alongside the main cluster of inhabitants, houses, and tourist hotels on the north side of the island. The San Andres airport was closed for business, the runway approach and taxiway lights unseen. But the airport, as my pilot well knew, was equipped with PCL—Pilot Controlled Lighting. Standard set-up at many lonely airports across the globe. It allowed aircraft pilots control over the lights through radio frequency. Tune the correct frequency, key the mike the appropriate number of times at a set interval, and—voila—runway lights turn on.

Both the sudden landing lights and the sound of a jet would draw attention. Not the best stealth approach. But dark night and an active drug trade in this part of the Caribbean were temporary friends. The locals would pay little heed to a late night landing and ask few questions. But still, enemy turf. And entry points were high risk.

The pilot kept the engines running, and I bailed near the airport terminal. My transport turned for immediate takeoff. He wasn't hanging around. I took cover near a line of baggage carts and waited for quiet. It came soon enough. The jet roared away, the runway lights flicked off, and calm restored for this middle-of-nowhere island airport.

I considered pulling the assault rifle but quiet and calm prevailed. So I skirted the side of the terminal structure in time to see an old and well-used vehicle pull up. The driver stopped at the small terminal and exited his car, hair unkempt. A small magnetic illuminated *Taxi* sign was slapped on the rooftop. The jet's noise had clearly woken him. He'd tossed on clothes and made an airport hustle for a potential fare before the competition could beat him. I admired his moxie.

I exited the shadows and waved his direction. A broad smile was returned along with a question in broken English. He'd sussed me as a Norte Americano.

"You need taxi?" He used both hands and straightened his hair, smiling.

"I do." I kept it Spanish, although I appreciated the attempted catering for a customer's preferences. And having exhibited this much get-go, the driver could prove invaluable. A potential provisioning of more and much needed services. Taxi drivers world-wide were a font of connections.

"You like hotel? Girls?" He kept to English as I approached.

"A place to sleep." I kept to Spanish. "Not a hotel. Away from town and private. Any ideas?"

"No hotel?" His brow furrowed.

"No hotel."

He returned to his native tongue. "I know of such a place. A friend. But it is quite primitive."

"I have a hammock."

"As you wish."

Excellent. We drove south along the western coastline. Town lights disappeared, a yellow haze across the northern horizon. Movement, isolation, safety. So far so good. The driver introduced himself as Paco.

"Are you here on a visit?" he asked.

The headlights illuminated the empty road ahead and moonlight reflected off Caribbean waters fifty yards on the right. Small collections of thatched-roof pueblos passed on the left, most of them dark, asleep. I sat in the front seat, leather bag between my legs, rucksack on the back seat.

"A tourism photographer. Canadian."

"I am taking you far from the tourists."

"I like solitude when I'm not working."

"This is clear. Will you require a ride during the day?" Paco asked.

Time for a mining expedition. Test the waters for this guy's other acquaintances.

"Yes. A ride and other things."

He turned, lower lip extended, a serious expression. And nodded as an opening gambit for a business opportunity.

"I can help. Be certain, I will find what you require and take you where you wish to go."

I took the plunge.

"I wish to travel tomorrow. To Providencia. On a boat. At night."

He nodded again and considered the request.

"You can fly during the day. Perhaps. It depends upon the schedule and the pilot. He is known to have problems."

"No. A boat. At night."

He shrugged, having done his good deed of presenting a better choice, and steered me toward his personal solution.

"I have a friend who can do this."

"A fast boat."

He chuckled. "Oh, it is a very fast boat. And very expensive. Are you sure you do not wish to fly?"

"Will you take me to your friend?"

A lift of his hand from the steering wheel. "Of course. Mid-morning."

We pulled over among a group of thatched shacks near the sea. Not a light on. He parked and asked me to wait. With a silent approach, he bent over and whispered into one of the shacks then straightened as a man emerged and walked toward me. The rucksack over my shoulder, leather bag in hand, I greeted him and asked if I might stay the night. I would, of course, pay. He pointed toward a thatched shack without walls, a local bar or restaurant now empty and dark. Perfect. Hammock strung between two support poles, I settled in.

The lonely quiet did little to dispel the mission's torn structure. A quest to ensure the safety of my family, and myself. Fair enough. But a quest tainted, overlaid, with aspects of a stone cold killer. I couldn't shake it, even weighing Stinnett's multiple attempts on my life. But while my concerns held sharp moral shards, commitment never wavered. I slept with the assault rifle loaded, safety off, as the Caribbean breeze blew and small waves lapped at the rock coast.

"Coffee?"

Daybreak. A man, the small open-air establishment's proprietor, stood at the edge of his own place and politely asked the question as I packed the hammock. His teenage son stood alongside him. Both wore shorts and T-shirts, no shoes.

"Coffee would be excellent. Thank you."

"Breakfast?"

"If it is not too much of a problem." I'd save the energy bars for later.

He turned and addressed his son. "Fish." He lifted his chin toward the open waters a few yards away. The two of them moved behind the crude counter—created from driftwood—and assumed separate activities. Dad turned on the propane and began coffee preparations. The son pulled a five foot homemade steel spear from behind the counter and strolled toward the water. I followed—a morning show not to be missed.

The kid pulled off his T-shirt, threw a "Watch this" look my way, took a deep breath, and jumped in. This section of the coast was rugged rock and formed a small subterranean ledge over the sea. The kid swam under the rock overhang and, while out of sight, he must have waved the spear about. Stirred things up. In seconds, multiple small Barracuda darted into the open sea. As one escaped its overnight sanctuary, the spear tip shot into view and pierced it. The kid swam into the open with his catch and rose for breath. He treaded water for a few seconds, smiled, and lifted the speared fish for my perusal.

"Will this do?" he asked, strutting his stuff.

"It will more than do," I said and smiled large.

Hot coffee served, Barracuda steaks frying, I checked the satellite phone and laptop. No messages. Good. As far as my brothers knew, the *Ace* and I sat in Charleston. If Jules had any additional information it would have appeared. It raised the confidence level of Stinnett's continued presence on Providencia.

Paco arrived at the appointed time, más o menos, and I enquired about the whereabouts of this fast boat he'd arranged.

"The other side of the island," he said.

"Could you be a little more specific?"

I would avoid the northern tip—the most populated portion of San Andres—if possible. The island's main docks were situated near there as well. High odds my proposed ride wasn't anchored in public view.

"The east side. South of town," he said with an expression of bemusement. "Why would it matter? This is a small place."

"Let's head south. Fewer people."

He shrugged. I left my rucksack and leather bag and handed the proprietor a hundred dollar bill, along with instructions neither were to be touched. He assured me they would remain unmolested and slid both behind the bar counter. His personal turf.

The narrow two-lane road hugged the coast around the southern tip, passing small villages along the way. A classic Caribbean day—bright, mild, stunning. Several miles up the east coast, Paco turned right toward the water. A two-track dirt path wove past dilapidated shacks and abandoned marine equipment and general refuse. This wasn't the yacht club.

A collection of boats were pressed inside a small cove against the thin sand beach, bow first. Lines trailed onto the beach, boat anchors as terminal points across the sand. The boats held a common theme. Low, long, and fast.

The low profile made for a poor radar reflection. The hulls, aluminum, light weight, long and narrow. Unloaded, one of these would ride high in the water. Loaded with drugs or other contraband, the freeboard would consist of but a few inches. Each was equipped with massive engines. Most with pairs of powerful outboards. Two boats held an automotive engine mounted amidships with a coupled driveshaft extended through the stern. Steering for those required dual rudders—you couldn't turn the engine as with outboard motors so the driver turned the boat. A bit of a downside, but for a screaming nighttime run across calm open water—uncatchable. I eyeballed the flotilla of drug-running and piracy vessels. All they lacked were individual Jolly Rogers flapping in the breeze.

Paco asked me to wait in the vehicle while he finalized arrangements. Miscreants, murderers, drug-runners and hangers-on wandered about the small cove. The Taurus pistol in my waistband pressed a comforting coolness against my belly.

Paco returned with a squat dark man, head shaved. He wore loose-fitting gray cotton pants, an unbuttoned sleeveless shirt, and no shoes. Scars were evident across his torso. Knife fights. A machete, sheathed, hung from his waist. A quick nod of acknowledgment between the two of us was sufficient as way of introduction. This was a business transaction and personal identities were not required. We strode toward the beach.

The squat man pointed toward his vessel. Over thirty feet long with twin 150 horsepower outboard engines. With Case Lee Inc. as the sole cargo, not much of the keel would touch water at full speed. I nodded agreement toward the smuggler and cast a head movement toward Paco, indicating we should step away. Time for negotiations, the routine well-practiced. Paco the intermediary, ensuring his cut of the trip protected.

"How much?"

"Five thousand US," Paco said.

"Roundtrip?"

"Of course."

"Two."

"He will not take two."

"Fifty miles one way. Hundred miles round trip. That's fifty dollars a mile."

"He will not take two."

"Tell him two."

Paco sighed and lifted both palms toward the heavens. Then turned and shuffled the dozen steps between us and the smuggler. He relayed my offer. The squat man spit, crossed his arms, and provided a counter offer. Paco returned, smiling.

"Four."

"I'll go three. No more." I waved my arm toward the other vessels and ensured the smuggler viewed the display. "I could find others here who would take three thousand for such a trip."

And present the potential of cutting Paco out of the deal. Which wouldn't do. So my taxi driver girded his loins and delivered my BAFO. Best And Final Offer. The smuggler spit again, bitched and moaned, and accepted the deal. I'd arrive at dark, the fifty miles covered in an hour, more or less. The smuggler insisted he wouldn't linger at Providencia more than two hours. Not a problem. A two by two mile island. Find Stinnett before he fled. Before the Chinese became aware of the situation. Find Stinnett and protect my silver. Find him and end it.

Chapter 35

The weather was decent. Not great but good, and I'd take it. An eastern breeze blew a chop across the Caribbean. My preference—a glass-like surface for hauling ass across fifty miles of dark sea. But at least there were no rollers, no waves to contend with.

We arrived at the pirates' cove after dark. Leather bag in hand, I slung the rucksack across my back and approached the vessels wearing fatigues, a webbed battle vest, and holstered sidearm. The assault rifle and high explosives would be produced once we hit Providencia, although there was no point hiding intent. Paco didn't care, although my battle attire ensured he'd demand his cut early. In case I didn't return.

The squat smuggler looked me up and down, grunted, and lifted the anchor off the sand. Several other boats made preparations for nighttime runs, a few with their cargo tarped while others remained empty. Drugs, contraband, human immigrants—the underworld trade displayed before me was replicated a hundred times across the vast swath of Caribbean islands.

As my boat driver stood with anticipation, a roll of Benjamins passed hands. Half the fee. The other half upon return. The smuggler handed Paco his cut, then pocketed the cash and dropped the small anchor into his vessel. I splashed through a few inches of water and climbed on board. Paco followed, carrying a string bag filled with water bottles and food.

"You shouldn't come," I said as he lifted a leg across the gunwale. "Wait here. I'll return in a few hours."

"I will come with you. It is part of our agreement."

A tacit agreement between the two of us or an understanding with the squat smuggler—didn't know and didn't care. Likely he traveled as investment protection and ensured his cut.

The smuggler toted a long canvas bag and dropped it alongside his feet once situated at the rear of the boat. A small clang accompanied the bag's placement. A familiar sound. This guy traveled with his own selection of weapons. Fair enough. A pirate, a smuggler—he wouldn't travel unarmed.

I settled at the prow, the front peak of the boat. Tucked the rucksack as a backrest and faced Paco and the driver. With the beach transaction complete, the smuggler, and Paco, knew I carried cash. Lots of cash. My back wouldn't face either of them, preventing a likely scenario. A few miles at sea, a quick head shot, rifle through my possessions, and toss my dead body overboard. A short, lucrative trip. I pulled the pistol and checked to ensure it was loaded. An act performed for the other two. I always kept my sidearm loaded.

The smuggler fired the engines and blue exhaust smoke wafted away with the breeze. He let them idle, warm up. Then lit a cigarette. Plastic gas tanks—their hoses jury-rigged to feed the engines—littered the floor of the vessel at his feet. Great. Just freakin' great. At least he wouldn't fire any more smokes once we were underway. Too much wind.

"Ready?" the smuggler asked.

Other boats fired their outboards around us. One of the boats with a mounted car engine roared awake. Calls and insults between smugglers, a bit of tight laughter. The pirate navy of San Andres came to life. Providencia fifty miles north, the Corn Islands off Nicaragua eighty miles west, Costa Rica and Panama an intrepid three hour fast boat trip south. All a pirate needed was plenty of fuel, weapons, calm seas, and brass balls.

"I have a question."

The smuggler cocked his head and waited. He'd know of Stinnett. A lone gringo as a Providencia resident. Plus the smuggler understood my mission. The battle garb, the sidearm, my own clanging leather bag. It didn't bother him—these guys worked under strict don't ask, don't tell policies. The risk lay in whether Stinnett had this guy on the payroll. The best practice in these situations—ascertain the answer early.

I rolled the dice and asked, "An American on Providencia. He lives there. Owns a big boat. You know where he lives?"

"Yes."

"Will you point his house once we arrive?"

Providencia consisted of steep hills, lots of tucked-away spots. A time-saver knowing where the guy lived, although he could have a favorite bar or eatery where he spent evenings. But he'd return home at some point.

The smuggler spit over the side and tossed his smoke into the water. "A thousand."

A positive sign. Either there was no love lost between the two or they didn't know each other as the smuggler sought easy cash for information. Unconcerned if a random rich gringo was whacked this night.

"Five hundred."

"Seven fifty."

"Done."

Deal struck, the smuggler eased backward into the cove, turned the boat, and goosed it. The bow lifted, the engines howled, and in short order we planed across the surface. The light surface ripples delivered the boat irregular bow slaps. The lights of San Andres faded, stars coated the sky, the freshest of salt air whipped past. Fifteen minutes into the trip I pulled the satellite phone from the rucksack and checked GPS. The smuggler was on a perfect track. He'd made this run more than a few times. Phone returned, I settled back and watched our wake and the boat's other occupants. Past the driver's head and to the left, a distant and sporadic light. Strange colors—a mix of yellow and blue, twinkling.

I stared for ten minutes and pondered as it approached. The strange lights maintained a parallel track to ours, off the right side. And catching us. It was difficult to fathom given we scooted at a speed hard for any decent-sized boat to match. Then realization came, without undue concern. It was one of the car engine powered boats from the smuggler's cove. Exhaust pipes, pointed skyward, popped blue/yellow flames as the boat flew across the water.

I lifted a pointing finger toward the approaching vessel. Our driver stared into the distance to his right, back ahead, and again toward the right. He studied the other vessel for a full minute. Then as one hand gripped the wheel, his other unzipped the canvas bag and produced an AK47 assault rifle. Concern arrived, and I followed suit. The Tavor rifle appeared and lay across my lap.

"What's going on, Paco?" I called above the engine noise. He'd observed both the approaching boat and the driver's actions.

He yelled a question at the driver, the words lost in the whipping wind and engine noise. They held a brief yelled conversation. Paco turned toward me and called over the noise.

"It is possible they are making the same trip."

"What else is possible?"

"It is possible they wish your money."

Hells bells. I had enough to think about without a ragtag pirate gang attempting a high-seas robbery. I hadn't hidden the cove beach transaction, the roll of dollars evident. A stupid mistake. It was a substantial wad handed over, visible even at night. One of my driver's competitors saw easy money flashed and decided low risk easy pickings this night. Wrong, asshole.

I checked them through the Tavor's night vision scope. The surface chop allowed irregular focus, their image bouncing in and out of my sight. But I could discern their makeup. Five men. A collective effort among the San Andres pirate community. Their distance, five hundred yards. And closing.

I put myself in their shoes. Get within a couple hundred yards and begin firing. Scatter sufficient bullets across the distance, count on several rounds hitting our vessel. Knowing we couldn't outrun them, we'd stop. Capitulate and quit and hope for robbery instead of murder on the high seas. Well, screw that noise.

My driver didn't appear in the mood for any form of quit. He kept the boat's throttle firewalled, no slowdown. At three hundred yards the nasty twinkles started. Muzzle blasts from automatic weapons. No tracers so I couldn't tell how close the bullets flew past. Until one, then two and three thwacked the side of the thick aluminum hull between me and Paco. The driver heard the bullet strikes as well and ducked tight behind the wheel. A critical moment. The driver held the option of stopping, perhaps save himself. And take his cut of the prize in the process. Time to take that option off the table.

Frustrated with the lack of aiming ability with the boat's jolting, I switched the Tavor's selection to full automatic, threw it to my shoulder, and fed hot lead their way. Short three-round bursts. I couldn't tell where or if they struck home, but the other boat's occupants would see my muzzle blasts and understand they were in a fight. My driver sensed we'd crossed a point of no return and joined the gunplay. He switched the AK47 to his right hand and drove with his left. One-handed, he too cut loose with short bursts aimed in the general direction of our enemy while screaming curse words at the top of his lungs. Better than nothing.

At two hundred yards as both vessels skipped across the sea's surface, numbers began to count. Five against one. I didn't rely on my driver's shots hitting their mark. Several of mine did, evidenced when the other vessel's occupants lowered their profile and fired behind the boat's protective hull. Paco huddled below the gunwale and yelled for updates. I yelled back a quick assessment. We were in deep shit.

Five full automatic weapons blasted our way. One and a half fired back, the driver now even lower in his seat. His AK rested and bounced on the gunwale as he cut loose with ineffective bursts. Another string of bullets splatted against our hull—the sound of hard-thrown rocks against a tin shed. Not good. Not good at all. The situation screamed for a change in dynamics.

All right, you bastards. Let's introduce someone new to the party. I laid the rifle back into the leather bag and pulled the Thumper. Breech cracked open, the heavy short barrel hinged downward. I slid a soda can-sized grenade into the barrel and slammed it shut. Commitment, accuracy, courage, and tactics. All critical components required for battle. But back them up with more damn firepower.

A simple weapon, I gauged the Thumper's aim. Eyeballed the appropriate elevation and distance ahead of the speeding enemy. Slapped the trigger. It kicked against my shoulder, a low *thump* sound instead of the sharp crack of a rifle. The grenade soared into the night. Two and a half seconds later it struck past and behind the other boat. A volume of Caribbean water geysered upward when it hit the surface. Too much elevation, not enough of a lead. Round two.

While loading, I glanced at the other occupants. Paco held a serious eyebrow-bunched expression and watched with great intent. The scarred smuggler exhibited a different response. He placed the AK back across his lap. His wide wolf-grin flashed a gold-tooth display in the moonlight as he gave me an enthusiastic thumbs-up.

Closing the breach, I aimed further ahead and with less elevation. Bullets continued to thwack against our hull as the enemy closed. A muted *thump* and a second and a half later the water exploded twenty feet behind the enemy, but on the proper line. Elevation good and with a bit more lead, party over. Two grenades left.

The other boat, their eyes aimed at us and ears filled with the howling engine and the crack of automatic fire, hadn't noticed either of my shots. That would soon change. I adjusted the Thumper's aim for a better calibrated distance in front of the speeding boat and lowered the barrel's elevation a small amount as the distance between us closed. I tugged the trigger.

The explosive round blew away the front third of their boat. The vessel's remnant hull dug into the warm waters and sent it flipping end-over-end in the Caribbean night. The yellow/blue engine exhaust flames continued their staccato pops as it tumbled through the air two, three, four times. Then an ugly landing as pieces of boat and men blew across the salty surface.

Paco shot me a tight affirming nod. The driver kept a predator smile, now tight-lipped, satisfied. We continued skimming the sea, full bore. Flying fish burst through the surface at our bow wake and glided off into the night. Millions of stars hung as bright pinpoints. And five more dead men were chalked up across the Caribbean Sea.

A quick slide of the Thumper back into the leather bag, the assault rifle lay across my lap. A preventative measure in case my personal pirate reconsidered the golden opportunity facing him across the boat's interior. Helluva way to live.

Chapter 36

We approached Providencia. A dark mass rising from the sea with clusters of lights along its coastline. The steep inland hills—rising as high as 1000 feet—held fewer signs of habitation. I'd studied the maps, the geography, and understood most of the island residents clustered around the north end of the island. Stinnett's yacht would dock there. But he would live inland, enjoying his personal slice of isolation and protection.

A single road circled the island. A mix of pavement and gravel near the coves and beaches and open air shacks offering beer and fresh fish. The less occupied villages carried the names of Freetown, Bottom House, Smooth Water.

Providencia held no large tourist hotels or developments. A Caribbean island throwback when simpler times ruled. No cell phone service. Two undependable Wi-Fi spots. Several dilapidated fortresses from the real pirates of the Caribbean days. A random ancient rusted cannon or two. Shorts and T-shirts were the official dress with bikes and scooters and sandaled feet the modes of transportation.

We headed west toward the leeward side of the island. The protected waters changed to flat calm, glass. The smuggler slowed, cruised, a half-mile offshore. A cluster of lights, a small town, appeared and we edged our way toward it.

"Fresh Water Bay." With the engines cut back and speed slowed, the smuggler's voice could be heard. "The Norte Americano lives above the village."

It made sense. Stinnett drew his posse from the village below him. And there would be a posse—guards, a protective gang—guaranteed. He'd crossed the line and now lived a lucrative and susceptible lifestyle.

"Take me south of the village. Away from people."

He took the opportunity to light a smoke and relax, a hand draped over the wheel and one leg thrown across the gunwale.

"There is a small road from the village to his house."

"I do not want the road. The beach south of the village. Drop me off there and wait."

I pulled the rucksack from the bow point and made a show of removing several fat rolls of Benjamins from an interior pocket. I took my time and shoved them into pockets of the webbed battle vest. Not doing so opened the door for my return ride making a hasty and lucrative exit after he dropped me off. An ass pain, but I *was* dealing with a pirate. And for all I knew, Paco would have assisted him.

We cut speed to a fast idle as the beach approached. Steep vegetation-covered hills rose ahead, the lone hardtop road at their base. No motorized traffic heard. Human noise drifted across the calm bay. Villagers ate, drank, socialized.

The bow eased onto the beach, and the engines shut off. I vest pocketed the four Ruag frag grenades and two extra rifle clips. A KA-BAR knife waist-strapped, shoelaces tightened, and knee pads situated. Good to go. I delivered a tight nod toward Paco, and he returned the grim gesture. A locked-eye stare with the smuggler constituted our good-bye.

Before I crossed the beach and made it through the fifty feet of brush toward the paved road, three boys appeared. They were hidden among the moonlight-shadowed palms at our arrival, playing, being kids. Unseen. Now they stood stock still, capturing the sight of a lone boat with two men. And a third man in fatigues carrying an assault rifle. Bad luck. Bad luck heightened when they took off, a mad dash toward the village a quarter-mile away. Oh man. They'd alert villagers of the situation. And word would reach Stinnett's posse. Damn.

No turning back, no reconsideration. I held no intention of engagement with local armed badasses, but the possibility had always existed. I moved forward. Dozens of black crabs at the intersection of beach and trees scuttled away. A spooked iguana, lurking in the vegetation before the road, dashed ahead, cut left, and disappeared. I checked both directions at the road. Still, quiet, no traffic of any sort. I crossed and scaled a steep brush-covered hill, topping out at a ridgeline running inland. Several more ridges showed on the left and right, steep brush-filled ravines between the jagged spines. I knee-dropped and gathered visual intel.

Above and along another ridgeline stood a substantial house. Not a mansion or estate, but larger and more prominent than a run-of-the-mill Caribbean dwelling. There were a few inside lights on, but no movement. No other houses or structures around. I scoped the vehicle parked in front. A Kawasaki side-by-side ATV, brand new. The polished chassis reflected moonlight. That wouldn't last long in a salt air environment. Then relief flooded as a shadow passed across the main room. Stinnett was home.

I wasn't adverse to a long-range shot. A sniper's shot. Cold, dispassionate. It also held the advantage of a quick kill and no trace of entry or conflict. So I sought a sniper position. The next ridgeline over offered a clean view of the house's large main room as well as several other rooms' windows. I crawled off the ridgeline—no silhouette against the sky—and made my way downhill. The steep ravine at the bottom was filled with scrub trees and brush—thick and unavoidable. Maintaining slow movement, I sidestepped through brush. A broken brush limb would sound a crack, a nighttime noise indicating animal movement. Or a hitter's progress.

Scaling the new ridge I searched for the best firing angle. Just below the top and on the other side held the most promise. As I crawled over the narrow ridgetop and dropped down several yards, noise. Brush moving, a few crackles of small limbs. And whispered voices below me in the bottom of the ravine. Stinnett's posse had arrived, searching for me.

Let them pass. It was a waste of time and energy engaging a motley bunch of armed amateurs. Instead, I'd take out their boss and haul ass. Flat on my belly, I waited. So did the posse. Two of them climbed the other side of the ravine, dark shaped movement working uphill. They crested and dropped to the other side. Where Stinnett's road lay. A hand-full remained, now quiet and eyeballing the terrain. The head-high brush and stunted trees filled the ravine's bottom and hid them well, but also obscured their vision. Fine. Boredom would set in soon, and they'd climb out—head either for Stinnett's house or for the village and a beer, excitement over. I bet on the latter. The testimony of a couple of ten or eleven year old kids wouldn't hold a great deal of water. They could check the parked boat a quarter mile down the beach from their village and find the smuggler and Paco. But they'd leave the smuggler alone, ask few questions. Unwritten rules, and ones they would avoid breaking.

A large fat iguana worked its way toward me. No stealth, an utter lack of concern regarding its environment. With no natural predators other than local dogs, it sashayed through the brush, its path marked with the sound of low brush scraping its tough hide. The distance from the posse was too great to draw attention. Until it came upon me. Insects buzzed, a few mosquitoes hummed, and the large lizard assessed the creature stretched before it. Me. For reasons I'd never know, the reptilian synapses fired danger and the stupid critter took off. Ran its waddling side-to-side gait and whacked against stiff brush during its exit. Which brought plenty of noise and the attention from the gang below me. This exercise wasn't going well. First the kids and now a stupid oversized lizard.

Maybe they'd never fired the automatic weapons Stinnett provided them and wanted to cut loose and give them a try. Or maybe they half-way knew what they were doing. Either way, the ridgetop became a hot fire zone. Bullets slammed into earth, ricocheted off rocks. They peppered my general area. A few bee-buzzed over my stretched-out body. Meanwhile Stinnett's house lights turned off. First the main room then the others. He'd make a dash for his personal arsenal. Given the CIA background, ownership of an assault rifle with night-vision capability was a strong possibility. It was time to vacate the current situation and reposition. Change assault tactics.

First, work fast and clear the area, then move. I didn't relish the idea of Stinnett scoping my position with his night-vision weapon. And doing so from a superior vantage point. It would take him sixty seconds or so to acclimate his vision and focus on the battle area. I produced three of the four Swiss grenades and rolled onto my back, allowing for a decent throw. Pulled the first one's pin and heaved it downhill toward the steep ravine bottom. Pulled the second pin and released it as the first one blew. Big bang, baby. The second one followed suit. The handful of Stinnett's men flushed like quail and hauled it up their side of the ravine, scrambling. A couple of them crashed through ravine brush toward the village, exit stage left.

I tossed the third grenade toward a different section of the brushy draw. Just to be sure. And to draw Stinnett's eye. The third explosion gave me one second, maybe two, for a scoot over the top of the ridgeline and a drop to the other side. Out of Stinnett's line-of-sight.

A quick flip onto my knees and a mad scramble the few yards uphill. I flung myself over the sharp-edged ridge and heard the wicked angry whine as a near-miss bullet whipped past. Immediately followed with the sharp crack of a rifle. A snap shot from the house. Well, it answered the question whether the enemy held a weapon with night-vision capabilities.

It was a new ball game. His stooges were out of the picture but the element of surprise now lost. So it was just him and me. And he knew who came after him. The grenades, the quick dash over the peaked ridgeline. He knew. Death stalked him in the night. And wouldn't quit.

A nighttime sniper-on-sniper approach was off the table, with its hours of waiting, scoping. I wasn't playing that game and would take him at short range. Inside his house, up close and personal.

Traversing below the ridgeline, I dropped into the ravine and up the other side. Then repeated the maneuver and followed another spine uphill, past his house. The plan—enter through the back. Stinnett would defend 360 degrees of potential assault. I planned one attack angle. Straight at him. Advantage, Case Lee.

Freakin' kids. Freakin' stupid iguana. The unexpected. Count on it. I pushed those thoughts away and focused on the approach. Scoping the rear house layout, several options presented. The most appealing—the structure's nearest back corner. A pinpoint route straight for it held the poorest view angle for anyone inside. I could nestle against the corner and slide along the wooden exterior toward several back entry points. A plan developed, odds in my favor. Execute, move, terminate.

I didn't know the guy's background but high odds he lacked great marksmanship. I counted on it. Three hundred yards behind and above the house, I moved fast and made a beeline toward the rear corner. A low jog, dodging dwarf trees and oversized scrub. The final twenty yards were across open ground—a high-risk stretch. I accelerated approaching the open area, headed downhill, and sprinted across the danger zone. Then pressed against the corner's exterior clapboards. No response from the enemy. Stinnett focused elsewhere—toward the front or off to either side. He'd cover the back at some point, seek his target. Too late, Stinnett. Nightmare time, baby. I'm at your doorstep. Say your prayers and prepare for Case Lee's stamp of *Expired* on your birth certificate.

Chapter 37

Cut and run was a possibility for my quarry. But he didn't know my position, and performing a hasty exit left the possibility he'd run into me. Bad news for my opponent, and he knew it. I gave his runaway low odds. He might move about, creep in the darkness and seek me through different vantage points. Or the most likely scenario—he would stay put. One spot where he felt safe, protected. A place which afforded him a strong sense of self-defense, forcing me to seek him. An activity that tilted odds more toward a level playing field. To hell with level playing fields. I wanted him moving, active. Inside a dark house, his movement and sound posted the highest vulnerabilities. I'd force him into both activities.

Four windows spaced across the back of the house. A door, centered, closed and likely locked. A poor choice for entry. Another option would become available soon enough. The key—aggression. Force Stinnett into a mindset of being under extreme attack. Create a mandate of movement. Maybe get the guy talking, open negotiations. Pinpoint his location. And take care of business.

Once the assault kicked-off, the key was speed and terminal violence. Move fast, hit my target. Start with the farthest window. I ducked low and dashed across the wide back wall. Settled in a squat under the glass windowpanes at the far corner. I lifted the assault rifle over my head and fired on full automatic. A short burst as glass imploded, the weapon's firing sharp and explosive. Then waited three seconds for a response—returned fire or the sound of movement. Nothing.

I pulled the final hand grenade's pin, tossed it through the window, and flew along the back wall, stopping under the window closest to my original corner position. The grenade explosion blew a chunk of wall outward and sent metal fragments throughout that corner of the house. Pretty much guaranteed it grabbed Stinnett's rapt attention.

Next the window above my head. The opposite side of the back wall from the grenade toss. I pulled the pistol and blasted five quick shots into the room, then hauled ass back toward the aftermath of the grenade explosion as glass shards collapsed to the ground behind me. Hit the blown-out wall area and entered the killing floor. Sought my target, the assault rifle shouldered.

"Lee! Lee! Listen up."

The voice was steadier than anticipated. It came from the left side of the house, near the front. Near the large great room. The room I'd entered, minus most of its back wall, was a spare bedroom. The doorway hung on one hinge. A splintered armoire lay on its side.

"I know you can hear me."

I avoided crunching across broken glass and edged toward the grenade-shattered doorway. Led with the weapon's barrel, sought my prey.

"What you're doing is murder! You can paint a pretty face on it, Lee, but it's still murder."

I focused on the sound source, not the words. A spook, playing head games, working me. A short hallway showed empty. Eased my way along it. It opened on the great room. The voice came from a space near the large living area.

"The reasonable thing is a discussion. We can talk this out. I can issue guarantees. Solid guarantees. You won't get that from anyone else."

I could issue a guarantee as well, you dumb bastard. Guarantee your sorry ass would not be among us much longer. I pressed against the doorjamb, focused on pinpointing his voice. The night vision scope sought movement or a portion of his body. Any target facilitating a trigger squeeze. A wounding shot, a hand or leg. It didn't matter. Punch flesh, keep firing, attack. Follow up with a kill shot.

"And money. Money like you can't believe. No more work, no more danger. You could retire. Think about it."

A quick scan of the floor for debris and a silent step across the opening. It allowed for a better firing angle and less body exposure. The large sliding glass door of the great room—opened to a small overlook porch—let in a Caribbean breeze. It ruffled long light curtains. Hillside insect sounds, silenced when my grenades went off, returned full chorus. Distant Caribbean waters glistened under moon and star light.

He'd show soon enough. Run out of one-sided dialogue. He knew I was close but had no clue of my location. He'd given his position away for the running soliloquy but held a plan close to his vest. A short-term plan—kill me. My existence held nothing but downside for Stinnett. He might blabber for hours, but sooner or later he'd try and kill me. One of us wasn't walking out of here.

"I know about the bounty."

226

Frozen. Movement and focus and intent—all frozen.

"And I know who funds it."

The one operational Hail Mary the guy could throw that would seize my attention. The sponsor of the bounty. Identify the sponsor—a Yemeni sheik or Chechen mafia boss or South American drug lord. Hunt him down. And cut loose the burden, at long last, on my family, Marcus, Bo, Catch. And me.

But I dealt with a spook. A spook who would say anything, do anything, to save his hide. I opted for a short Q&A. A stay of execution. Clemency was still off the table but facts delivered, hard facts, extended Stinnett's life a few more minutes. But only a few.

Speaking identified my location, so I slid further from the great room's doorway. I had no idea what type of weaponry Stinnett held.

"Tell me."

The great room's lights flicked on. And pinpointed his location. A half-wall between the kitchen and large room held light switches. I'd scoped the area seconds ago. He'd reached around the interior wall and threw the switches, exposing just his hand. He now stood behind the same wall, in the kitchen.

"Simply tell you?" A low chuckle followed. An affectated, ballsy move. This guy raised the bar on fatal game-play. "It's my hole card, Lee. Let's work out a few details first."

"Such as?"

"Such as how this ends. Then work backward to the information you want."

"This ends how and when I say it does." I launched a quick probe. "How many of us carry the bounty?"

"Five."

His answer lent credence to a claim of paymaster knowledge. My CIA dossier *did* contain information about myself, Marcus, Bo, and Catch having a bounty on our heads. As well as Angel. But Angel lay buried in Montana. A fact unknown to anyone but us remaining four.

Marilyn Townsend, a few months earlier, claimed the Company didn't know the sponsor. She may have lied. A leverage point for future use. But Stinnett could have other knowledge. Maybe. Maybe not.

"What part of the world? Give me that. A sign of goodwill and brotherhood, asshole."

If this little chat went sideways quick, at least I'd have acquired a morsel. Anything to narrow the sponsor search. Otherwise, it was a big world and neither I nor my brothers knew where to begin.

"No can do." Another chuckle. "Let's first talk about how we both walk away from this. The end game."

The explosive *boom* shocked the crap out of me. A single shot from a high-powered pistol. What the hell? On the heels of the deafening gunshot, two concurrent sounds. The rattle of a weapon dropped on a hard surface. And the thud of a dead body. I slapped the assault rifle against my shoulder, heart rate soared, senses cranked.

"What the hell was that, Stinnett?" My voice loud, demanding, although my gut told me I wouldn't hear anymore from Stinnett. Ever. I applied trigger pressure, sure of immediate gunplay. The adrenaline pump redlined.

"Relax, Lee. It's over."

Mind reeling, I tried piecing the immediate together. I knew the voice. Not the inflection or accent or rhythm. But the sound of the voice.

"Paco?"

"Yeah. Whatever. Step out. My pistol is in my right hand. Pointed at the floor."

My taxi driver. Speaking perfect English. With a Midwest accent. Iowa, or Indiana. What the hell?

"You gotta be shittin' me."

"No you moron. I'm not shitting you. Get out here and lower the high-caliber hackles."

The Company. Played me like a freakin' Stradivarius once again. Pissed, relieved, confused—and the adrenaline pump still fired on all cylinders. First things first—a visual assessment of the situation.

"Coming out."

I dropped to a knee and, leading with the Tavor assault rifle, popped a partial view of my body around the doorjamb. Locked the weapon's sight on Paco's chest. He stood at the edge of the illuminated room, pistol pointed down. Breath blew rapid through my nostrils. Son of a bitch.

"I'm going to place this pistol in my front right pocket. You got that?"

His voice was calm, sure, and directive. He'd occupied this position more than once. A CIA wet work operative.

"Yeah. Got it."

He did. A seasoned, relaxed, smooth move. I lowered my weapon and stood. Kept the rifle battle-ready, finger on the trigger, barrel aimed knee-cap high. Moved toward him. He understood my immediate goal and backed farther into the kitchen, allowing me space for a quick view. Stinnett lay crumpled as blood pooled. A head shot.

I locked eyes with Paco or whoever the hell he was. His voice changed. No longer conversational, it was now flat, definitive, etched in stone.

"We take care of our own business."

I nodded in response. Yeah, Paco. Yeah. I guess you do.

Chapter 38

"I need to collect a few things and could use your help," Paco said.

The wheels turned but the gears didn't mesh. The mental clarity this guy held wouldn't arrive for me. Except for one thing. Paco was a hitter extraordinaire. A Company hitter. And I wasn't releasing my rifle grip. Or turning my back on this guy. He sensed the attitude.

"If it will help, I'll lay the firearm on the counter. So you can relax. And help gather a few items."

Again, I nodded as response. He used thumb and forefinger, pulled on the pistol's exposed grip. Then laid the weapon on the counter.

"You're not in any danger." He displayed a wry grin. "Unless you run into more pirates on the way back."

"Okay." I noticed he didn't use the plural regarding the return occupants on the smuggler's boat.

"You've got friends in high places." The grin disappeared, replaced with dead seriousness. "I received specific instructions not to harm you unless necessary."

Marilyn Townsend. Fine. But the caveat of no harm my way unless necessary drew a cold interpretive line in the sand. A line subject to this wet work specialist's immediate situational view.

"Good to know. But I'm keeping a grip on my weapon."

He shrugged, said, "Whatever," and strode toward Stinnett's body, flicking on more kitchen lights along the way. Paco checked his pockets, found nothing, and wandered down a hallway, turning on lights as he went. I followed.

He searched room to room. Banged walls, sought hidden stashes. In Stinnett's office he dumped a laptop, thumb drives, and papers into a leather satchel he'd snatched off a doorknob.

"Lobbing those grenades into the ravine provided great cover." He pulled open another drawer. "And blowing the back of the house off sure drew his attention. No one is going to accuse you of being subtle, Lee."

"He might have told me something of value. Big-time value. You could have waited."

I stood in the office doorway and watched him work. He was thorough, fast, professional.

"He fed you BS. Waited for his shot."

"He knew things. The number five, as an example."

"He had access to your dossier. Anything beyond that was pure conjecture. BS."

Mr. Wet Work found a hidden compartment under the desk. Removed more thumb drives and rolls of cash. Everything was tossed into the leather satchel.

"What do *you* know?" I asked.

He glanced up, shook his head, and returned to rifling through drawers.

"If you're talking about the bounty, I don't know jack."

The truth or a lie? I'd never know.

"So that's it?" I asked. "Over and done?"

"You want a parade?"

I stepped aside and he returned to the kitchen. Eyeballing me, he reversed the two-finger process of pocketing his pistol.

"I'm out of here. Going to borrow his ATV for a little ride."

"You're not taking the boat back." An affirmation we were parting company. He'd drive the ATV to a pick-up point. Maybe the small unlit airstrip. Or an isolated spot where a long-range night-capable helicopter would retrieve him. Either way, he would soon disappear.

"No thanks. Good luck, Lee." He turned, satchel over one shoulder, and laughed. Switching back to Spanish, he said, "You might want to avoid turning your back on that smuggler waiting for you."

I cast a glance around and turned off lights, remaining in the dark. In too damn many ways. The ATV started out front. Oh man. Alone and twisted and numb. The Company figured I would head toward San Andres. They placed their hitter there a couple of days ago. Long enough for him to get the lay of the land. Assume an identity and prepare for me. I took minor solace knowing he'd played the part well. Still. Should have picked up on it, sensed a vibe. I'd let my guard down. Then they used me as the prime distraction for Stinnett. Opened the door for a quiet, efficient hit. Great. Just freakin' great.

I held a spark of gratitude toward the Company. They took care of their problem. And mine. Kept my hands semi-clean. So they took care of business with one of their own. Used Case Lee for misdirection. As a tool. Oh man.

I side-hilled the ravines and worked toward the boat. No interference, no sign of Stinnett's now unemployed posse. My personal pirate sat among the gas containers, smoking.

"Where's your friend?" he asked.

"Gone."

He ruminated on this development—not out of concern, but gratitude. He wouldn't fork over a slice of the pie to Paco, the arranger. All good by him. I pushed the boat off the beach and jumped in. Kept the rifle across my lap and faced the smuggler. He flicked his smoke into the still waters.

"There was a great deal of shooting."

I didn't respond.

"You must be a tough hombre, no?"

"Tough enough."

He laughed, spit into the sea, and started the engines.

"You have the look. I have seen it often and still do not understand," he said, speaking over the idling engines.

"What look?"

"Sadness. Doubt. Why is this? You are alive. Others are dead. These are the only two choices in life."

"Sometimes it's not a choice."

He spat again. "It's always a choice."

He turned the vessel toward San Andres and firewalled the throttle, ending all conversation. We arrived an hour later. I paid up and took Paco's vehicle. Stripped off the vest and stuffed the rifle into the leather bag. Returned the way we came, around the southern tip of San Andres. No other vehicles on the road. Two customers remained at the bar shack where I'd spend the night again. A single naked lightbulb cast a yellow hue across the sand floor. My rucksack—unmolested.

The proprietor and two customers spoke of local things, life. Relationships with wives and family and friends. Where the best fishing could be found at this time. The ongoing repair of the village's water tank. Not once did they enquire of my activities. I asked for his finest rum from a selection of a half-dozen bottles. He held a bottle of Guatemalan rum, two-thirds empty. I asked for the entire bottle. No glass.

"It is expensive," he said. "The others are also fine and cost less."

"How much?"

He stated an amount equivalent to ten bucks. I folded a Benjamin in my pocket and palmed it. Passed it via handshake across the driftwood bar. He received it in the same manner, giving a quick glance at the amount before it slid into his pocket.

"For everything," I said.

He thanked me. The exchange would constitute a major topic of discussion for weeks among the small bar's clientele. I excused myself and pulled a chair into the sand and opened the laptop. The rum bottle nestled alongside me. I acquired a satellite signal and considered exit options. Another charter jet couldn't be arranged until morning, with availability uncertain. I checked commercial flights. Direct shots for Cartagena, Bogota, and Panama City. The first two headed the wrong direction. And the Panamanian flight left the earliest. Panama, Atlanta, Savannah. I could smell the barn.

At daybreak the assault rifle went into the Caribbean, as far as I could throw it. I kept the pistol until security at San Andres airport. Dropped it in a bathroom garbage can. The magazine, loaded with bullets, deposited in another. Both wiped clean prior to disposal.

The Panama layover afforded an opportunity for a great cup of coffee and laptop catch-up. No report filed with Global Resolutions—this mission was personal. But it stamped a hard period on the end of the Caribbean job. Over and done, loose strings tied. No sense of job well done or personal satisfaction. Just over. I sipped coffee and read an email from Marcus. He chastised me about a Montana trip confirmation.

But I couldn't shake the post-events blues. Case Lee, Inc. had made a concerted and unsuccessful effort to engage contracts of the more mundane variety. I'd failed the sniff test of geopolitical implications associated with grand plans and big money. Perhaps Global Resolutions' business model didn't offer plain vanilla contractor gigs. Which left the alternative of finding my own investigative work. A concept dead on arrival. Advertise, market, spread the word—activities leaving me more exposed, more public. No thanks. Developing a better nose and exhibiting greater discernment when considering Global Resolution contracts constituted a more viable path. Stay away from arenas and venues where spooks played. Deal with non-clandestine situations. Unless I chose to enter Spookville. Then do so with eyes wide open.

Choices and decisions were weighed while I sipped black coffee and grappled with a white picket fence existence and life partner floating out of reach. In part due to the bounty. Another opportunity lost with Stinnett, although the wet work operative may have been right. BS on Stinnett's part. So cue the blues but temper the post-gig malaise with a degree of satisfaction at, once again, having departed the realm of spies and lies and obfuscation. Man, was I wrong.

He slid into the chair opposite me at the coffee shop table. The dude was mid-thirties, Chinese, and dressed like a preppie. No smile but no appearances of hostility either. Benign, perhaps, although the word "spook" might as well have been printed across his forehead.

"You are an interesting man, Mr. Lee."

No accent. Spoke like he'd graduated from UCLA. Hell, he probably had.

"I'm a simple man. You got a name? Since you know mine."

"I am Mr. Lee as well." He smiled. I didn't.

"You going to fire a poisonous dart across the table? Or can I relax and drink my coffee."

He continued smiling. "Please relax. And as you claim to be a simple man, allow me to speak in simple terms."

MSS. The Chinese Ministry of State Security. Their version of the CIA. Wanting a little chat about events of the last week. Less so about Stinnett— they understood the Company would sooner or later figure it out and take care of their guy. A permanent solution. Last night or earlier this morning they tried contacting Stinnett. Perhaps took satellite images of his house when he failed to respond. Noticed a back corner of his house blown away. Put two and two together.

And they understood I was involved. Not the details, perhaps. Details such as me starring as the dumbass providing Company misdirection. No, these people played the long game. Years forward. And wouldn't dwell or agonize over small items such as their Company guy getting whacked. A loss, sure, but this was about the big picture. Panama. Costa Rica. Trillions of dollars in world trade. The down-the-road perspective.

"Have at it. I like simple." I sipped coffee and stared across the table over the porcelain cup's rim.

"We are always looking for exceptional people such as yourself."

This guy was trying to recruit me. Didn't see that coming.

"I'm retired."

"A short stint with us would ease your retirement plans. Lessen the burden of money concerns."

"No thanks."

"A few years. No more than five. And it would allow you to continue using your special skills. Most impressive skills."

"No thanks."

We entered the danger zone. Money hadn't worked. If he had any leverage, personal leverage such as family and friends, it would play now.

He cocked his head, the pleasant countenance remained. "I understand. You are tired and such a decision requires considerable thought." He reached into the pocket of the button-down pressed shirt. Pulled a business card and placed it before me. "Please contact me when you wish to discuss such an opportunity. The remuneration is, truly, quite spectacular, Mr. Lee."

He stood, shot a quick head bow, and strolled away. I pocketed the business card, worth a chunk of change on the Clubhouse ledger. And let relief flood. He'd stuck with money. No leverage, no threats, no indications he knew all *that* much about me or my private life. Still. A simple cup of coffee in the Panama City airport and another damn clandestine player plops down. It was like I splashed on spook attractant each morning after a shower.

On the upside, he—and MSS—clearly held no deep animosity toward me or my actions. Unlike the Russians, who kept me high on their shit list. But MSS could change their mind at any time. A closed door office, several of their operatives sitting around a conference table. After tea was served, the seventh item on the meeting's agenda broached. Take out Case Lee. It could happen any time.

Yeah, well, I wasn't operating a popularity contest. The sit-down with MSS cranked the engine, cylinders fired, hackles raised. And blew away the blues. Fine and dandy, Spookville. Bring it on. Screw with me and reap the whirlwind, boys. Just bear in mind there was a long string of alleged badasses who, if they could still talk, would speak with one voice. You'd best not mess with Case Lee.

Epilogue

CC and I strolled among palm trees and massive old moss-draped oaks on Jekyll Island, Georgia. The *Ace* was tied along Fancy Bluff Creek, Tinker tugged at the end of his leash, and all was well in the world. We were on our way toward the Sea Turtle Center.

"Turtles," she said. "Turtles and Tinker Juarez and you and me."

"That's right, my love."

It was the sixth day of our adventure. Mom and Peter visited Yellowstone Park and the Tetons. Mom called every day under the guise of a CC check-in. The reality—revealed with Mom's statements of continued health among Rocky Mountain wilderness—was her assurance they'd so far avoided being the prime entrée for a grizzly bear.

Marcus called and confirmed my date of arrival in Montana. We also confirmed a few other items.

"How'd the mess we spoke of work out?" he asked.

"The Company took care of it."

A pregnant pause while he digested the statement.

"And just how do you know that?"

"I'm a man of mystery."

Another pause. "You're bullheaded. You dived in. And opened the door for more of the same in the future."

"Things were dealt with. Important things."

"I swear I'm dealing with a teenager half the time."

"You putting me to work on the ranch, Dad?"

"You wouldn't recognize work if it drove over you."

"I'm a delicate flower, Marcus. Let's not forget that."

"About as delicate as a wire-bristle brush. Tell CC hi for me."

The Sea Turtle Center captivated her. I paid for a behind-the-scenes tour and CC interacted with injured sea turtles in rehab. The technicians allowed her to feed one and touch and rub others. Her response was wide eyes and a mouth open with wonder. She kept shooting quick glances toward me, ensuring this shared moment was stamped real and magical and etched in our common experiences. I returned loving smiles each and every time.

JJ emailed me a link to a short blurb from the Bay Area press. Jordan Pettis was killed in a hit-and-run accident. Dollars to donuts he'd re-initiated the Costa Rica deal. Killed by greed and stupidity and hubris. And by another office closed-door session, perhaps attended by the guy who met me at the Panamanian airport. Above the email link she asked, *Coincidence?*

Could be. I wasn't elaborating on the subject, and finished my short reply with, *Hope all is well.* I couldn't shake the badge aspect when interacting with her. Maybe time would leaven our trust factor. Maybe not. But her email prompted a Bo catch-up call.

"What's shaking, castaway?" I asked.

"Caribbean sand, my brother. Gotta shake it out of everything. Sandals, shorts, hair. An irritating constituent of this time and place. One I have yet to sidle up next to and embrace. How's my Georgia peach?"

"CC and I are on a boat trip. Mom and Peter traipse around Yellowstone as we speak. Avoiding bears."

"Bears take many forms. We have one in Portland."

He meant Catch. Blood brother and bear of a man with a bear's attitude.

"Speaking of bear country," I said. "Why don't you join me in a couple of weeks? Montana. We can drive Marcus crazy."

"I'll pose the question to JJ. She does have this thing called a job. Me too. An ugly imposition on life schedules."

"You have a job?"

"I escort bundles of visitors on snorkeling trips."

Bo with a job. It wasn't for money. Perhaps a signifier for JJ he wasn't a ne'er-do-well. A man capable of honest work. Hard to say, but good hearing.

"How's the job working out?"

"It's interesting. Folks seem to enjoy my perspectives on sea critters. And life."

"I'm pretty much a fan as well."

"You're a grounded goober. My sea anchor. Although JJ partakes in that role to a lesser degree."

"And how's *that* working out?"

"Better than good."

He elaborated on his relationship, voice filled with growing satisfaction. Fine and good to hear.

CC and I untied Tinker from outside the sea turtle building. He wasn't enthused about being left behind.

"Case. Can you believe?"

"The turtles?"

"The turtles. And turtle doctors. Did you know about turtle doctors?"

"I did not."

"Would Tinker Juarez like turtles?"

It required some thought. "I think maybe dogs and turtles don't pay much attention to each other."

"Why?"

"Well, they're just different. They *might* like each other, but one lives in the water, one on land."

She chewed her lower lip. The ocean breeze ruffled her hair and prompted Tinker into a nose held high gait, capturing scent.

"I wonder if turtles like snow cones?" I asked. A summer snow cone shack was situated between us and the *Ace of Spades*.

"Maybe. Maybe the turtle doctors know." We strolled several more yards. "But *I* like snow cones. So does Tinker Juarez."

Melinda Whitmore called late one evening while CC and Tinker were sleeping below deck. I occupied the foredeck throne with stars and a half-moon and a vodka-rocks my lone companions. I'd forgotten to disengage the Omaha phone exchange, but did remember leaving Melinda a Jack Tilly business card. The chat was light, fun, casual. We touched on a variety of conversational subjects, her low laughter appealing and infectious. And she formed a solid touchpoint outside my shadowed world. The conversation ended with her asking me to call her some time. Keep in touch. Left it on my side of the court. Fair enough and the desire to take her up on it pulled strong.

We turned onto an old brick-lined path. Massive live oaks lined both sides, their branches forming a shaded tunnel. Spanish moss hung as blue-gray stalactites and moved with the breeze. CC and I held hands and took our time. One of those stab-in-the-heart moments, poignant and captured for storage in personal treasure boxes.

"How many snow cone colors?" I asked.

CC liked two or three flavors, colors, on her snow cone.

She took her time. "Three. But Tinker Juarez wants one."

"Sounds great. I think I'll get two."

"Two is good. But dogs like one."

"Then that's what we'll do. Three colors for CC, two for Case, one for Tinker."

"Tinker Juarez."

"Of course. Tinker Juarez."

She squeezed my hand in affirmation, with a love clean and pure and precious.

On the return leg to Charleston, I received a message from Jules.

Status?

A bit of a surprise. Not the arrival of a Clubhouse message, but the intimation she wasn't aware of recent outcomes. Company wet work was buried too deep for her spider web network. I shot a short reply.

Over and done.

Her return message marked another benchmark on my life's path, neither welcomed nor shunned.

Huzzah. But remember the big item, dear boy. It is seldom over. And never done.

THE END

Dear Reader,

I hope you enjoyed the experience, and thank you for joining me on the trip. The sights, sounds, and textures of exotic places around the world are part and parcel of the Case Lee series. I've been fortunate to have lived and worked around the globe—from the Amazon to New Guinea to the Congo. And love incorporating those backdrops into my tales. The next page—**About The Author**—details some of those adventures.

If you would like to get updates and insights on the next Case Lee book, please join my newsletter list by simply copying the link below in your browser.

http://eepurl.com/cWP0iz

And I need to ask a favor. If you are so inclined, I'd love a review of *The Caribbean Job* on Amazon.com. Reviews mean a lot to potential new readers.

Other Case Lee adventures:

The Suriname Job: A Case Lee Novel Book 1

The New Guinea Job: A Case Lee Novel Book 2

Again, thank you so much for dedicating the time to spend with me and Case in *The Caribbean Job*. Here's hoping you and yours are doing well. And remember, we're all in this together.

Sincerely,

Vince Milam

ABOUT THE AUTHOR

I've lived and worked all over the world, traipsing through places like the Amazon, Congo, and Papua New Guinea. And I make a point of capturing unique sights, sounds, and personalities that are incorporated into each of my novels.

The Suriname Job

I worked a contract in that tiny South American country when revolution broke out. Armored vehicles in the streets, gunfire—the whole nine yards. There's a standard protocol in many countries when woken by automatic gunfire. Slide out of bed, take a pillow, and nestle on the floor while contemplating whether a coup has taken place or the national soccer team just won a game. In Suriname, it was a coup.

There was work to do, and that meant traveling across Suriname while the fighting took place. Ugly stuff. But the people were great—a strange and unique mixture of Dutch, Asian Indians, Javanese, and Africans. The result of back in the day when the Dutch were a global colonial power.

Revolutions and coups attract strange players. Spies, mercenaries, "advisors." I did require the services of a helicopter, and one merc who'd arrived with his chopper was willing to perform side gigs when not flying incumbent military folks around. And yes, just as in *The Suriname Job*, I had to seek him out in Paramaribo's best bordello. Not my finest moment.

The New Guinea Job

What a strange place. A massive jungle-covered island with 14,000 foot mountains. As tribal a culture as you'll find. Over 800 living languages (languages, not dialects) making it the most linguistically diverse place on

243

earth. Headhunting an active and proud tradition until very recently (I strongly suspect it still goes on).

I lived and worked deep in the bush—up a tributary of the Fly River. Amazing flora and fauna. Shadowed rain forest jungle, snakes and insects aplenty, peculiar ostrich-like creatures with fluorescent blue heads, massive crocs. Jurassic Park stuff. And leeches. Man, I hated those bloody leeches. Millions of them.

And remarkable characters. In *The New Guinea Job*, the tribesman Luke Mugumwup was a real person, and a pleasure to be around. The tribal tattoos and ritual scarification across his body lent a badass appearance, for sure. But a rock-solid individual to work with. Unless he became upset. Then all bets were off.

I toned *down* the boat driver, Babe Cox. Hard to believe. But the actual guy was a unique and nasty and unforgettable piece of work. His speech pattern consisted of continual f-bombs with the occasional adjective, noun, and verb tossed in. And you could smell the dude from thirty feet.

The Caribbean Job

Flashbacks of the time I spent working in that glorious part of the world came easy. The Bahamas, American Virgin Islands, Jamaica, San Andres, Providencia—a trip down memory lane capturing the feel of those islands for this novel. And the people! What marvelous folks. I figured the tale's intrigue and action against such an idyllic background would make for a unique reading experience.

And pirates. The real deal. I was forced into dealing with them while attempting work contracts. Much of the Caribbean has an active smuggler and pirate trade—well-hidden and never posted in tourist blurbs. Talk about interesting characters! There is a weird code of conduct among them, but I was never clear on the rules of the road. It made for an interesting work environment.

One of the more prevalent memories of those times involved cash. Wads of Benjamins—$100 bills. The pirate and smuggler clans, as you can well imagine, don't take credit cards or issue receipts. Cash on the barrelhead. Benjamins the preferred currency. It made for inventive bookkeeping entries.

About Me

I live in the Intermountain West, where wide-open spaces give a person perspective and room to think. I relish great books, fine trout streams, family, old friends, and good dogs.

You can visit me at www.vincemilam.com to learn about new releases and writer's angst. I can also be visited on Facebook at Vince Milam Author.

LFW
JP

71146937R00139

Made in the USA
Middletown, DE
29 September 2019